ST. LOUIS
Secrets

SIZZLING CITY SERIES
BOOK 3

ZIZI HART

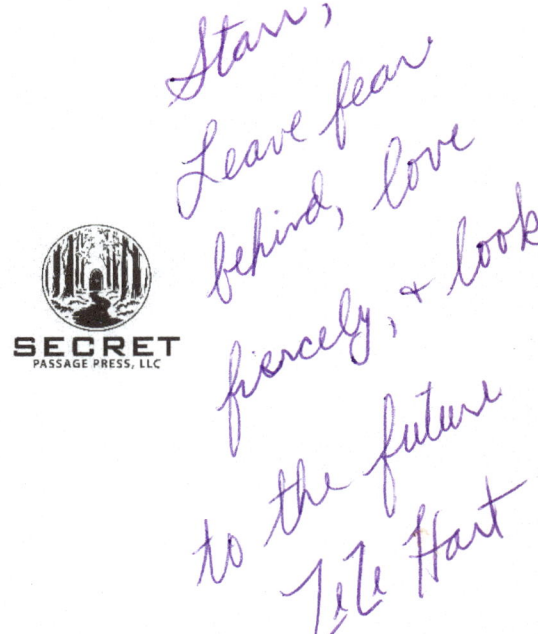

St. Louis Secrets
Copyright © 2025 by Zizi Hart.
Published by Secret Passage Press, LLC

This book is a work of fiction. Names, characters,
places, and incidents are either products of the author's
imagination or are used fictitiously. Any resemblance to actual events
or locales or persons, living or dead, is entirely coincidental.
All rights reserved. No part of this book may be used or reproduced
in any manner whatsoever without written permission
except in the case of brief quotations embodied
in critical articles or reviews.

For information contact:
www.zizihart.com
www.secretpassage-press.com

Cover design by Miranda Lexa
Editing by Cyndi Rule

ISBN: 978-1-9644-6004-8 (paperback)
ISBN: 978-1-9644-6005-5 (eBook)

First Edition: April 2025

Secret Passage Press, LLC
Canon City, CO

Disclaimer

This book contains adult language, themes,
and sexually explicit scenes.
It is intended for readers 18+.

*To my incredible St. Louis crew.
I could not have done this without you.
Thank you for helping me uncover
the hidden secrets of St. Louis.
So many people provided insight and inspiration.
From the underground tunnels, spectacular sights, and
delectable food, it was hard to narrow down the places I wanted
to share with my characters.
I had such a fun time exploring the city.
St. Louis is one of the top cities I'd call a foodie paradise.
My waistline thanks you.*

Prologue

Rosa

I stared down the barrel of a Glock and felt numb down to my core. The man threatening my life was my cousin, Luís Lorenzo. We held no love for one another, even though we were family. I knew I would go out like this one day. Bold and Bloody. It was inevitable. I had no illusions of how my life would turn out, but I did have regrets, plenty of them. I cringed thinking of how my body would be found. Why had I delayed changing out of my Club Cuervo uniform at the end of the night? My skin-tight next-to-nothing outfit barely contained my figure. While it might work great for tips, it sucked at providing any warmth in a vacant warehouse in the middle of the night. I shivered.

    The evil grin on my cousin's face was sickening. He enjoyed my fear. I wanted to scream that I wasn't afraid, I was freezing, not that it would do any good. Luís would call me a liar. I had long ago wished for a world where good would conquer evil. Then again, good was relative, especially, if you worked for my family. The Lorenzos were Colombian Mafiosos. Our money came from drugs. Cocaine was our bread and butter, but we had diversified over the years. Each branch of the family was involved in the process; cultivation, manufacturing, exporting, distribution, and selling. I was low-level, and a cousin of the Lorenzo Brothers on their father's side. I worked for Luís, the youngest of the three brothers.

Another cousin of mine, Ramón, fell to his knees beside me. He was only 21 and had lived a sheltered life. Ramón was the reason I was in Santa Fe. His mother, Maria Lorenzo had been my best friend growing up. On her deathbed years ago, I had sworn to protect Ramón and keep him out of this life, and away from the family business. I had failed. His uncle Luís had been trying to recruit the kid despite his sister's wishes. Luís had promised me that he would leave the kid alone if I agreed to come work at Club Cuervo in Santa Fe. He had lied. The kid arrived in town a month ago. Ramón had been hired as a barback for the club.

The kid cowered in front of his uncle.

He shook his head, sobbing.

"Nunca. Nunca. Never. Never. I swear."

"On your feet Ramón," I said, my voice low. "You're a Lorenzo."

The kid climbed to his feet, sniffing. It filled me with pride. I needed him to remain strong. Reminding Luís of the family connection might save us. It was a slim chance since he wasn't always rational. Luís knew that someone betrayed him, and needed someone to blame. Cruz stood on my other side. He was a bartender at the club. We had worked together for the past six months.

Luís pointed the gun at each of us in turn. Ramón, me, and Cruz.

"Two of you are family, and the other a trusted employee," he said. "How. To. Decide."

Luís' phone buzzed. He slipped his gun into his holster while he smiled at the message. He signaled for several guards to follow him over to another part of the warehouse. My breath hissed out when he walked away. Cruz cleared his throat, and I gave him a sidelong glance. He was trying to tell me something with his eyes. We had worked together and had developed an unspoken way of communicating. He needed a distraction. Did

ST. LOUIS SECRETS

that mean he had a plan? At this point, I was up for anything. I scrutinized the two men left guarding us. One I had flirted with back in Colombia. I focused my attention on him. I shifted my stance and waited for Cruz's signal.

He fell to the ground like his knees had given out.

"The whole thing's a mistake. I would never do anything against the boss."

Cruz sobbed like he was falling apart. It was an act. I knew that Cruz was made of sterner stuff, but the two guards didn't. They were fresh from Colombia.

"This one is no Lorenzo." I scoffed, nodding at Cruz. The guard I didn't know well stepped closer, poking him with the tip of his gun, trying to get him to stand back up.

I took a step toward the other guard.

"Hey Pablo, can you itch my shoulder? With these ties, I can't reach it."

I wiggled my left shoulder. "This one." My breasts bounced with the movement and Pablo was more than willing to inch his way closer for a better view. Typical pendejo.

"Por favor. It's been driving me loca," I said sweetly.

The second guard swatted Pablo away and jostled me in the process. I stumbled but caught myself. Cruz suddenly did something the guard didn't like. He rushed forward and slammed Cruz against the van. In the collision, I noticed Cruz's hands were free. Neither of the guards seemed to realize. I was blocking Pablo's view, so I'd make sure he kept his focus on me.

"That was uncalled for," I said.

We heard arguing from the other side of the warehouse. It was Luís. He was not happy. The voices rose in pitch. Then a gunshot was fired. Not a big surprise. That's how he ended most arguments.

The next sound, however, was unexpected. It was an explosion. The bay doors blew inward in pieces. Floodlights blasted through several windows and the open space that used to be a door. Pablo and the other guard stared at the chaos.

"DEA. You're surrounded." I heard over a megaphone. The staccato sounds of gunfire drowned out the voice. Cruz tackled me to the floor. The impact made me gasp. My hands were still tied behind me, so my knuckles took the brunt of my fall and dug into my back. Somehow, I managed not to break anything. Either Cruz had been careful, or I had been lucky. Not something you could usually say about me. I did not live a charmed life.

Our two guards were still focused on the commotion by the trucks. Cruz knocked Pablo to the ground, grabbing his gun in the process. The other guard was shot from above and collapsed in front of Ramón. Cruz cut my zip ties and did the same for Ramón. The kid was splattered in blood and shaking violently. My poor cousin. He was not used to this kind of thing.

I watched as Luís made a run for his limo. He was limping. Blood stained his Armani slacks. La policía were everywhere. Normally that would fill me with dread, but tonight I was grateful. I'd take them over Luís pointing a gun at me any day. I watched as Luís aimed his Glock at one of the officers, and pulled the trigger. He had to realize there was no escape. Although, I didn't expect him to go quietly. That wasn't his way. Like his nickname, El Lobo Rojo, the red wolf left a path of blood in his wake. The policía fired at him, but he used one of his guards as a shield. After the barrage of bullets, Luís tossed his shield to the ground. Finally, someone tackled him to the cement. The policía issued a series of commands in Spanish demanding surrender. The whole thing was over before I knew it. Cruz appeared to be shot in the shoulder. Ramón sprinted to a corner, heaving up his last meal. I glanced down at my body. I had a few bumps, some scrapes, and a broken nail. I felt lucky.

"Jac," Cruz yelled to a large officer in a tactical vest who was cuffing Pablo.

The man grinned at Cruz. It was clear they knew one another.

ST. LOUIS SECRETS

"You were in on this?" I asked.

Did that mean that Cruz had been working with the police this whole time? Was he an informant?

"I was undercover," he said.

"I knew it."

Everything Cruz had done these past months. It all made sense now. Cruz had that good guy streak he just couldn't hide.

My attention focused on Luís. He was screaming promises of revenge, while one of the officers arrested him, trying to lead him away to one of the vans. Luís fought back. The man wouldn't give up. Many colorful obscenities in Spanish spewed from his lips. I couldn't help but grin at his predicament, even though I would be arrested too. But arrested was way better than dead.

Luís' eyes turned feral.

"You. I will get you!" He roared.

I shivered. I knew that look. He thought I had betrayed him. Luís was going to make me pay. Even if it wasn't true, it wouldn't matter. His mind was made up. Logic never played into his decisions. As soon as he got out of jail, it would happen. And with his political contacts, I knew that wouldn't be long. I inhaled a sharp breath.

Suddenly this huge man came out of nowhere and punched Luís in the jaw. He fell to the floor with a thud. I sighed with relief. Someone shouted a reprimand at the mysterious hero with an unrepentant grin.

"What?" He yelled. "He was swearing, and there are ladies present."

The man stared at me. I gulped. This handsome stranger started walking straight toward me. I briefly wondered what expression he saw on my face. Awe? Gratitude? Shock?

Jac blocked the man's progress.

"How the hell are you, Taz?" He asked and gave Taz a slug on the shoulder. It barely moved the behemoth of a man. Taz reached out to shake Cruz's hand. He knew them both. I stared at the three men standing together. All stunning in their own right. When had the policía started recruiting straight from Chippendales?

"Howdy ma'am." Taz nodded. Clear concern on his face. "You all right?" He said with a Texan drawl.

I nodded. My mouth was still open. There was something about this man. He pushed all my buttons. Big and protective. Ruggedly sexy.

"I don't want Rosa arrested," Cruz said. "She's been through enough."

"Ramón either." I managed to say. I finally found my voice. "I'm calling in my debt."

Days ago, I had helped Cruz rescue some girls from the club. He had promised me a favor to be named later.

"What do you think?" Cruz asked.

"I'll see what I can do," Jac said.

"What if I..." I glanced between the men. "I know things."

"She's a Lorenzo," Cruz said.

Taz was listening intently. His stance stiffened when the name was mentioned.

"Luís already thinks I betrayed him. As soon as he lawyers up." I crossed my arms over my chest and tried to keep the quiver from my voice. "I'm dead."

"We can't have that now, can we little lady?"

The Texan charm disarmed me.

He stood close. I had to look up and up to stare into his dark eyes. The man must be 6 and a half feet tall at least. Was he making fun of me? My brows furrowed. His words were calm and soothing, but something was off; like it was all an act. He held an edge behind the gentle attitude like he was moments away from exploding. I wondered if his friends realized. I had a radar for repressed rage. It was a hard-earned skill developed from working with Luís.

I shivered. The events of the day were finally catching up to me. Or maybe there was a draft from the now open bay doors.

ST. LOUIS SECRETS

Taz took off his jacket and bundled me up with care. I'm sure I looked ridiculous. I wasn't used to people being nice. It confused me.

"Let's get you out of the way," he said and started leading me to a set of cars and SUVs. My legs gave out, and I stumbled. Before I even knew what was happening, he swept me up into his arms like I weighed nothing.

I yipped. "Put me down. I can walk." I didn't appreciate being manhandled, even if it was by the sexiest man I had ever laid eyes on.

Then he whispered something to me in Spanish. I always had some witty comeback, but the comment left me tongue-tied.

"You're mine to protect."

It was possessive and filled with heat. His eyes glittered with some emotion that I didn't understand. I didn't believe it was love. We had only just met. But it wasn't lust either. I was too tired to figure it out. After almost dying, I needed something to cling to; something to hope for. I held on tighter, enjoying the warmth and safety this man offered. Cuddling into his chest I smelled his earthy scent, a mixture of sweat and cologne. I allowed my body to go limp, relaxing for this moment in time. I knew it wouldn't last; nothing ever did.

Chapter 1

Six months later

Taz

I approached the safe house checking out the surroundings, following standard operating procedures. A deputy was on duty watching the witness. We had several witnesses for a high-profile case against Luís Lorenzo, aka El Lobo Rojo. But this one was critical. She was family. That meant she had the potential to do the most damage. The trouble was she was a pain. For multiple reasons. I didn't like how she made me feel. I had always been protective especially where women were concerned, but my feelings for her went beyond job responsibilities. It didn't make sense. While it was my job to protect the bastards that came through WITSEC, I didn't always like it. At least this one was easy on the eyes. She was also a pretty tough cookie. Rosa played the part well, but I could see a vulnerability that she didn't reveal to others. I noticed how her behavior changed when she was with me.

I hated the Lorenzos and had good reasons for that. That family caused irreparable harm to someone I loved. I would never forget or forgive.

Deputy Williams buzzed me in after I knocked and then texted the correct code. The door opened and the deputy shook his head.

"She's in a mood today. I think she's gone stir-crazy."

A pot was launched across the living room.

"I said spices, pendejo. This isn't what I need."

She hurled a spice bottle at his head."

"I couldn't find what you asked for." The deputy complained.

"What kind of backward-ass place have you brought me to?"

A plastic stir stick sailed through the air. I stepped in the path, and I caught it.

"Now Ma'am, we talked about this."

The deputy took the opportunity, to scurry out of the apartment while he had the chance. I locked up behind him before making my way into the kitchen.

"What's with all the fuss?" I asked.

Her nose tilted up, and Rosa crossed her arms over her chest. Her V-neck T-shirt showed an obscene amount of cleavage. How could she make a simple T-shirt look so darn erotic?

"I need things," she blinked deep chocolate brown eyes at me.

Her slow perusal of my body felt tactile. Rosa's lashes were thick and dark. From her lust-filled gaze, they matched her thoughts. She had shared some of her fantasies with me. I'm sure it was to get a rise out of me. It had succeeded. In fact, I needed to adjust myself right now.

"You showing up like that, looking the way you do doesn't help matters."

She approached me slowly. Rosa didn't walk, she strolled, with seductive swishes of her hips.

"What does that mean?"

ST. LOUIS SECRETS

She slid fingertips over my pecs and down my abdomen. I caught her wrist before she went too far. The woman loved to play games.

"All sexy and macho, when I have no chance at you know."

"Know what?"

"Getting a release," she sighed dramatically.

I released her wrist.

Rosa stood back and gestured to my body. "It's not fair."

I grinned. She was always saying outrageous things to rile me up.

"Well ma'am, you can always take matters into your own hands."

"You think I don't?" She wiggled her eyebrows.

I had been teasing, but she sounded serious. The image of her had me swallowing hard. To know that she was doing something like that in the bedroom when I was in the living room guarding her, my neck suddenly got hotter than Hades. I went over to the thermostat and turned down the AC.

I cleared my throat.

"What is it you were looking for specifically, ma'am?"

"Call me by my name. Stop calling me ma'am. It makes me feel old."

Rosa told me that repeatedly over the last six months. I had ignored her request to keep things professional.

"I need a treadmill," she said with hands on her hips.

"I thought you needed spices."

"Yes. I need those too. Cooking relaxes me." Rosa walked over to the cutting board filled with fresh vegetables. She slid a chef's knife from the block and chopped peppers and green onion.

"When I get irritated, I want to stab things," she pointed the knife in my direction and grinned. Her eyes sparkled with mischief.

My eyebrows rose. I walked to the other side of the island and relieved her of the knife.

"Not much of an incentive to let you play with knives."

"Oh please. If I wanted to stab you, I could have done so dozens of times."

I tilted my head.

She huffed. "Ok. Maybe once. You're fairly alert. The others not so much."

"That would violate your agreement.

She rolled her eyes and walked to the icebox pulling out a few chicken breasts that had been marinating.

I finished cutting up the vegetables she had laid out, wondering briefly if I needed to warn the other deputies. Rosa liked to make threats, but I knew they were mostly empty. She had a flair for the dramatic.

"Why do you need a treadmill, Rosa?" I asked.

It felt personal using her name, but I rather liked how it sounded.

She froze staring at me with raised eyebrows.

"This body was not honed into shape without working out regularly. I've gained twenty pounds since I've been stuck here. You and your gang keep bringing me fast food."

"We can change up the menu if you like. But I thought you enjoyed the selection."

"I do. Obviously. St. Louis food is fattening as hell. Delicious, but fattening. I need to start cooking my meals. Less fat. More flavor."

I glanced at her body. I didn't mind the extra weight. I thought she looked better than before. When I had initially gotten her into the program, I thought she was too skinny. Working as a cocktail waitress, I knew she had to watch her figure, especially considering the amount of skin she had to show in her club outfit. At first, I thought she might have taken drugs to stay thin. I had worried we might need to send her to detox before putting her in the program, but her blood work came back clean. Even though she had been selling drugs out of Club Cuervo, she hadn't been taking them herself.

I blinked. "That's a mighty big item."

"This is a mighty big ass," she grabbed her behind. "And I need to get rid of it."

I tilted my head for a better view and grinned. I thought her ass looked fine. More than fine. I imagined taking her over my knee on more than one occasion when she'd get all uppity.

She huffed at me. "Then get me a gym membership."

"Now Rosa, you know that will never happen."

She shrugged. "Then you will just have to deal with my outbursts. I can't help myself."

I knew what we both needed. The sexual tension between the two of us had been building to a point where I could barely stand it. Not that I could do a darn thing about it. I needed this trial over, so I could relocate her and move on. I didn't have the luxury to get attached. There was something about Rosa that got under my skin. I was equal parts attracted and irritated.

My phone rang, and I looked at the number. It was the district office. They usually just texted, so it had to be important.

"Is your witness secure?"

It was Sandi Summers. She was an administrative support assistant.

"Affirmative," I said, glancing around the apartment. I still started re-checking windows, doors, closets, and under the bed. I shoved a complaining Rosa into the bathroom, shut the door, and locked it from the outside. It was something I had implemented because of her outbursts. She banged on it and swore at me in Spanish. Rosa had quite the vocabulary.

"What happened?" I asked, sitting on the edge of the bed.

"A witness was killed. One of Luís' men."

"Which one?"

"José."

Another essential witness for the prosecution. Although I had serious doubts he would make it to trial. Not that I thought he'd end up dead. I believed he would back out of testifying at some point. He was one of Luís' sicarios. José knew where the bodies were buried because he helped bury them.

"How?" I asked.

"The man snuck out of his room. We assume it was to buy cigarettes. He had been complaining earlier that his handler had gotten the wrong brand." Sandi blew out a breath. "He climbed out the bathroom window and down the fire escape."

"Didn't the deputy follow security protocols?" I asked. We had a series of checks. All entry and exit points were wired to set off an alarm if they were opened.

"The wire was tampered with. He figured José circumvented security."

"Where was he killed?"

"At the convenience store around the corner from the safe house. The local PD thinks it was a robbery gone wrong. There was a hold-up. The shooter escaped. We are waiting for security footage now."

"Does the SI believe it was just an accident?" I asked.

"No. The senior inspector thinks it was a targeted hit. The PD found a cell phone and cash on the body," she said.

These things didn't happen randomly. They were orchestrated. I had been doing this long enough to know. The deputy should have been better at his job. But this incident also identified a risk to other witnesses in the case. Whoever had targeted José had gotten the address to one of our safe houses.

"Do we have the phone?"

"Not yet. They are still processing it, but it looks like a burner."

"We need the last number called."

"Already on it. The Inspector is at the scene."

ST. LOUIS SECRETS

Not that I figured it would yield much. It was probably from another burner. But we could get lucky. Oftentimes criminals weren't overly bright.

"And the deputy?"

"Being questioned now."

"Has the accountant looked over his records? Does he think he might have been paid off?"

I didn't want to think along those lines, but it was necessary. If the deputy was compromised, then we needed to change passwords, locations; everything he might be aware of.

We had safe houses all over the city. If he was a threat, this could jeopardize more than just one witness. It could potentially risk our entire operation.

"He hasn't found anything unusual in his bank accounts."

She sighed heavily.

I knew what was coming, but I asked anyway.

"Is there anything else?"

"Why are you guarding her?"

It was my turn to sigh, "Ms. Summers, you know good and well that I don't need to justify my actions."

I had recently been appointed Chief Deputy US Marshal for the Eastern District of Missouri. Before that, I had been a Deputy Marshal for the Southern District of Texas. Over the past decade, I worked in various positions within the USMS. I was currently one of the youngest Chief Deputy Marshals in the U.S. The last thing I needed was staff questioning my command.

"It's just that you have so many deputies that could handle that sort of thing. It's beneath you."

I knew what the real problem was. The witness was attractive and just my type, ballsy and beautiful. Sandi knew this. We had gone on a few dates early in my career when I was young and dumb. It had been a mistake. Office romances didn't work, especially in my line of work. But she still occasionally pushed for more.

"Call me when you know more," I said.

She hung up. Sandi was moody, just like another woman in my life.

I sighed, staring at the bathroom door. As soon as I unlocked it Rosa would raise hell. She had every reason to. If I were in her shoes, I would too. I couldn't stand feeling cooped up and out of control. I scrolled through a list of treadmills. It was an excessive expense, and I didn't want the finance guy raising his eyebrows. I might just pay for it myself, just to get Rosa to calm down. I unlocked the door and she was ready for it. She launched herself at me and tackled me to the bed. I wrestled her easily, flipping us over, and pinning her body.

"Enough of this. I know you are unhappy. But this is the way it has to be. You agreed to the terms."

She squirmed beneath me, but her smoky kohled eyes had dilated. Rosa was turned on. She rattled off a mixture of curses and compliments in Spanish. I grinned. I couldn't help myself.

Her chest pushed against mine. I held her wrists together above her head with one hand and balanced my body with my other arm. I didn't want to crush her with my weight, but I was still unwilling to move, afraid she might attack again. I wasn't worried that Rosa would hurt me, but she could injure herself, and that I wouldn't allow. Feeling her soft body beneath, I tried to focus on something, anything other than her pouty lips, and silky hair. Those dark eyes. The same ones I dreamed of when I slept. She rolled her hips and my jaw ticked.

"Don't do that," I whispered.

"Or what pendejo?" She pursed her lips. "Will you tie me up? Or will that just turn you on more?"

I was hard. She could feel it. There was no concealing my erection.

She rolled her hips again, and I thrust. It was automatic. We were aligned perfectly and it made her gasp. Rosa's eyes rolled back in her head.

"Again. Por favor."

ST. LOUIS SECRETS

It brought me to my senses. Still, I hesitated. I didn't want to move. I wanted to give her what she needed, what we both needed. I climbed off, eyeing her with caution. She reacted more like a wild animal most days. She did nothing for a moment and then curled into a ball.

"I hate you," she said. "Get out of here," she threw a pillow at my head.

I caught it and tossed it back on the bed. I turned and closed the door. My breath hissed out. I had almost done something unforgivable. She was temptation personified. As it was, I had stepped over the line. That wasn't like me, but there was something about her. She pushed all my buttons. I should be focused on her safety, not worried about how she felt beneath me, warm and willing. Was Luís Lorenzo orchestrating the elimination of witnesses? Or was his family? I needed a risk assessment on the deputy guarding José. Was he somehow involved? There were too many questions. I glanced back at the bedroom door and came to a decision. I wouldn't allow her to be next. Those bastards would have to go through me to get to her. From here on out I wasn't letting her out of my sight.

Chapter 2

Rosa

"We have to change locations," Taz said marching into the bedroom.

He started shoving my things into a duffel. I stood with my arms crossed watching him. I wasn't about to help. Not when I was so angry. He had left me hanging. I was sexually frustrated. It didn't matter that I knew it would have been a horrible mistake to sleep with the man. My body didn't care. My temper was usually on simmer these days. I clung to my anger, stoking that emotion, letting it build while I watched and waited. My clothes were strewn about the room. I didn't put my clothes into drawers or on hangers. It was in defiance of a certain overly organized US Marshal. I knew it drove him crazy, and that was the point. My life was in chaos right now, so my room reflected that. Choosing where to put my stuff was something I could control, and I needed some control right now. This man had stripped me of that.

He rushed about the room whispering things under his breath. Taz stopped momentarily as if the item he held gave him pause. He stared at the sexy lace push-up bra as his thumb rubbed the intricate pattern over and over. I had worn that underneath my club uniform the first night I met Taz. I didn't really need a push-up bra for lift. My breasts were large enough without any assistance in that department. But if distraction was your goal, then every little bit helped. The more cleavage the better. It was a tool when working at the club, and I'd take every advantage I could get. I probably should have tossed the thing or burned it after joining WITSEC, but on a whim, I had kept the bra and matching panties. It made me feel a little like my old self. Most days I felt depressed or frustrated with my current situation. Any emotion other than that was a good thing. It also gave me a small thrill to be wearing something sexy beneath the simple T-shirts the US Marshal Service had supplied me with.

"It's from Paris."

"What?" Taz asked.

"The lingerie you're holding is from a famous French designer." I cocked out a hip. "Planning to do something kinky with it?"

Taz cleared his throat and shoved the bra into the duffel.

I smirked at his expression. His jaw ticked.

"You're always trying to rile me up."

I walked over and blinked up at him. I slid a hand down his chest. A feather-light touch that had him rocking back on his heels.

"It's so damn easy to do."

He grabbed my chin and made me look into his smoky gaze. Taz allowed me a glimpse of his concern. He was normally so carefully shielded.

"I need your help. Please."

The words didn't register for a moment. Taz was asking for help? What exactly was going on? He didn't ask. He ordered. Taz moved about the rest of the apartment with speed.

I huffed and started gathering up everything I might need.

"Don't forget toiletries," he said from the living room.

I grabbed an empty garbage bag and used one arm to swipe all the lotions, and hair products from the bathroom sink. I dumped drawers filled with makeup that I had acquired after much debate with the Deputy US Marshal who had worked with me in

ST. LOUIS SECRETS

those first few days after joining WITSEC. I remember the first discussion like it was yesterday. I wrote a list of things I needed on a slip of paper and handed it to the deputy. 'Makeup is a luxury item he had said, not a necessity'. I had responded with a phrase mi mamá adored. 'Antes muerta que sencilla'. I'd rather be dead than plain. Mi mamá would prefer death rather than go outside the house without her war paint. It seemed I was now the same. I shoved everything into the duffel and carefully slid the nail file into my boot. I peered out the door into the living room. Taz was preoccupied. He was concentrating on his scanner. I quickly went to the closet, popped loose the floorboard, and snatched the few items I had stashed.

"What is this?" Taz asked from behind me.

Mierda. My shoulders tensed. I didn't even hear him come in. How could such a big guy, move so silently? I needed to put bells around his neck. I plunked the board back into place and stood not bothering to hide the items still clutched in my grasp. I had been caught. Denial wouldn't work. I had to give him the truth. Or at least a partial one.

"Emergency fund?" I shrugged.

He crossed his arms over his chest.

I couldn't come up with anything better. I was losing my touch. Too much time in protective custody.

Taz scrutinized the items in my hand. It was a few pieces of jewelry and some cash.

"Where the hell did you get this?"

My lips pressed together. Nothing I could say would help my situation.

He pried the diamond and sapphire necklace from my fist and held it up to the light. I didn't want to let it go, but he didn't give me much of a choice. I wore the necklace on occasion when Mr. Grumpy wasn't around. One of the Marshal's team had given it to me or rather retrieved it for me a few months back. This shy IT guy called Sam had witnessed me crying early on when I had first joined this off-tune mariachi band they called WITSEC. I had fallen apart in front of him. I hadn't realized I had an audience at the time. I never would have lost it if I had known. Sam had patted my shoulder awkwardly and it had made me laugh. After getting over my embarrassment, we struck up a conversation and the two of us had formed a friendship. He was in charge of network security and had been checking surveillance cameras at the time. Sam made excuses to come visit me mumbling that he had to run updates or check wiring. I think the deputies knew it was BS. Sam was sweet on me. It was obvious. Of course, I didn't mind the attention, and he really was a good listener.

After joining WITSEC, I was drowning in self-pity and feeling vulnerable. One time I had mentioned to Sam all the things I had left behind, my jewelry and clothes and several family keepsakes. Mi Nana, Teresa Lorenzo had left me a few things in her will a few years ago. Luís had stolen the necklace from me when I moved to Santa Fe, saying I didn't deserve it. I spoke with Luís' brothers, Esteban and Juan, but they refused to do a thing about it. We all shared the same grandmother since we were cousins. A few weeks after I had shared the secret about mi Nana, Sam arrived with a present. I had smiled half-heartedly at the plain brown paper bag wondering what it contained. It looked like one of those bags from a bakery, so I expected a scone or maybe a cookie. He had blindsided me. Sam had managed to find my grandmother's necklace. Apparently, Luís kept it at his place, and since all his assets had been seized from his Santa Fe home when he was arrested, my necklace had been sitting in a storage facility marked to be auctioned off after he was convicted. Sam said something about returning it to the lockbox after the trial so he wouldn't get in trouble, but I was only half-listening. Mi Nana's necklace was back. I was so excited at that moment, I had kissed Sam, smack on the lips. He had been so flustered at the time, that Sam practically ran out of the apartment.

"Did you steal this?" Taz dangled the necklace in front of me.

My eyebrows raised. How dare he accuse me?

"No, it was a gift."

"From who?"

I pursed my lips. I wasn't about to snitch on Sam.

"Some of your deputies are not complete dicks," I shrugged.

Since many deputies had paraded through on babysitting duty over the months, he'd have to dig to narrow it down.

"This looks expensive."

"It's just costume jewelry," I shrugged, "but I love anything that sparkles."

"What about the money?"

He pointed to the twenties I still had in my hand. I shoved my hands in my pocket and bit my lip.

"I might have borrowed a few bucks."

"So stolen?"

I shrugged. "Nothing noticeable."

"That's not the point. Stealing violates your agreement."

"Only if I'm caught."

I snagged the necklace from Taz, threw it in the duffel, and zipped up the bag in one move.

"But you were caught. By me," he stood with his hands on his hips and one eyebrow raised.

"You don't count," I said, flipping my hands in the air.

He didn't say anything further, but I knew by his expression he was ticked off. It seemed inevitable that I do things to irritate the man. And it wasn't always on purpose.

Taz scanned the duffel with a handheld device and seemed satisfied. He was checking for bugs. My cousin used similar equipment at the club.

"Where are we going?" I asked.

I couldn't help keep the quiver from my voice and I hated it. I was stronger than this.

Taz hesitated for a moment like he debated sharing the information.

"A hotel," he finally said.

"Really?" I grinned.

"It's just temporary."

My mind spun through the possibilities. A hotel gave me the opportunity I needed. I had to get a message to my cousin Ramón. To verify that he was safe. I owed it to his mom. I couldn't ask anyone from the US Marshal Service. Not only would they not allow me to call, but they would learn just how badly I wanted to contact my cousin. That could give them leverage, and the power balance was already so far one-sided, I could barely stand it. I refused to give them another thing they could use against me. Of course, there was that other little fact. Ramón was wanted by the police. Reaching out to him put him at risk. If they found him, he'd be arrested. Reaching out to him through the feds was a mistake. At least now, they weren't looking for Ramón that hard. At least I hoped not.

I wondered briefly why we needed the change of scenery, and why it seemed so urgent. No reason I came up with could be good. Not that I'd get much out of Taz. He was like a locked vault when it came to information. I had more of a chance with one of the other guards. I'd just have to wait until he switched off babysitting duty with someone else.

"Will this hotel have a gym or a spa?" I asked, my eyes wide with anticipation.

Taz shook his head and chuckled. "It doesn't matter. You won't be using the facilities even if they do have it."

I shrugged. I didn't expect him to say yes. But it was worth asking just in case. I'd figure out a way to escape somehow, and I could use finding the gym as an excuse. Plant an idea, and then pivot. It's how I had stayed alive so long. I was a master at misdirection. Or at least I used to be.

Taz received a text and went to the front door while I searched the room for anything left to pack. I didn't have that many things. I frowned at the duffel. It was sad that my life could fit into such a small bag. Not that I was one of those people that gauged success by my possessions. I wasn't superficial in that way. Of course, I didn't mind expensive things, but it was more for the value they could offer. Having a stash of loot that could be traded or sold might be the only thing between life and death. Staying alive was my priority. As sentimental as I was about my Nana's necklace, I might need it when the time came to make my move. I'd say a prayer and ask for her forgiveness. Mi Nana would understand my dilemma. She may have given it to me for just such a reason.

Taz walked back in with a large shopping bag, that I don't remember him having earlier. Did someone drop something off when I was packing up? He dumped it on the bed. It was a bunch of clothes. He took off his shirt and threw it to the floor. He muttered under his breath as he unbuckled his pants. I stared at him, wondering if I should pull up a chair and watch the show. I wouldn't mind the distraction right now. I grinned at the way the day was turning out. Maybe all the teasing was going to pay off. Was he finally going to do something about the electric chemistry between us?

Taz scowled at me.

"Strip," he demanded.

My eyes widened. I didn't expect him to be so direct or quite so rude. But I was game if he was. Not that I was going to make it easy for him.

"At least buy me a drink first."

"You've got two minutes to change or I'll do it for you."

He was serious. I frowned. This wasn't foreplay. I grabbed the items he gestured to and headed into the bathroom.

"Two minutes or I'm busting down that door and whatever you're wearing is what you leave in."

It took a minute and a half to change. If he was this serious, I wasn't about to take chances. I knew what was at stake. I didn't need him to spell it out for me.

"I want to meet the person at the Marshal's office who shops for WITSEC," I said through the bathroom door. "Someone at your office has a serious fetish for sexy librarians, and they got the wrong size."

"It was a rush job," he replied.

I flipped the long blonde locks over my shoulder. The wig looked decent but the outfit made me look fat. The black pencil skirt, while boring and unassuming was way too tight for my backside. It made movement difficult. I worried about splitting a seam. The white button-down blouse might have looked dowdy on other people, but because of the small size, it pulled across my chest. I had no choice but to wear a bra. My sexy black push-up bra was visible underneath. Since the pair of Mary Jane flats didn't fit, so I swapped them for heels. I slid on the fake glasses to complete the costume.

"Can you get my bag?" I asked coming out of the bathroom. "If I bend down, this skirt might self-combust."

I came up short on the man in the room. What the hell? Did another agent get here in the last two minutes? I glanced in the living room, but no one else was here. The man in front of me wore a plain black business suit with a crisp white shirt and dark tie. When I looked closer, my jaw dropped. It was the outfit Taz had laid out on the bed. The man in front of me had slick-backed black hair and thick glasses. It was Taz, but it wasn't. He didn't look anything like himself. The man in front of me appeared to be shorter by a half foot, and way less intimidating. Taz seemed smaller somehow. I was shocked by the transformation.

"How?" I asked.

"The simple way you hold yourself. Your posture. If you slouch or stand tall. Even ill-fitted clothing can change your appearance dramatically."

show it to me. I sighed. Maybe he thought I might run if I had an ID. It would be tempting, but I knew better. WITSEC provided protection. It was something I desperately needed until I testified. Once that happened, my cousin would go to jail, and I'd be able to start over. If I could stay alive long enough. Some days I wondered if the boredom would kill me quicker than a bullet.

A grand staircase heading down was directly in front of us, but Taz veered to the right to another staircase leading up. There were two on each side of the entrance, equally impressive. My gaze focused on the barrel-vaulted ceiling above us as I carefully climbed the steps. We had shown up during a light show in the Grand Hall Lobby. The massive room was relatively dark except for the dazzling display of colors dancing across the ceiling. It reminded me of stained glass inside a cathedral, but then the images transformed, morphing into butterflies, and then changing once again. The music and colored lights were soothing. The metaphorical leash that had been tightening around my throat the past few months loosened just a bit. I let out a deep breath. It was sad that getting out to see a fricking light show somehow made me feel a little less trapped.

As Taz led the way through the hall, I noticed several people sitting at an old-fashioned bar and I wanted to join them. I licked my lips, imagining the selection of cocktails they might offer. It was something I missed from Club Cuervo. Probably the only thing. Working there had been scary. You never knew what to expect from my cousin, Luís. The man was insane. Taz steered us past the bar to the check-in desk and I wanted to tell him to turn back. I hadn't had a drop of alcohol in six months. That may have been a record for me. Not that I was an alcoholic. But I sure could use the liquid balm for my nerves right about now. The fact that the bartender was also cute didn't hurt matters.

Chapter 3

Taz

"This is serious." I whispered, "No shenanigans."

I remember the last time Rosa had switched safe houses. I had given her the same warning, but it had fallen on deaf ears. Between the entrance lobby and elevator of the apartment building we had moved her to, she managed to start half a dozen conversations with strangers. It's like she didn't know how to stay silent. This time would be worse. Rosa had been cooped up too long in that apartment. She was a social animal and craved chaos.

"Whatever you say," she said with glittering eyes.

I sighed. Maybe I should have explained the reason why we were relocating. It might have scared some sense into the woman. Rosa pushed and prodded. She was as stubborn as that mule I had grown up with on my family's ranch in Texas. I doubt she would ever change her ways, just like that darn mule.

I glanced at her outfit not being able to keep my eyes off her body. Rosa was right. It was ridiculously tight. She had every reason to complain. Sandi knew that Rosa had gained some weight. It was in the report. I wondered if she had sabotaged Rosa's outfit on purpose, or if it had been one of the deputies. I knew of a few that made lewd comments about Rosa behind her back. Not that I believe any of them had pursued things with her or done anything improper. Rosa probably didn't even notice how they reacted to her. Flirting was like breathing to her. Well, in between throwing things. You never knew what you were going to get with her. Rosa's eyes took in everything at once. I bet she was mapping the place out in her head. She had done it before. Plotting exit strategies seemed to be second nature. Rosa gave me a cheesy grin, turning her attention back to the light show. Nice try, but I saw through what she was doing.

Rosa gave a long lingering glance to the guy standing at the concierge desk. My eyebrow raised. What was her game now? She gave him a dazzling smile, and the guy blushed. No. That wouldn't do at all. I needed to make things clear from the get-go. I pulled Rosa into my side and glared at the man. He visibly gulped. I realized I wasn't playing my part very well, but in that moment, I didn't care. Rosa stared at my expression from inches away. We were next in line, so I brought her along with me to the counter. At least she stayed silent.

"Mr. and Mrs. Connor checking in."

I handed the desk clerk a fake ID and credit card. Multiple aliases were sometimes necessary in emergencies.

"If you wouldn't mind, it's our second honeymoon, so we don't want to be disturbed. No newspapers. And we won't need much in the way of housekeeping either."

Rosa's eyes went wide and her jaw dropped.

I hadn't told her that part of the plan, and I couldn't help but smile at her expression. I had been concentrating on the way over to make sure we weren't followed, so I hadn't been able to fill her in yet. That's another reason, why it was essential she not talk to anyone and risk blowing our cover.

I pulled her into my side and whispered in her ear. "Close your mouth, sweetheart." I tapped her lower jaw. "And don't look so shocked."

She shivered. "I thought we were business executives. Co-workers," she whispered back.

"No one would believe that in your outfit."

ST. LOUIS SECRETS

She glanced down at her figure and nodded.

That wasn't the reason, but it was a good enough excuse. The problem was that co-workers wouldn't be sharing a suite. I needed a reason to be in the same room, and still have enough room where we weren't on top of each other. Although... My mind started imagining that, and I knew I was in trouble. I had to focus and get us to safety before I could breathe easy. Deputies were posted around the hall and would watch for suspicious activity. I didn't like being out in the open. The hotel lobby and grand hall felt too exposed. I needed to rely on my security team to research locations and suggest a temporary safe house until a more permanent one became available. We also needed to remain close to the federal courthouse to meet with the Assistant US Attorney. He'd be prosecuting the case. I didn't know St. Louis as well as I should in order to pick the location myself. I had to rely on my team and their expertise. Not that it was easy for me. I had trouble letting go of control. I was a feet-on-the-ground kind of Chief Deputy, which is why those who worked with me in Texas respected and trusted the decisions I made. I didn't have the same rapport with those here in St. Louis. At least not yet.

Rosa managed to extricate herself from my arms without making it look like she was angry, but I could tell she was. I frowned. I hadn't considered the possibility that she might be uncomfortable with the situation. With all the sexual heat between us, I thought playing a couple wouldn't be difficult to pull off. She stood slightly apart from me looking lost, almost sad. Had I caused that? I rubbed my chest not liking how that made me feel. The desk clerk slid over some papers and I scribbled my fake signature. She smiled and handed me the room keys.

"Oh Todd, can you take up the Connor's luggage?"

The man at the concierge desk bounced over with a cart. My jaw ticked.

Rosa's eyes lit up and I scowled. What was the woman plotting? She was a Lorenzo after all. Todd started wheeling the cart over to what I assumed was the freight elevator.

"I'll meet you at the suite. Feel free to take your time."

I sprinted over to him and jumped in front of the cart. He pulled on the cart so it wouldn't run me over. Todd grunted with the effort. While Rosa's luggage was light, mine was not. I had brought a lot of electronic equipment with me.

"Sorry sir. Is there a problem?"

"Can't we all fit into an elevator together?"

"It might be a little cramped. You'd probably be more comfortable traveling in your own car."

My eyes narrowed.

"Or not," he said.

I wasn't about to let my gear out of my sight. Since I had been insistent, he changed directions and we took a more elegant elevator up to our floor.

He opened the double doors to our suite and put the luggage just inside the doorway. Todd looked like he might offer to show us around until he noticed my stern expression.

"Uh. I'll just let you get settled in. If you need anything… Anything at all, don't hesitate to call."

He gave Rosa a nod and she smiled.

I used my body to back him out of the room. The kid took the hint and nearly tripped on his way out. I shoved a twenty in his hand just before slamming the door in his face. When I turned, I caught Rosa blowing him a kiss.

"What the hell are you doing?"

"Being friendly," she shrugged.

"Well, I could use a little less of that."

"No problem where you're concerned," she said under her breath.

I ignored the comment and unzipped my bag. I found the file with our temporary identities and handed Rosa's file to her. There was a zipper pocket that contained two gold rings.

ST. LOUIS SECRETS

"Wow. You shouldn't have," she slid the ring on her finger. "Could they have come up with cheaper wedding bands?" Rosa asked as I slid the matching band on my finger.

She scanned the file briefly and then glanced around the room.

"I notice there's only one bed."

I grinned. "We're married."

"Even some married couples sleep in separate beds."

"Not in my marriage."

"You do realize this is a fake marriage," she put her hands on her hips and glared. "Exactly how realistic do you expect this to be?"

I was just about to tell her she didn't need to worry, I'd be sleeping on the couch when a vase from one of the shelves flew past me and shattered on the wall.

"What in tarnation? We have to pay for that."

I quickly strode over to Rosa and put her in a bear hug so she couldn't grab anything else. She fought like a cat in heat. Her claws came out and she scratched, kicked, and swore up a storm. It was like trying to hold a greased pig. I guarded the family jewels so she wouldn't nail me in her attempt to get free.

"Little filly, you best settle down right now."

"Or what, Tex?"

"It's Taz."

I knew she was poking fun. My Texan drawl would come out from time to time. Usually when aggravated, which was often around Rosa.

After a full minute of squirming, she gave up, growing limp in my arms.

"If I let you go, do you promise to behave?"

"Fine. If you want an obedient wife. I'll play along."

I didn't trust her, but it's not like I could hold her like this forever. I loosened my arms until she could stand on her own. Backing up, I glanced at the broken vase. I picked up the larger chunks tossing them in the bin. After a few minutes of cleaning, I decided housekeeping would have to sweep or vacuum up the rest. Rosa stomped to the bedroom and stared at the divider. It was an eight-foot wall that separated the living room and bedroom. By her demeanor, she was clearly frustrated. Maybe it was the lack of a door separating the rooms or the situation in general. Who knew with her? I watched as she investigated the walk-in closet and then marched over to the dresser. She started opening and slamming the drawers shut.

"Easy on the furniture," I said. I didn't want her to damage anything else.

"The drawers were stuck, pendejo."

"You can put your stuff away wherever you like," I said walking back into the living room. "But remember we are sharing this space, so keep the mess to a minimum. The last place was a pig stye."

She popped her head around the dividing wall and glared. If looks could kill, I would have died on the spot.

An angry barrage of Spanish words blasted me. I heard the words pig and skin somewhere in the mix and decided, it was probably better not knowing the exact translation. I knew some Spanish, but I wasn't fluent, and certain phrases eluded me. The conversation ended with her slamming the door to the bathroom.

My stomach took that opportunity to growl loudly. We had missed dinner.

"I'll just get us some room service," I said. "You want anything?"

"Vete al diablo," she responded.

I grinned. She told me to go to hell. Yeah, she was a firebrand alright. This was going to be an interesting couple of weeks.

I called my team while Rosa freshened up in the bathroom.

It took longer than I wanted, but there were too many things that needed to be addressed. I was skilled at seeing the big picture and coordinating all the moving pieces. That's why I was given the job as Chief Deputy. I probably should have handed off more responsibilities to others on the team. I just didn't know them that well, except for Huck. I had worked with him back in Texas. His real name was Tom Sawyer, but everyone called him Huckleberry or Huck for short. He was quite the character.

"Everyone has their stations. Get to it." I said.

Several affirmatives in various forms responded and I disconnected.

One thing I knew for certain was that Rosa's protection was critical to this case. I wanted to limit the number of people who knew of her whereabouts, which meant I wouldn't be switching guard duty with one of my deputies. I was with her 24x7 until the trial was over. I'd handle her personally. I grinned, thinking what snappy remark she'd have if I told her that. The bottom line was we couldn't have any more screw-ups, otherwise I'd be out of a job. The drug lord had already weaseled out of the murder charges in state court. Luís' political contacts and money had somehow swung the jury in New Mexico. He claimed his shooting of the man was in self-defense. Somehow there were no witnesses at one of Santa Fe's largest drug busts ever. The sicarios that made deals for federal protection had been looking elsewhere at the time. It was way too convenient if you asked me. No one within twenty feet would testify against Luís.

The undercover detective César Ramirez, going by the alias of Cruz Diaz had been in another part of the warehouse at the time. I had hoped that his or Rosa's testimony might ensure that Luís do prison time for the shooting. Even the sniper's testimony wasn't good enough for the jury. The locals in Santa Fe knew Luís Lorenzo's reputation as a philanthropic pillar of the community. They thought the drug charges at his nightclub, Club Cuervo, were all just a setup. At least that is how the defense attorney had spun it. Maybe the jury was blackmailed, or bribed. We were still investigating, but we hadn't found any evidence of jury tampering. That case was supposed to be a slam dunk. It's why it had been rushed through the court system. With the amount of evidence against Luís, the prosecution thought they had it in the bag. But Luís had hired a slick lawyer, and it had paid off. That's why the federal indictment for drug trafficking was taking place in St. Louis. He didn't have the same pull here. Since the drugs had traveled by land and sea internationally from Colombia through the Gulf of Mexico, and through multiple states and cities including St. Louis, it was decided to try him in the U.S. District Court for the Eastern District of Missouri. We needed to convict him on federal charges, or the bastard was going to get away scot-free.

There was a soft knock at the door.

"Room Service."

"Hang on," I said through the door. I glanced at the bathroom. The door was still closed. What was taking her so long?

A woman came in with a cart.

"Where would you like it set up sir?"

I pointed to the dining table. She nodded and set the trays down. I tipped her and she left.

I lifted off one of the covers and the aroma of peppered steak and roasted potatoes made my eyelids nearly flutter. I couldn't wait to dig in.

"Where are your manners?" My conscience said, ringing in my ears with my mother's voice.

I glanced at the bathroom door and grumbled.

I banged on it hard, rattling its hinges.

"Come out already. I want to eat."

There was no response from inside.

"Rosa," I said softening my tone, "Are you ok?"

I started to panic. My mind swirled with possibilities. She might kill me if I came in there and she was undressed, but at the same time, it was my duty to protect her. What if she had fallen or hurt herself? I debated for about three seconds before busting down the door.

Rosa wasn't in there.

ST. LOUIS SECRETS

Where was she hiding? It's not like the hotel room offered many places to go. It was a two-room suite, with a closet, a small dining area, a living room, and a bathroom. When I was done scouring the place, my blood ran cold. She wasn't here.

Somehow, she had managed to slip out when I was on the call. I didn't understand why she would run now. Rosa had been in custody for six months. Was it our heated discussion before the call? I knew she was angry, but this was reckless even for her.

I shook her luggage onto the bed to see if she had taken anything that might give me a clue where she was heading. Her jewelry and money were still there. That was a good sign at least. I needed to take that back from her at some point. I hadn't bothered earlier because all it would have done was start a fight and delay when we didn't have the time. Normally I wouldn't shy from a fight. I enjoyed pushing her buttons and bantering back and forth. I thought she felt the same. We might have plenty of differences between us, but in that, we matched. Both of us had explosive tempers and preferred a fight over silence.

Grabbing my gun and the key card, I charged for the elevators. Since she left wearing heels, stairs wouldn't be her friend.

Todd stood at the concierge desk. He took a step back when I approached. I probably had a nasty scowl on my face because his eyes got wide. I couldn't help that I didn't like the man or the way his sight lingered on Rosa's cleavage, and backside. Although if I were honest, the guy would have to be dead not to notice her assets.

"Mr. Connor. Can I help you with something?"

"I'm looking for Mrs. Connor. Have you seen her?"

"She's in the Grand Hall at the bar."

He pointed to the blonde chatting up the bartender and my breath whooshed out of me. I stomped over to her. I wanted to wring her neck. Of all the stupid, idiotic things to do. Why would she never listen to me? Didn't she realize the danger?

She laughed loudly at some joke the bartender had told her. Relief flooded me that she was all right. Not that it soothed my anger.

"I thought I told you not to talk to strangers?" I whispered in her ear through gritted teeth.

Surprisingly Rosa didn't flinch.

"But he's not a stranger. This is Matt. He's been telling me about all the sights in the city. I have a list of must-hits for our vacation."

"Do I have to tie you up?" I whispered. My words were harsh, but my hand moved up her back gently.

She leaned back. "Oh, don't be like that Jim," she giggled. "You'd enjoy that way too much."

At least she had read the file on our aliases. I was Jim Connor and she was my wife, Susan.

Matt had walked away to serve another customer. I glanced around the room. There weren't that many people here at this hour on a weekday.

"Susan, honey, our room service will be getting cold upstairs."

"She leaned back against my chest, blinking dark curly lashes up at me.

"I needed a drink."

"We could have ordered one to be sent up."

"Like you would have let me," she sighed. "I needed to get away from you. Ok. You frustrate me."

"Back at you," I replied.

It's like we really were married.

My phone vibrated and I glanced at the message.

'WTF Chief? Why didn't you tell me that you'd be in the bar? I was doing a perimeter search.'

I rubbed my eyes. None of the others on my team would call me out like that, but I had worked with this one in Houston.

'Plans change Huck. Adapt.'

'FU. She ditched you.'

ST. LOUIS SECRETS

'Report.'

Huck was my POC while I was inside and couldn't be on the radio without blowing my cover. I didn't want to admit that he was right. He'd be razzing me about this later, weeks from now when the threat was over.

'Perimeter clear. Nothing suspicious. But you need to lock her down.'

I agreed. The trouble was without duct-taping her to a chair or physically sitting on her, that was going to be nearly impossible.

"Let's finish your drink upstairs, sweetheart." I grabbed her glass and slid the bartender some cash.

She glared at me but allowed me to escort her to the elevator. Todd was paying way too much attention to our interaction. He averted his eyes when I glared at him. Todd might become a problem. I wanted some intel on him. I made a mental note to have someone at the office do a background check. He could just be an overzealous and highly observant hotel employee, but I wanted to make sure.

Once I got us settled back in the hotel room, I heated our meals in the microwave. I set the table finding the domestic routine soothing. Calm settled over me. The adrenaline always ran high when we were out in the open. It was too easy for things to go wrong, too many variables. There was only so much I could do if someone was really determined to take her out. I was confident in my abilities, but I knew the risk. I had made a rookie mistake not contacting my deputies as soon as I noticed her missing. My mind had been distracted. Rosa distracted me. My nickname Taz had been earned over the years. At times, I could go Tasmanian Devil when riled up or backed into a corner. Rosa excelled at doing just that.

"Earlier I was teasing you about sharing the bed. Is that what made you so upset?"

She sighed and stared at the food, getting cold once again in front of her. She sipped her cocktail. "My nerves are frayed. Ok. I'm sorry I took it out on you. I know you're just doing your job."

Rosa glanced around the suite. She eyed the bathroom door, tilting her head. It was hanging by its hinges. I'd have to fix that later. Her gaze continued to the bedroom. "Where will you sleep?"

"I'll take the couch in the living room."

She eyed it suspiciously. "I don't think you'll fit on that thing."

Rosa might be right. I'd probably hang off the bottom, but it didn't matter. I wasn't here on holiday. I was here to work. I'd make do with the accommodations. The floor would be fine. It's not like I'd be getting much sleep.

ST. LOUIS SECRETS

The normal bad-ass superhero had been transformed into a geek.

"Well come along Clark Kent. Our hotel is waiting."

He grinned and the Taz I had spent months getting to know peeked through the facade. We spent our drive in silence. Taz's spine was ramrod straight. His eyes went everywhere at once. I wanted to say something to lighten the mood but I wasn't sure how Taz would react.

"There is to be no talking with anyone," Taz said when we arrived at the hotel.

I had been nervously playing with my new hair, twirling golden locks from my wig. I stopped mid-twirl and saluted him.

"Yes sir."

I knew it was flippant and uncalled for, but that's how I rolled. And something had to give. The overwhelming tension during the car ride had been almost unbearable. If I had to think seriously about my situation, I would start screaming and never stop. By Taz's exasperated sigh, he was growing tired of my attitude. Right back at you buddy. I wanted this over too.

He pulled up to the curb and handed his keys to the valet. I needed help getting out of the car and I hated it. Waiting for him to come around to my door felt like an eternity. I couldn't move fast and it aggravated me to no end. I wanted to swear in Spanish, but one look at Taz and I bit my lip. I wasn't the only one frustrated.

"Are we supposed to be executives at some conference?" I asked as we walked toward a very large historic building. I noticed a sign that said St. Louis Union Station Hotel.

"Hush," he said as the doorman opened the door for us. I frowned. Thanks for not answering my question pendejo. I kept the remark to myself, but I had to bite my tongue, to bottle it in. Taz should have given me a clue about our cover, or at the very least given me a name. Was that too much to ask? They had printed up a new ID for me. That much I knew. He just refused to

Chapter 4

Rosa

I woke to an electric whizzing sound and blinked up into the sunlight peeking through the hotel curtains. I threw a pillow at the sound. It bounced off some guy on a short ladder. He was using a cordless screwdriver to put up surveillance cameras.

"Does he have to do it at this hour?" I complained to Taz.

"It's after 11, sweetheart."

I glanced at the clock and groaned. This bed had been way too comfortable and I had slept hard. I climbed out of the softest bed imaginable and stretched, noticing the sound had stopped.

Both men were looking in my direction.

I shuffled my way to the bathroom half awake. After doing my business, I glanced in the mirror with horror. Wearing the wig yesterday had flattened my hair and it stuck up in odd places. I had the worst bedhead imaginable. No wonder they had stared at me. Even my thin nightie had bunched and twisted leaving it in wrinkles. I found a robe on the back of the door and put on the wig I had left on the counter. I'd have to fix my own hair at some point, but at least if I had the wig on, there was a chance Taz would let me out of the room. Last night had been a reprieve from the daily monotony. I needed to explain that for my sanity's sake, he had to allow me out once in a while. Even prisoners got one hour of recreation a day, and I needed my sunshine. Maybe I'd finally be able to use that swimsuit, I had demanded as a necessity. This place had to have a pool and a jacuzzi. I brushed my teeth and put on my makeup and felt somewhat presentable minus clothes, but the robe would do for now. I ignored the men as I exited and made my way to our makeshift kitchen, a counter with a coffee pot, and a tray of snacks. I selected one of the pods for the coffee machine and pressed the button.

"What's for breakfast?" I asked.

"The room service menu is over there," he pointed. "I've already eaten."

I glanced at his bloodshot eyes. I knew the couch would be uncomfortable. The man looked like he hadn't gotten a wink of sleep.

After my first cup of coffee, my eyes could finally focus. Taz was on a call with the office. This was my chance. I went to corner Sam. I stood behind him as he was climbing down the ladder. He bumped into me and the gear he was holding clattered to the floor.

"Shoot," he said.

I helped him look for screws that bounced onto the carpet and rolled under the bed.

"I got you something," Sam whispered in my ear.

I grinned, thinking of the last time.

He pointed to the edge of the bed. I sneaked a peek between the mattress and the box spring. It was a newspaper. I frowned. That was one of the items Taz had on his list of things I wasn't allowed. Taz said I might see something in the paper and get upset. I thought it was one more way he could control my life.

"Page 3," he said quietly.

I nodded and stood up. I'd take it into the bathroom and read it later.

He glanced over his shoulder. "It's important," Sam whispered. "Your safety depends on it."

Intriguing. Why was he keeping this from Taz? He was still on the phone, scowling at whatever was being said.

"Thanks again for retrieving Nana's necklace."

Sam grinned. "About that."

I knew what he was going to say, so I silenced him, pressing my fingers to his lips.

His eyebrows raised.

I leaned forward and whispered in his ear.

"I might need another favor."

He tilted his head.

"A burner."

Sam shook his head. "Out of the question. It's completely against the rules."

"I didn't tell on you. Taz has no idea it was you who got me the necklace from the Luís' seizure stash."

Yeah, I might have been emphasizing his misstep as a bargaining chip. What's a little blackmail among friends?

He licked his lips. I could see his Adam's apple bob up and down. I made the guy nervous. I blinked up at him.

"Come on Sam. Please." I begged.

He cleared his throat and took a step back. Taz had hung up the call and was standing behind me.

I turned around and smiled. I was trying for innocence and probably epically failing. Sam was moving quickly gathering his gear and getting the hell out of Dodge. I watched him leave the hotel room and I wished I could go with him. To be stuck with Taz and his mood swings was not going to be fun.

"Why were you bothering Sam?"

"Is that his name?" I asked.

There was no reason for Taz to know how close we had become.

"I was just asking where the video feed was going to see if I could get a copy. Maybe I'll put on a show." I loosened the belt on my robe, baring one shoulder and showing some leg. I still had my PJ's on so it didn't have the same effect as being nude underneath, but Taz reacted just the same. He closed my robe and tightened my belt for me.

"Put some clothes on," he said through gritted teeth. "And do it in the bathroom."

I grinned. Showtime for those watching would have to wait. His response told me the bathroom didn't have cameras.

I decided to poke the bear because I was bored, and let's be honest, it was in my nature. Plus, I had gotten a taste of freedom last night and I wanted more. I realized what had been missing in my life these past few months. I just needed to convince my jailer.

I had hung up my clothes in the closet late last night in my effort to accommodate his neat freak nature. Maybe that had provided me with a little goodwill. I flipped through my meager selection and sighed. There was nothing I wanted to wear, so I switched to searching the dresser drawers. Ah ha. Something bright and eye-catching. Perfect. Taz was playing with the laptop, probably ensuring the cameras worked perfectly. I stuck my tongue out at one, and I heard a chuckle from the next room.

After a quick shower, I put on my colorful swimsuit and matching coverup and marched into the living room. I took a seat on the couch and crossed my legs, flipping through the hotel magazine that was sitting on the table.

"What do you think you're doing?"

My eyebrow raised.

"Finding something to eat. There is quite a range of dining choices here. Do you remember Matt? He's the bartender from downstairs. Last night, he provided me with a few suggestions."

"What's with the outfit?"

I shrugged. "It's not like I'm naked." I rolled my eyes.

"Close enough," he mumbled.

I smiled and flipped the mostly transparent cover over my exposed leg.

"Is that better Marshal?"

ST. LOUIS SECRETS

He grumbled some incoherent response and went back to his computer.

After paging through the magazine, I decided I wanted to go to the pool and get some sun.

"I need some vitamin D. Maybe I can sit out by the pool for a bit."

He shook his head. "The pool is closed for the winter."

"What?" I threw my body back into the cushions. Dramatic I know, but I was upset.

"Is it under repair?"

"It's an outdoor pool."

Oh. From the pictures it looked like there was a glass dome covering it. I frowned. That was going to ruin my plans.

"It's the end of November. Why would you have thought the pool would be open?"

"From the picture." I showed him the magazine. "Well, this is useless." I grabbed the edge of my coverup and whipped it over my head.

"Woah. What are you doing?"

"Taking this thing off."

"Bathroom!" He commanded.

"Oh, don't be such a prude." I stormed off. I went into the bedroom and found some slacks and a blouse. Taz had turned on the TV, so I snuck the newspaper from under the bed and slipped it into the bag with the clothes.

"I'm going to take a nice long bubble bath," I said.

He didn't look at me, just grunted his approval while flipping through the stations. Not that I wanted his attention, but it ticked me off that he was ignoring me. I pulled the string on my bikini top and tossed it at his head. By the time he turned around, I was already inside the bathroom with the door locked.

Take that Taz.

I filled up the tub squeezing out nearly the last of my French lavender bubble bath. I had gotten it a few months back. I wondered if Taz would allow me to get a replacement bottle. He was probably angry enough to refuse. I put the toilet seat down to sit while I waited for the tub to fill. I flipped the newspaper to page 3. I found the article that Sam must have been referring to. The picture of the victim had me shivering despite the heat from the bathwater warming the room. It was José, one of Luís' sicarios. He had somehow gotten shot at a local convenience store. The journalist didn't mention that the guy was due to appear in federal court and had been in protective custody. I wonder if the feds killed that part of the story, or if the person who wrote the article didn't realize the connection to the Lorenzo case. José was supposed to testify against Luís. He had probably gotten a deal similar to mine, dismissal of all charges, in exchange for testimony. José had critical information for the prosecution. This must be a big blow for them. That meant my testimony was even more important now. It also meant I was an even greater target. I gulped. That must be the reason we moved locations. They thought I might be next.

    I slid into the bathwater trying to warm myself, but the shivering didn't stop. I was afraid. Luís was a madman. Just because I had never seen him kill anyone didn't mean I was oblivious to the clues around me. I knew exactly what he was capable of. He often had bloody shirts at the club. Luís would hand them to his sicarios to burn. I'd witnessed enough bodies wrapped in plastic, to have an unhealthy fear of saran wrap. I wondered if there was a name for my phobia. Maybe I'd ask my therapist when I finally settled into my forever home. That is if I made it through the trial in one piece. I still couldn't believe Luís had been acquitted of the murder charges back in Santa Fe. There must have been at least a half dozen men, maybe more that witnessed Luís pull the trigger and kill the truck driver during the drug bust. He even managed to sneak out of the police assault charges. I mean he shot a guy from SWAT. True the guy survived, but still. His lawyer had gotten those charges dismissed. Luís only had to pay a fine and community service for resisting arrest.

ST. LOUIS SECRETS

That's it. His PR team would probably spin the community service into something that made him look good instead of it being a punishment. Every time I thought about it I wanted to throw something. How had he weaseled out of it? I sighed, knowing the answer. It was his political contacts and PR team. The jury saw what the media printed about him being a businessman and how much he gave back to the community. They didn't know his true self like I did. At least in St. Louis, he didn't have the same level of contacts. His public relations pal wasn't going to be a problem here. The feds had learned their lesson. They made sure the firm he had used came under obstruction charges. It probably didn't mean much. A bunch of lawyers would battle it out and get rich. In any case, the damage had been done. At least the firm dropped Luís as a client. Although it was more than likely only temporary. It meant the federal court district had a chance. At least Luís' assets were frozen, and he had an ankle monitor. That must be driving my cousin nuts right about now. They were tracking his every move. Luís might have run back to Colombia if they hadn't done that. I finally gave up on the bath. It wasn't working. I wasn't relaxed at all. In fact, I was exactly the opposite. I didn't bother changing into my clothes. I walked back to the bedroom in a robe.

I needed to get out of this hotel. I felt like I was in a cage. I kept pacing back and forth, like some wild animal. Something was going to break inside my chest. I re-read the article from the paper and the tears threatened to fall. Taz took that moment to come into the bedroom to find me. At least he didn't say a word. Maybe he was learning. I wanted to rail at him, scream and curse but I knew this whole situation wasn't his fault. I got myself into this mess. I couldn't blame others for my own mistakes. Why had I trusted Luís? Why had I made that promise to his sister? He stared at the crumpled piece of newspaper clasped in my fist. He was going to ask for it. I knew it. There was no way I could get away with trying to hide the thing. Not now. I marched up to him and thrust the paper into his chest. He didn't move an inch, even though I put my whole weight into the shove. All it did was make his brow quirk in that adorable way that made me hate and want him equally. At least I could still surprise him somehow. He should be used to my attitude by now. I took a deep breath but it was no use. I was going to lose it. I rushed back into the bathroom slamming the door behind me. I refused to let him see me cry.

Chapter 5

Taz

The shower and fan were blasting in the bathroom. I knew Rosa was sobbing. I could still hear it. The woman didn't do anything quietly. The fact that she was trying to mask the sound at all said a lot. Rosa usually didn't give a rat's ass what anyone thought of her, especially not me. The fact that she was also not a woman to cry didn't go unnoticed. I took the wadded-up paper and headed to the dining room table. I straightened the article, flattening the torn edges until it was smooth. It was about José. One of Luís' sicarios. The one that died in a 'robbery gone wrong'. I knew that was bullshit. There was no robbery. It was a hit. The Lorenzos were eliminating threats.

What must be going through her mind right now? She hid her fear, but Rosa wasn't stupid. She knew exactly what this meant and the implications. I had kept this from her on purpose. That's also why I had asked Sam to put a device on the TV that restricted news channels from coming through. It wasn't just for legal reasons to keep her testimony untainted. I simply didn't want her to panic. Witnesses under emotional distress often made poor decisions in the heat of the moment. How the hell did she get hold of a newspaper? I'd have to call the front desk and emphasize the importance of this. Rosa's life had been hard. I had read about it in her files, and the few things she let slip over meals. Rosa didn't need this on top of everything else she had been through. I rubbed my palms over my eyes and sighed.

I knew how upset Rosa had been these past few months, and it seemed like the closer we got to her testimony, the more vulnerable she became. It ramped up my need to protect her. It was instinct, I kept trying to tell myself. A wounded woman with a tough-as-steel attitude masking a tender heart. That got to me. She was ballsy and brash. My mother and sister both had that same fiery attitude. From the moment we met, there was something about Rosa that set something off within me. The fact that she was a Lorenzo was the only thing holding me back. Well, that and compromising work ethics. I needed to remember her family. Even if she was fighting against them at every turn. She was a witness. A job. Nothing more.

I dialed the hotel's concierge and put the phone on speaker while checking the camera feeds that Sam had installed.

"Good afternoon, Mr. Connor."

It was Todd. Did this guy ever leave the hotel?

"Todd," I said trying to keep the disdain from my voice. "I don't want any newspapers sent to the room. Is that understood? No media whatsoever."

"Of course. Sir." Todd cleared his throat.

I could almost picture him at his desk downstairs, face red, his whole body rigid just like he was when I caught him staring at Rosa when we checked in.

"Make sure that doesn't happen again."

I didn't say or else, but the threat hung in the air.

"Um," he squeaked. "Did you and Mrs. Connor need something set up? Perhaps for tonight?"

"No. The missus and I will be dining in this evening."

"How about a couples massage after dinner? I could send up a masseuse."

Rosa stepped out of the bathroom.

"A massage?" She asked.

ST. LOUIS SECRETS

Her eyes were red and swollen but she had put on fresh makeup to cover most of it.

I took the phone off speaker.

"If the missus wants a massage, I'll be the one to put my hands on her, not some stranger."

"O-of course. Sir. I- Uh. Sorry. I didn't mean to."

"That will be all." I hung up on him trying to apologize.

Rosa's mouth quirked. She thought I was bluffing. I really wasn't. If she wanted a massage, I would give her one. I could keep it professional. Somehow. I knew the women needed to relax. From the rigid way she stood, Rosa looked ready to break.

She carefully walked over, brushing against me as she reached over to grab the phone I had just hung up. She did it slowly and deliberately. I think in her own way she was daring me to stop her. But I didn't. Rosa dialed room service.

"A fifth of rum and some fruity liquors, and the best tequila you have," she said.

"What are you doing?"

She gave me raised eyebrows and turned away ignoring me, like I had done to her earlier.

I sighed.

"Food? Hmm. Yeah. I guess so. How about some tortilla chips and the hottest salsa you got." Rosa gave the room number to the person she was talking to and hung up.

I didn't want to address the no liquor rule, instead I'd tackle the elephant in the room.

"You shouldn't have read that," I said softly.

"Really," she whipped around. "That's what you're going with?"

I sighed, guessing I owed her the truth. "I thought it would only make you worried."

"Well, I am." Rosa pointed to the paper. "This was El Lobo Rojo."

"We don't know that for sure."

She put her hands on her hips and raised her brows.

I grimaced. Yeah. I knew the probability of it being her cousin too. That's the only reason we left that apartment. Staying at this hotel until the trial would cost a fortune. Normally I couldn't justify that type of expense, but the circumstances were dire.

"Room service said they would bring it up in about thirty minutes. You can get the door. I'm going to lie down."

Rosa was still in her robe. The locks on her dark hair were wet and wild. She hadn't put back on the blonde wig. Even with all that was going on, she was still trying to follow my rules or at least most of them.

"Don't you dare turn them away," she warned me.

"I won't."

She huffed and crawled under the covers, robe and all. I wondered if I looked as guilty as I felt. I should have told her. Rosa had a right to know. Protocol and all be damned.

After the alcohol and chips arrived, I sat with her at the dining table. She proceeded to get completely shit-faced. Rosa still hadn't dressed. It was unnerving. That single belt was all that prevented her from exposing herself to the room. I knew I was the only one physically there, but others were watching on the cameras. We had constant video recordings in case security was compromised. I wasn't taking any chances. It also meant I needed to remain on my best behavior. I wanted to say something about her attire, but it was as if she was testing me. Rosa glared every time I focused for overly long on her robe. I ended up joining her in a few shots, in her effort to polish off the liquor.

"Waste not," she said pouring shots for us both. "There are poor people all over the world right now. Isn't that what you Americans always say?"

ST. LOUIS SECRETS

"You know that only applies to food. Liquor doesn't go bad. And besides you're not American."

"I'm South American, and I rather like that custom."

We clinked glasses and pounded the shots.

"You know you're pretty hot for a cop," she slurred the words. "And trust me I've known plenty."

I wanted to ask what she meant by that, but Rosa walked away from the table. Well, walk was a strong word for the serpentine way she staggered to the couch. She fell and the robe split open. I joined her on the couch, quickly flipping the robe closed, not wanting any of my deputies to get a free show. The trouble was it broke that proximity barrier I had managed to keep while we were at the dining room table. Rosa took that as an invitation and launched herself at me. She pinned me to the couch with her body. It took tremendous effort to control my movements. Rosa felt too right in my arms. She kissed up my neck and I groaned trying to extricate myself from her octopus arms. My ethics and body fought one another. If I were honest with myself, I wasn't trying all that hard. I spent more time keeping her robe in place than pushing her away. My phone buzzed and my senses returned.

"Stop." I managed to say.

I picked her up and set her to my side. She looked confused. Her hair was in disarray and her makeup smeared. I must have a healthy bit of her lipstick on my face, by the clear lack of it on Rosa's lips.

I glanced at my phone.

'You need any help in there?'

I sighed. It was Huck.

'FU.'

'Seems like it was heading to be a FH.'

I shook my head at the camera. I knew he was correct. I might have wanted to take things further with Rosa. Not that I'd let my wants come between me and what was right.

"I don't understand." Rosa slurred. "I thought you were starting to like me."

I was, but I wasn't going to muddy the waters with feelings.

"Come on. Let's get you to bed." I pulled her to her feet.

Her eyes lit up, clearly hopeful.

"Keep that dirty mind of yours in check. You're going to bed alone."

"What fun is that?" She responded.

I chuckled.

When her head hit the pillow, she all but passed out. I debated loosening the robe so she would be more comfortable sleeping, but ended up just putting the soft blanket on top and tucking her in tight.

Another message came through my phone when I sat down on the couch in the living room.

'I've nominated you for sainthood.'

Oh, Huck. I shook my head at the camera. He cracked me up. Always the character. That was for sure. He always added comic relief when I needed it most.

Chapter 6

Rosa

I was in hangover hell. At least no one was here with power tools. Taz was padding around the hotel room quietly. He had kept the drapes closed. Thank goodness.

"Tengo un guayabo terrible." I rolled over and groaned.

"Here take this." Taz stood beside the bed, handing me ibuprofen and Gatorade.

I sat up gingerly. My stomach felt like I was trapped on one of those spinning carnival rides. I hadn't gotten this drunk in a very long time. Even at Club Cuervo, I'd do shots during or after work, but never to this extent. I always had to keep my wits about me when dealing with my cousin Luís. I took a step toward the bathroom and lost my balance. Taz was there to catch me. The room went off-kilter. Great. I had a hangover, and I was still drunk. My life sucked right now. The only thing that would make it worse, is if I threw up.

"Did you need anything to eat?" Taz asked. "I got room service."

Maybe soaking up some of the alcohol might help. After a quick trip to the bathroom, making sure to avert my eyes from the mirror, I decided to attempt breakfast. Maybe something light like toast. Yeah. I could handle that with no problem. Taz was standing there at the bathroom door waiting to escort me to the dining room table. It was cute how he was trying to take care of me. A smirk formed on my lips before I could help it. I hadn't had someone take care of me in I don't know how long. Taz whisked the silver dome off the platter. When I saw the runny eggs, well-done hashbrowns, and greasy sausages, my stomach lurched. I realized too late, that I had made a horrible mistake. One glance was enough.

    I sprinted back to the bathroom, making it to the toilet just in time. I heaved my guts out for the next few minutes while Taz leaned over holding my hair. He rubbed my back gently, telling me repeatedly it was ok. I wanted to scream at him, that in fact, it was not ok. Not remotely considering the position I was in. However, I was too busy with my face in the toilet. I refused to look Taz in the eyes. I was wallowing in self-pity and embarrassment. I was a grown woman, nearly forty years old, and my babysitter slash bodyguard had watched me get black-out drunk and was caring for me in the aftermath. I felt like some wayward teen. Why did he have to see me like this, at my absolute worst? I finally couldn't take it anymore. My humiliation was complete. Pride forced me to my feet. On weak knees, I forced my body to move, backing him out of the bathroom. I closed the door, wanting nothing other than to clean myself up and pretend it never happened.

    When I finally made an appearance after some time, I had taken a shower, washed my face, brushed my teeth and gotten dressed in the clothes I had set out on the counter the day before. I blinked at the sun's rays streaming in from the living room. I put a hand over my eyes. Taz jumped up to close the curtains. I slowly sat on the couch. The next thing I knew, Taz had placed a hot cup of coffee in my hands. He came back with a large tray with one of those silver domes on top. He presented it like a server at a high-end restaurant. I shook my head not wanting a repeat of what had just happened earlier. But he swiped off the lid anyway. It had saltine crackers arranged in a smiley face on the plate. A bubble of laughter came out before I could help it. It was incredibly sweet. I smiled gratefully and proceeded to nibble on the crackers and take small sips of the coffee.

"Here's some more Ibuprofen and Gatorade when you're ready."

"You're pretty nice you know that."

"Shh. Don't tell anyone," He grinned.

"I feel like I owe you an apology," I said, my eyes closing. "I normally don't do things like this."

"Get drunk, or get sick after."

I shrugged. "Both, believe it or not."

"I do. Believe you that is."

"Why? You have absolutely no reason to."

"Well considering I've known you for six months. I think I've gotten to know your character."

I snorted. "Character?"

"What you're made of. Why you do what you do."

"I haven't told you a thing about me."

"Maybe not, but you can tell a lot about a person by how they carry themselves, what they find important. What they spend their time doing."

"I've been petty and demanding. My temper runs hot, and I tend to lose it regularly. Why are you defending me?"

"Because I think you're in a crappy situation and you've made the best of it."

I was shocked that he felt this way. It was as if he saw me as a person not just as a witness that would get him something his side desperately needed.

"Do you think people can change?" I asked.

"Not really," he shook his head. "I think that what you have inside shines through. Situations arise and your true self whether good or bad is magnified by the circumstances."

My shoulders slumped. That's what I figured. I might be an ok person for a criminal. But he'd always see me like that. Not that we'd know each other long-term. After my testimony, they would throw me somewhere and forget about me. It was just nice for a moment to think he might be different. But I knew better. He had a cop's mentality. Taz saw things in black and white, and my whole world was gray. A moral compass was something I didn't possess. I didn't have the luxury. He probably thought I was a lost cause. Taz was just a good guy offering his pity. I wanted to tell him I didn't need it. But instead of getting defensive which was my usual MO, my curiosity won out.

"So why do you protect witnesses that do bad things?"

"I have a code, an oath I've sworn to uphold."

"Would you believe I have something similar?" I asked.

Taz looked at me like he was trying to work out a puzzle. "You don't say? Want to talk about it?"

Did I? It would feel good to share a little. Maybe I was vain and didn't want Taz to see me in a bad light.

"I'm loyal."

"To your family?"

Of course, he'd go in that direction. He wanted information about the Lorenzos. This was a perfect opportunity to get me to spill family secrets while I was feeling weak and vulnerable.

My face hardened. "I'm loyal to those I care about."

"Testifying doesn't violate that loyalty?"

"Against Luís? Ha. He's a psychotic asshole."

"But he is family."

"Unfortunately, you can't choose your relatives."

"So you are saying some of your family is ok?"

There were those in my family I would die for. Like my cousin Ramón. Not that I'd give Taz those details. That would be dangerous. If he or the feds knew about the promise I had made to his mother Maria, they could use it against me. Or the fact that Ramón was not just related to one drug empire but two. Certain secrets needed to remain buried, no matter what the cost.

ST. LOUIS SECRETS

"What about your family, Taz?" I asked. "Got any Bennett family members you'd rather not see around the holidays?"

His back stiffened. I seemed to hit a nerve.

"We were talking about you."

"I'll make you a deal. I'll share something if you do."

There was a long pause in the conversation as we stared at one another. I finally looked away. Taz must not be in a sharing mood.

"Fine," he sighed.

A thrill ran through me. Getting background on this man seemed like discovering hidden treasure. I doubted he shared much with others.

"You start," I said.

"My mom and dad are divorced, so family holidays are a bit of a battlefield. Growing up, both families celebrated together, so the kids wouldn't have to choose. Holidays were always chaos."

"I can just imagine. How many siblings do you have?"

"One brother and one sister. How about you?"

"No brothers or sisters. I'm an only child, which is a rare thing to find in Colombia, but it's because both my parents died young. I grew up mostly with my aunts and uncles bouncing from house to house. Holidays were always fun." I couldn't help smiling. "Most of the family tended to behave especially when the grandparents were there. I loved Nana Teresa. She was my great-grandmother. Nana was hilarious. Anyone causing trouble and she'd start waving her cane around like she was dueling an imaginary demon. She'd swear she would do God's work and smack the devil out of anyone acting up. And it wasn't just idle threats. She would too. And no one was off limits. Everyone was scared of the woman. Big, strong men would run from her." I laughed. "Everyone in the family thought she was a little loca, but that woman loved fiercely. You couldn't find someone more loyal to the ones she loved."

"I take it you were on that list the way you talk about her."

I grinned. "I might have been one of her favorites. She said it often enough to anyone who'd listen."

"I thought grandparents were never supposed to have favorites."

"Not in the Lorenzo family. Competition is encouraged. But Nana knew when you weren't being sincere. Anyone who tried to sweet-talk her would fail miserably. The woman had tons of money, and people always asked for things. Except me. I didn't come from money, even though I was born a Lorenzo. Maybe that's why she was constantly showering me with gifts. Luís hated how close the two of us were. Whenever he would complain, she'd tell him he'd get exactly what he deserved, which was usually nothing."

"So testifying against Luís is no hardship?" He asked.

"It's an absolute pleasure."

"What about the rest of the family?"

I glared. "That wasn't part of the agreement."

"But what if you are asked in court?"

"I will say I don't know."

"Is that the truth?"

I made my face blank and shrugged.

There were many things I wasn't willing to share, but I knew better. If I brought up Ramón that would just encourage the feds to seek him out. I was hoping he had dropped off their radar. Right now, no one thought he was important, and it was going to stay that way. Revealing just how much the boy meant to me would tip my hand. It wouldn't matter that the kid was barely involved in the business. They'd use his bloodline against him, and assume the worse. I needed to get to him, not just to warn him, but also because I knew how the kid thought. He was gullible and loyal. He idolized his Uncle Luís. Once I knew that Ramón was safe with the Mendozas, I could talk to him and make sure he didn't do anything stupid. I hadn't told him all the horrible things that Luís had done because I hadn't wanted to scare the kid. He didn't have the same kind of hard upbringing that the rest of us did. His mother had kept him sheltered. Ramón had a tender heart. He deserved a happy ending. I had done things I wasn't proud of to give him that life.

Taz said he didn't think people could change. Did that mean that the blood of a Lorenzo or a Mendoza was destined for crime? I don't know that I could convince someone who saw only black and white, that we aren't all bad. Or at least not as bad as Luís. Some of us just wanted to get away from it all. That's what I was hoping to do. I knew there was no happy ending for me. I had no illusions, no dreams of a fairy tale ending. But if I could save Ramón, then everything I'd done would somehow be worth it.

Chapter 7

Taz

Rosa glared at me from across the room. Our conversation the day before had done the opposite of what I wanted. I had hoped that by opening up, she would do the same. It had worked for a while, then she had clammed up tight. Whatever was going on in that mind of hers was making her not trust me. Not that most of the witnesses in protective custody were open books, but I thought Rosa had been different. In between swearing and throwing things, she had a warm heart and a sharp mind. It was almost as sharp as her wit. I enjoyed our conversations, even when they turned into fights.

Rosa rattled the page of the book she held with deliberation and slammed it down. I grinned. Only Rosa could figure out a way how to read loudly. There was a knock at the door. Rosa huffed and retreated to the bedroom. I checked my weapon and looked through the peephole. I knew what to expect. Todd had arrived with something I ordered the day before. It was a surprise for Rosa, the woman who carried the weight of the world on her shoulders. I opened the door, grabbed the package and bag from Todd's grip, flipped him some bills, and slammed the door in his face. It was over and done in seconds.

"This. Uh. Wah-" Todd said.

I watched him from the peephole looking flabbergasted. He picked up the bills that had fallen to the carpet and walked away with slumped shoulders. I was such a jerk. But Todd was far too nosey and I didn't want him to see things he shouldn't. Dealing with hotel management on broken decor and wall damage from mounting brackets and shelves for all the electronic equipment was not something I was prepared to deal with at the moment. Of course, we'd pay for everything when checking out, but right now I didn't need the hassle. It wasn't a priority. I set the boxes on the far side of the couch.

"Can I come out yet? Or are you still visiting with your boyfriend?"

"Ha. Ha. It was actually one of your boyfriends. But he's gone now."

Rosa joined me in the living room.

"I don't have a boyfriend," she said wistfully. Rosa walked to the window to stare outside at the cold and bleak cloudy day. "I haven't for quite a while."

I didn't want her to be sad. That's why I got her something. Rosa needed to be cheered up, and I was just the man to do it.

"Stop moping and get your pretty little behind over here."

Rosa turned her glare on me and stomped over to the couch. She huffed and sat down.

"What? I can't look out the window either. I'd be better off in prison."

"Quit your bellyaching and open up your present."

I put the giant box that I had been hiding from view on the coffee table in front of her.

Rosa's eyebrows rose.

"You got me a gift?"

She shifted in her seat. Her lips curled ever so slightly. Rosa was trying to fight off the smile, but I could tell she was pleased.

She bit her lip and untied the satin bow. Rosa lifted the lid and gasped. It was an elegant velvet evening gown in deep purple.

ST. LOUIS SECRETS

Rosa's favorite color. She pulled out the gown and stood, swirling it around.

"Dios mío. The fabric. It's so soft."

"There are two smaller boxes too." I placed them on the coffee table next to the dress box.

She placed the gown carefully back in the tissue and unwrapped the bows on the other two gifts. One held matching purple pumps, and the third box held a black faux fur shawl.

"This one feels like a blanket," she wrapped herself in it and closed her eyes.

"I could easily be content wearing this and nothing else."

I started imagining just that and I had to clear my throat.

"I don't think they would allow that at the restaurant."

Her eyes popped open and she sat up quickly.

"We can go out?"

I nodded.

"Not too far. It's right here at Union Station. It's out by the lake underneath the train shed. We have a reservation at Landry's Seafood House."

"When?"

I smiled.

"Tonight."

"Isn't it Thanksgiving?"

"Yes, it is."

She chewed on her lip. And her eyes teared up.

"Now don't be doing that," I said.

Rosa turned away wiping her eyes. "I'm sorry. It's just," she hiccupped. "I didn't expect you to be so nice."

"My Texas charm comes and goes. Better take it when you can get it."

She laughed and kissed my cheek. Rosa ran into the bedroom with the boxes.

"I'm going to try everything on right now. No changing your mind. I'm holding you to it."

ZIZI HART

"Do you want the lobster or crab? Or maybe a filet?"

"My mouth is watering right now. Everything sounds so good."

"Normally for Thanksgiving, they have a small menu, but I happen to know the chef, and they are willing to do me a favor, so sky's the limit."

"How about cocktails?"

"Are you sure you want a repeat of two nights ago?"

"That won't happen again. I can control myself."

A text message came through from Huck.

'Can you take a picture of what you're eating? Or better yet, bring me a doggy bag?'

I chuckled.

"What are you laughing about?"

"My team is complaining that they are hungry. They are just razzing me that we are having dinner and they are stuck watching."

"Can't they take a break?"

"They are keeping you safe."

"Aren't you already doing that?"

"Yeah. But I make the rules, and I say they stay until we get back to the hotel room."

"Tú eres el jefe."

"I am," I said grinning.

I knew she was being sarcastic about me being the boss, but I wasn't taking the bait.

Rosa shook her head and let out a sigh.

After ordering our meals, the fire and light show started and Rosa's eyes widened with excitement. We watched it from the window of the restaurant and seeing her smile made me realize how few times I had seen her do that in the last few months. I realized that while keeping her safe, I had overlooked an essential part of her well-being. For someone so vibrant and energetic, being stuck in one place must have been the equivalent of sensory deprivation.

When our meal arrived, Rosa's overwhelming enthusiasm was almost comical.

"You must try this," Rosa said, holding up her fork with some of her crab cake.

I had little choice but to take a bite or risk insulting her.

"Isn't that amazing?" She grinned.

Before I knew it, we were sharing our entire meal like that, describing every little detail like we were discovering the mysteries of the universe.

"Did you try the lobster tail? Dios mío. Deliciosa. It is so juicy and tender. My mouth has gone to heaven."

We had steak, crab, and lobster along with mixed vegetables, potatoes, and salad. We even shared dessert, not being able to decide between the New York cheesecake and the triple chocolate cake.

Rosa groaned with every bite. She took pleasure in everything she did.

"Do you want anything else?"

"I can't eat another bite. Everything was so good, but I'm about to explode."

"Isn't that the tradition? To go into a food coma after a huge Thanksgiving feast."

"I wouldn't know," she shrugged. "We don't have Thanksgiving in Colombia."

"Well, I'm glad that you were able to experience it with me. When we get back to the hotel, I have another tradition to share."

Her eyebrows rose.

I was hoping all this sharing might encourage her to give me more details about the Lorenzos. There would be a meeting with the AUSA; the Assistant US Attorney on Sunday for the upcoming trial and I wanted to get her talking. Plus, I really enjoyed getting to know her. She was genuine and sweet, underneath the loud, ballsy no-nonsense exterior.

"So, what is this tradition?" Rosa asked. "Does it involve clothes?" She grinned.

My eyebrows rose. Was she hitting on me? I chuckled. When wasn't she hitting on me? I had already sent my team home to spend time with their families. We weren't going anywhere, and with no one watching the camera feed, I felt a little more relaxed and willing to flirt back.

"Clothing is entirely optional," I said, almost daring her.

She chuckled. "I meant, can I put on pajamas? But I like how your mind works. Seafood makes you frisky and bold."

"Maybe it's just the company."

"And now you compliment. What happened to the real Taz? Are you his mischievous twin?"

I grinned. "Go change, and I'll get everything ready."

"Give me two minutes," she said and raced to the bedroom.

I slipped into a cotton t-shirt and thin sweatpants. Grabbing two pens and a notepad from the desk, I tore the pages into slips and waited.

She sprinted back in and came to a halt.

"I missed the strip show? That's just wrong. Plain wrong. What's a girl gotta do to get some entertainment around here?"

"If you want entertainment, I've got a game we can play."

Her eyebrows wiggled and she rubbed her hands together. "I like where this is going."

"Keep your mind out of the gutter."

She frowned. "What's the fun in that?"

ST. LOUIS SECRETS

"First, we write down all the things we are grateful for. Even the stuff we are angry about. Especially the stuff we are angry about." I pointed to the slips of paper on the coffee table.

"Boring," she blew a raspberry.

I ignored her.

"We take turns, sharing them with the room."

"You mean each other?"

"Well, in this case, it's just the two of us, but when I play the game with my family there are a lot of us. And remember this is after we have been fighting and arguing, so it's an opportunity to make amends by the end of the evening."

"You do this after dinner?"

"Yep."

"Then after everyone reads their gratitude list, each person gets a gift. Not a physical item, just a hug, or a promise. It's a way of thanking everyone for being in our lives and sharing the day together."

Rosa bit her lip. "Ok."

The two of us spent some time writing down a few things on the slips of paper.

"I'll begin," I said. "I'm grateful for a wonderful meal shared with an amazing woman with a great sense of humor and an incredible zest for life."

"Nana would say you are laying it on pretty thick."

"But I speak the truth."

Rosa licked her lips and picked up her slip of paper. "I'm grateful for the best meal I've had in a very long time. And the company didn't hurt either, even if he is a US Marshal."

"Ouch. It sounds like I was a burden to bear."

"Well, I wrote it before you quoted poetry to me."

"What does it really say?"

Rosa put the paper behind her back. It looked like there were only a few words on the slip. "I expounded on the basic premise."

"Hmm." I grinned. "Here's my next one. I'm grateful for Rosa's explosive outbursts and flying objects, they provide me with entertainment and exercise."

"Wow. I had no idea I sounded like an actress from a soap opera. And how exactly is thrown objects exercise?"

"A lot of this," I said as I animatedly showed her my duck-and-weave moves.

She laughed.

"Here's mine. I'm grateful for Taz's snoring because it tells me I'm not alone."

"I don't snore."

"Now who's fibbing?"

"Ok. I got another one." I swallowed. This was a personal share. It was the reason I was here on this case and why I took the St. Louis position. "I'm grateful for Rosa giving testimony to put El Lobo Rojo behind bars, and get justice for wrongs done to my family."

Rosa's eyes went wide. "Care to explain?"

"In a bit. It's your turn."

She licked her lips. "I'm grateful for being alive long enough to keep a promise. Luís will pay for the things he's done if it's the last thing I ever do."

"Sounds like we are both on the same page."

Rosa nodded. "I didn't know you had a history with my cousin."

"I don't. At least not directly. Unless you count socking him in the jaw at the drug bust."

Rosa grinned. "That was pretty awesome."

"It felt good too."

"So are you going to tell me what happened to your family? What did Luís do?"

My hands shook. It was the anger. The anger always wanted to come out. It would often bleed out into my personal life. It's why I hadn't dated in over a year. I needed to lock it away like I was putting it in a vault. I took a deep breath. In and out. In and out. Until my pulse slowed and I regained control. "My sister Brenda, she's the youngest of the three of us. She just turned twenty-two this summer. All her college friends wanted to do something fun over break last year. They decided on a trip to Santa Fe. They went to Club Cuervo. They got your bottle service."

Rosa's eyes closed. She must have known what was coming.

"The girl that was driving had a severe reaction to the drugs. She had a seizure while driving on the interstate. The car swerved and smashed into a truck."

"Your sister?"

"She was in the back seat. Brenda hadn't been taking any, but she had been drinking. There were four of them in the car."

"I remember reading about it in the paper," Rosa said.

I tried to keep my voice steady.

"Brenda's spine was damaged in the accident. She's in a wheelchair. The doctors say she won't ever walk again, or ride horses." I turned away from Rosa not wanting her to see the emotion on my face. "God, my sister loves horses" I blew out a breath. "The doc said Brenda was lucky. Two of the girls were killed in the accident. Brenda was one of the two that survived. I bet this Thanksgiving she'll be saying she's grateful. Brenda's like that. Always positive, despite everything that's happened to her. I can't stand seeing her like that." I turned to face Rosa. "All I want to do is kill the person responsible."

My eyes were probably wild. I wasn't trying to mask the turmoil within. Rosa's eyes were as wide as saucers. She clasped her throat.

"You blame me?"

"No." I shook my head. "I blame Luís. He's the one that opened the club. It's his drug business. That's why I was at the drug bust, even though it wasn't anywhere near my normal district. I had flown up from Houston."

"Wait. I thought you worked here, in St. Louis."

"Well, I do now. I took the job here because there was an opening. I wanted to be here for the trial."

"And after the trial?"

That was the question. My position was temporary, but it could be permanent if I wanted it. I just wasn't sure if I did.

"You must hate me."

"Of course not."

Rosa shook her head. "I could have been the one to bring them the drugs. That was part of my job," she hung her head. "So many regrets," She whispered.

"Hey," I put a finger to her chin forcing her gaze to meet mine. I didn't want her to be sad. This day was supposed to bring a smile to her face. Rosa had been depressed as it was, and I refused to undo all that good work.

"It's time for the gifts."

She sighed. "I don't deserve one."

"That's not for you to decide."

She shook her head.

I pushed aside my role in the US Marshal Service. I was no longer simply trying to protect my witness. As a brother, I sought revenge. I set that aside as well. In this moment, I only wanted one thing, and that was to replace the anguish in Rosa's eyes, with something else. Anything else. So, I did the only thing I could. I kissed her. It started simple. A peck on the lips. It wasn't supposed to be more. But the moment our lips touched it was like an inferno that had been blazing beneath the surface suddenly exploded. Rosa moved to take off my shirt, but I captured her hands. She groaned against my lips clearly frustrated. As much as I wanted Rosa, I refused to take advantage of her. She didn't deserve a rough night of meaningless sex. That's all I was capable of at the moment. My anger was too high. Rosa was right. At some level, I did still blame her, even though logically I knew I shouldn't.

Chapter 8

Rosa

"Get dressed." The demand came when I was having a perfectly lovely dream. It wasn't a request. It was an order. I thought we were past this.

I growled. It was too early on a-. What day was it? I realized I didn't even know the date. Being in relative captivity did that to a girl. I thought we had fun the last couple of days. Something had broken down the barriers between us over Thanksgiving. I seemed to understand him a little better. We had both shared a little of our pasts. And that kiss. Wow. Electric. Even though my body wanted more. A lot more. I wouldn't push. I knew better. He had reasons to hate the Lorenzos, to hate me, and somehow he was still here, doing his job and being so damn nice. Well, at least most of the time. Maybe not now when he was ordering me about and being all surly. I wanted to head back to my dream world. I could imagine that I was here on vacation, traveling with a handsome man who would kiss me until my toes curled. Why did Taz have to ruin that? Why must he remind me exactly why I was stuck here?

I threw a pillow at him, and he caught it.

"Come on. I let you sleep as late as I could, but I know how you like to get all dolled up."

"I'm not moving." I clutched the sheet around me, knowing exactly what Taz would do.

He stripped off the covers for a surprise.

I was nude.

"Rosa," he said, voice hissing out.

I stretched lazily on the mattress.

"What?" I said innocently.

Even if I didn't want anything serious with this man, that didn't mean I couldn't have some fun. The shocked look on his face was worth it. I pushed his body back with one of my feet, and he looped his wrist around my ankle. It was automatic. Probably an instinct to protect himself. Not that I had planned on kicking him. He stared, swallowing hard as he looked his fill. His thumb circled the pad of my foot.

"Stop that. It tickles," I said.

Taz cleared his throat and released his hold on me, dropping his hands to his side.

I climbed to my feet grinning. The man still didn't get me. But very few did.

"What am I getting ready for?"

"You need to meet with the Assistant US Attorney handling the case."

I nodded and gathered my clothes.

On my way to the bathroom, I made a few rude hand gestures to the camera and whoever was watching the show. I knew several obscene hand gestures. I was multi-lingual, just in case they didn't get the Spanish references.

After showering and applying my war paint, grumbling that Taz did know me in that regard, I went to sit on the couch and wait for the blood-sucking lawyers to arrive.

"We're going downstairs to a conference room in a few minutes. There is no need for anyone to know what room you're staying in, so don't offer that information even if asked. As far as the US Attorney's office is concerned, we could have driven here, so take your coat."

ST. LOUIS SECRETS

Why were all these precautions necessary?

"Do you really think they could have been involved in José's death?" I asked.

"They shouldn't," Taz said.

A long pause of silence hung in the air.

"What? That's it. That's all you're going to say."

He shrugged.

"Why would the prosecution want their witnesses dead? It doesn't make any sense."

"I agree."

Another long pause. I threw my hands in the air, swearing at him in Spanish. I don't think he knew most of the words. But he must have known enough to raise his eyebrows at a few of the more colorful ones.

"Ok. Fine. Where is my coat?"

He slipped the white puffer jacket on my shoulders. It made me look like a shapeless blob. I hated the thing, but it's not like I had other options. We walked down to a different elevator. It was one we didn't normally use. Not that I had been up and down in the elevator that many times. Every minute or so Taz checked his phone, probably getting word from the eye in the sky. I knew there were cameras somewhere keeping track of my movements but I didn't look at them. Taz knew what he was doing. His body was on high alert. The conversation in our hotel room did nothing to relieve my nerves. I rubbed my hands together. I'm glad he suggested the coat. I was freezing.

"Don't worry. I'll be in there the whole time."

I blinked up at him.

Concern etched his stern face. It had softened his eyes ever so slightly.

I nodded, unable to say anything without my voice breaking. It was finally happening. Six months of waiting, and the end was almost here. I'd miss Taz when I finally got settled. He had told me that the 24x7 protection would end after the trial, once they got me into my new home. That realization more than anything had me shaking. When had I gotten attached to this man?

We walked into a small room set up with a single table and a few chairs. Two people in dark suits stood. I hadn't met either of them.

"You must be Rosa Lorenzo." The man said. He was six feet tall, with sandy blonde hair and deep blue eyes, handsome in that sophisticated clean-cut sort of way. The wrinkles etched around his eyes crinkled when he smiled. It was obvious that juries would love this man.

"Dick Chambers, Assistant US Attorney," he reached out to shake my hand. "It's a pleasure. I'll be prosecuting the case," he gestured to the woman standing next to me. "This is Lisa Winters, my paralegal."

I wondered if this was unusual to make a change this late in the case. I had worked with another lawyer up until now. Maybe this one was better. I shook both their hands. The woman looked like she could be his daughter. Same color blonde hair and blue eyes. She gave me a brief smile, but it didn't reach her eyes. The woman was definitely not my fan. Not outright hostile, but not exactly friendly either. Or maybe she didn't like anyone. I knew people like that.

"Crazy weather we're having," Dick said. "Do you need some coffee or tea to warm up?"

He saw me clasping my hands, my body fighting off the chill. I glanced at Taz, remembering what he said. The man didn't need to know that I hadn't been outside.

"I'm fine."

I took a seat and the two became all business, flipping through the files that were spread out on the table.

"Ok. Let's begin. We've got a lot to cover and not a lot of time."

Dick read the witness protection agreement I had signed, outlining my obligation to cooperate with law enforcement by providing testimony.

"We may be asking questions about crimes you committed, but this agreement prevents any prosecution against these matters. The defense may accentuate some of your wrongdoings to make you uncomfortable."

"I'm not ashamed of anything I've done." I sat up straighter in my chair.

Lisa clicked her tongue, and I turned in her direction, but her head was down reading through the file she was holding.

I pursed my lips. I didn't want to admit that wasn't exactly the truth, but these people didn't need to know that. I had plenty of regrets, but these slimy lawyers didn't deserve that level of soul-searching. They weren't here to protect me. They wanted to get my cousin, and given the chance, they'd be more than willing to send me to jail too. Luckily, I had made a deal, one that guaranteed no jail time, not to mention I could get rid of my cousin, the bane of my existence for as long as I could remember. I was more than willing to give them anything they needed for that.

"Do you have any qualms about testifying?" Lisa asked.

My eyes widened. "Qualms? Do you mean fear?"

"Ms. Winters, this is not the time."

I looked between the two of them. That was interesting. They weren't on the same page about something.

"You want me to be honest with you, Luís needs to go to jail. He's a stone-cold killer and an asshole to boot. It's in everyone's best interests to get his ass tucked safely away for a very long time."

"But he's your cousin. Your family," she said.

"By blood? Yes. But you can't pick and choose your relatives. And he certainly never treated me with respect. Women are lower than dogs to him."

"That's something I wanted to ask you about. The women in Luís' life. Does he have a girlfriend or wife?"

"No recent serious girlfriends that I know of. As for a wife, yes, he did have one, but she died."

I didn't want to tell this story, but it made sense that they'd be curious. Or maybe they thought of using his relationships against him. It wasn't going to work. My cousin was psychotic. He didn't feel things the way normal people did.

"Rumors say it was a rival family," Lisa said, "why she died."

It figures she asked me a question she already knew the answer to. Typical legal tactics.

"It wasn't. I think he killed her himself. She wanted to leave him. He had been abusive for years. The women in our family tried to help her, but in the end, it wasn't enough." My voice had gotten soft.

She reached a hand out to me. "I'm sorry."

"Is there anyone you're leaving behind? Any boyfriends or children?"

I shook my head. "After seeing how Luís treated his wife and girlfriends, I had decided long ago, not to make the same mistake. I don't let anyone get too close."

She frowned. "That's a little sad."

"Life is brutal. You learn to deal with it." I gave her serious eye contact. Whatever she saw in my expression made her flinch.

Dick cleared his throat. "We know that Luís was acquitted of the murder charges in New Mexico for the truck driver of the drug shipment that took place on May 25th. Since murder isn't a federal offense-"

I raised my eyebrows at that.

"What I mean is that normally the federal courts don't handle murder cases. It has to be a special circumstance, like the murder of a federal official, or if it takes place in a federal building like a bank. If the murder is outside those parameters, the state judicial system handles the case."

"New Mexico loves my cousin. He's untouchable there."

ST. LOUIS SECRETS

My cousin had control over politicians and judges back in Santa Fe. His spider-like infrastructure pulled at their strings. He had loads of dirt on everyone. My cousin scared me for what he'd done, but worse for what he could do and get away with. For him, there were never any consequences. He covered his tracks. And if he didn't, I knew what he did to those who betrayed him. If it weren't for Taz and WITSEC, I would have already given up and accepted my fate. As much as I complained about protective custody, I did appreciate everything they had done for me. It meant I had a chance.

"That's why this case is so important. Luís doesn't have that same pull here," he said.

I nodded. I sure hoped they knew what they were doing.

The lawyer and his assistant reviewed the facts of the case to make sure they had everything covered. They asked me loads of questions, both from the prosecution's standpoint; and anticipated questions from the defense. I practiced my answers like I was rehearsing for a play.

"Pause if you need time to think. Don't get rattled."

"We can even get an interpreter." Ms. Winters suggested.

I scowled. "My English is good," I said.

"That's not the reason," she shook her head, "I didn't mean anything by it. Sometimes that extra time to think about the question can help."

"You can also ask the defense to rephrase the question. Saying I don't know is perfectly ok as well, but if you answer it that way too many times, he'll use it as an excuse to say you aren't a credible witness."

"The defense's lawyer is good. Luís Lorenzo managed to get one of the best attorneys in the US."

"It doesn't surprise me," I said.

"I don't how he can afford the man," Lisa said. "I thought his accounts were frozen."

"He has money stashed away in little holes for a rainy day. My cousin is like a rat."

"I thought his nickname was the red wolf."

"That too. The man is an animal. Plain and simple."

"Since Luís was acquitted of the murder charges, this trial for drug trafficking is all we have. It's the main reason we are having the federal trial held here in St. Louis where he doesn't have the same connections."

"Oh. I thought it was the weather," I said.

Lisa laughed. I think she was warming up to me.

"The defense will try to tear your testimony apart. You mustn't lose your temper."

I glanced at Taz. Was he feeding the attorney information about how I was behaving in custody?

I pursed my lips. "I don't know what you've heard about me, but let me reassure you, nothing is more important than this. That cabrón needs to go to jail. To be put away as long as possible. I won't be the one to blow it."

They talked amongst themselves for a few minutes and seemed satisfied.

Taz walked me through the hotel. We were taking a different route, but I wasn't paying close attention. I didn't realize how stressed I would feel talking with the lawyer. Everything felt all the more real. I'd have to face Luís in the courtroom. He'd be watching me up on the stand. I suddenly felt like an emotional wreck. My heart was pounding and I was starting to panic. I couldn't seem to take in enough oxygen. When we stepped outside into the cold, I clutched my coat and looked around. Taz grabbed my hand and my inner thoughts quieted.

"Where are we going?" I asked.

"Bird's eye."

I tilted my head. What did that mean?

We started walking to a giant Ferris wheel and he handed the man a ticket. We climbed into one of the gondolas and out of

ST. LOUIS SECRETS

the freezing weather. The temperature inside the car was a toasty seventy-two degrees.

"Hope you're not afraid of heights."

"And if I was?"

"Then I'd tell you to close your eyes."

I laughed. "Luckily, I'm not."

"Good then shut up and enjoy the ride."

In moments we were up and going around. I looked over the city. St. Louis was stunning. A clear blue sky that was marred by only a few clouds. The cityscape was beautiful. It felt almost magical. Taz pulled out binoculars. He was looking for something specific. I ignored him the best I could and forced my shoulders to relax. The beauty of the landscaping and the soft music in the car released some of the tension that had been crawling up my spine during the interrogation.

Taz put away his binoculars and sent a text. His phone pinged.

"I wanted to check on the paralegal. We're good."

"So, she's trustworthy?"

"She's not setting you up."

"That didn't answer my question."

Taz smiled. "Did you learn anything from the meeting?" He asked.

"That lawyers suck, and not to throw anything in the courtroom. It's bad etiquette."

He laughed. "Then it wasn't a waste of time."

Chapter 9

Taz

Rosa needed a distraction. I could see the worry etched in her brows when the lawyer was questioning her. I hoped that I hadn't made a mistake by inviting over some guests this evening. The last thing I wanted to do was aggravate the situation further. But I should have known better. Rosa treated it like a reunion. When César stopped by with Mari, Rosa came out of nowhere and slugged him. Then she hugged him with such exuberance he lost his balance and knocked over a piece of pottery from the shelf in the living room. I shook my head. We were racking up quite the hotel bill.

"What's with the blonde hair?"

"I'm incognito," Rosa said flipping back the long locks of her wig.

She turned to Mari. "You look fabulous." Rosa gave her an equally big bear hug. "Are you keeping this one in line?" She gestured to César.

"That's a full-time job," Mari grinned, "But yeah, I am."

Rosa's eyebrows rose. "And you Cruz, I mean César," she wiggled her eyebrows. "You were policía the entire time. I still can't believe it. Luís checked your background before you were hired."

"My alias was solid. I've been working undercover as Cruz Diaz for years."

"You had everyone fooled. Why didn't you tell me? I thought we had become friends."

César shrugged. "I wish I could have, but it's not allowed. Plus, the risk," he licked his lips and the two shared a serious expression.

I knew they were thinking of what Luís would have done if he had found out sooner. César had been working undercover at Club Cuervo for six months gathering evidence before the big drug bust in Santa Fe.

Rosa glanced over at me. "So many rules with you guys."

She tried to play it off like it was no big deal, but I had seen the concern in her eyes.

"Hmm. Whatever. So, are you locking this one down?" Rosa asked Mari.

César cleared his throat. "What does that mean?"

Rosa shoved him. "You know exactly what it means man whore."

César had an unrepentant grin. "Hey, no name calling."

"We're trying to take things slow," Mari said.

Rosa tilted her head. "Weren't you trying to seduce him after barely meeting him?"

"Not one of my finest moments," Mari muttered. "I was drunk."

"Oh, we've all had nights like those." I caught her winking at me, sharing a sly smile, "Come let's catch up. Apparently, your seduction skills finally paid off."

Rosa dragged Mari to the dining room where they poured wine and started talking in hushed voices. They giggled in between snacking on hors d'oeuvres and polishing off a bottle of wine. They were cracking open another bottle when Jac and Sofía showed up.

"It's good to see you," I said to Jac giving him a side bro hug. I patted his back hard.

"Same here," he grunted.

Jac was a big guy like me. He was just a few inches shorter, so we tended to shove each other around when we worked together. He knew about my sister. It's why he had asked if I wanted to be there for the drug bust.

"I see César's already here with Mari. Let me introduce you to Sofía. She's César's sister."

"Really?" I grinned. "How did this work out?" I pointed at the two of them.

"My brother is overprotective. Kind of like a pit bull." Sofía reached to shake my hand. "But Mari's training him."

"Hey, I heard that," César yelled.

"It's the truth."

"Is that what you're doing to me?" César asked Mari.

He whispered something in her ear that had her blushing.

"You're dating a Casanova," Rosa shrugged. "Embrace it, girl."

"A one-woman Casanova," César corrected, "My exploits ended with her."

He gestured to Mari, who was trying to bury her face in her arms on the table.

I chuckled. It was clear Rosa and César often ribbed each other by their easy camaraderie.

Rosa stood and hugged Sofía. "It's so good to meet you. I'm sure you have some juicy stories about your brother," she rubbed her hands together.

Sofía grinned. "Oh, the things I could share," her eyes twinkled with merriment.

"Hey guys, can you come over here? I need to discuss a few things."

Jac, César, and I huddled in the living room, while the girls sat in the dining room gossiping.

"Are you aware that José was shot?"

"Yeah, man. How did that happen?"

"He escaped custody."

"You think it was a hit?"

"It could be. That's why we're taking extra precautions."

"I read the police report. He had a burner on him when he died?"

I nodded. "The last call was incoming from another burner, just before he escaped. Nothing else. No text messages or voice mails. The phone was bought with cash from a store that had no cameras. It's a dead end."

"Do you think it was a setup? To get him away from protective custody?"

"We still aren't sure." I grimaced. "Just be careful. We don't know if it's Luís or the Lorenzo family, or just karma catching up to the sicario bastard."

"Is it safe for the girls to be here?" Jac asked.

"The place is being monitored. Video surveillance. My team is on it. If you stay at the hotel, you should be safe."

"Emphasis on should." César frowned. "Mari's testimony is coming up in a few days."

"I know. And I don't want her concerned. There's no reason for her to think she's a target."

Jac, César, and I shared grim expressions.

"None of the other witnesses have had any issues. But I'd still like to be overly cautious, just in case."

"So, what's the plan? Hole up in the room until it's our turn to testify?" Jac asked.

It meant something for him to ask. He didn't have to. The man didn't report to me, but he did respect my skills and valued my input. We had worked together over the years, and I appreciated him allowing me to take the lead without a contest of wills. That often came about when local police and federal agents worked together.

"I think we need to visit the aquarium."

"What?" He asked with a chuckle.

"The girls would enjoy it. They need to keep their minds occupied and not focus on the trial."

"You mean Rosa," César said.

I nodded.

"How's she holding up?"

"Pretending she's not scared senseless. Acting tough."

I glanced at Rosa and she met my gaze. The woman was way too observant. She knew something was up, but she kept talking to the girls. Rosa must have said something funny because Sofía and Mari started howling with laughter.

"It's not an act. Rosa's had a rough life." César said. "Has she told you what it was like for her growing up?"

That gave me pause. How much did César know about Rosa? They had only worked together for six months, about as long she had been in WITSEC. I hated that Rosa might have shared more with the man than she had with me. Was it jealousy? Not that I wanted to poke at my emotions. I had no right to feel anything for the woman. I just didn't like how close they had been.

"It's not like I have Rosa's whole life story. But from the tidbits of information, her life hasn't been easy."

Rosa was the same with me. She was particular about sharing. I had to reveal something about my own life before she was willing to share secrets of her past. That didn't come easy for me.

"Did you and her, ya know?" I asked.

The question came out harsher than I wanted it to. He threw his hands up and backed up a step.

"Woah. No man," César said, "It was never like that between us. I mean. Well, it could have been, given my tendencies," he chuckled.

His grin faltered as he stared at my stern expression.

He cleared his throat. "But I was way too focused on the case."

"I read some statements in the police reports," I said rubbing the back of my neck. I felt awkward asking because it sounded like I was jealous, which might have been true, but I needed to know for other reasons. "Most of the club workers said you and Rosa were having an affair. Is there anything that might derail your testimony?"

"Oh, that," he laughed. "It wasn't real. Anything we did at the club, was only for show."

My eyebrows rose. Exactly what did they do? Did I really want to ask? As it was, I felt entirely self-conscious about questioning him. It wasn't my concern. This shouldn't affect the case. But I gave the universal hand gesture for him to continue. Maybe to appease my curiosity more than anything.

"When Rosa rescued Mari from Luís' office, we had to figure a way out. His goons were standing guard. With my reputation at the club, we pretended to hook up. In the supply closet. The ruse worked and we were able to sneak Mari out in a rolling suitcase."

"Sorry?" I asked trying to muffle my laughter. "I hadn't read that part of the report."

"Haha. I get it, I'm small." Mari said. "Laugh it up, boys."

The girls were listening from the dining room.

"We might not have shared that little detail." César cleared his throat, glancing over at Mari. "We didn't have enough evidence to prove he had drugged her, otherwise we could have charged Luís for that as well. Getting her to safety was my priority. Well that, and keeping my cover. Mari's brother was Jac's CI. He worked at the club. BJ died trying to get the evidence we needed. His coded journal is the reason we have all the dates, names, and locations for the shipments. There was a secret panel in Luís' office that led to a supply closet. BJ would sneak in there to gather intel. It's the same closet where Rosa and I pretended to have sex."

ST. LOUIS SECRETS

I didn't want to think about that. Even as a ruse, it made me want to pound César with my fists until he was a bloody mess. I needed something else to focus on. Anything else.

"Who's up for room service?"

The guys both held up their hands.

"We just got in, so we haven't eaten," Jac said. "I'm starving."

"You're always starving," Sofía complained.

"What do you all want?" I asked the girls.

"Wine." They all yelled in unison.

They broke into a fit of laughter.

"Several bottles," Sofía said.

"And nothing cheap." Rosa grinned. "Since the feds are picking up the bill."

"We can drink to Luís' incarceration," Mari said.

"He certainly has it coming." Rosa's eyes narrowed. "At the bare minimum."

"And with all the evidence against him, it can't fail."

The two girls clinked glasses.

"Wait let me join in," Sofía said clinking her glass with the others. "I'll cheer you on from the gallery."

I popped open some beers and handed them to the guys. "What do you say? "Down with El Lobo Rojo."

"That bastard's gonna pay." César grinned.

"To justice." Jac nodded.

As much as I said I lived for justice, I knew deep down that wasn't exactly true. At this moment all I wanted was revenge for my sister. If justice was served in the process, so much the better. I looked around the room. Most of those here had been wronged by him in some form or another. We were going to make sure El Lobo Rojo paid for his crimes. He wasn't escaping this one. Not this time.

Chapter 10

Rosa

We walked into the giant train shed from the hotel and I felt a thrill run through me. I was excited to be out of the hotel room. Thanksgiving had got me thinking about all those things I was grateful for. Being alive was at the top of my list. The past few days I had more external stimuli than I had in months. Sad but true, simply walking into the sunlight felt like a fantasy come true. I still hadn't said thank you to Taz. Every time I got close to uttering those words, Taz would inevitably do something bossy, or say something condescending. Although he had started eyeing me a little less like an insect and more like a person lately. In fact, on occasion, he was downright polite.

I was still infuriated about that smoking hot kiss from a few days ago. Not the actual kissing mind you. It was the abrupt halt just when things got interesting that I had a problem with. Taz frustrated me. The hot and cold flip-flop attitude was driving me crazy. Taz would give me a heated stare, and then just walk away, leaving me all hot and bothered with no relief in sight. Oh, I knew getting involved with Taz was a mistake. I wasn't a fool. But life wasn't worth living without a string of regrets. Los arrepentimientos demostraron que viviste. Regrets prove you lived. Another Lorenzo family motto. That's why I lived life to the fullest every chance I got. When Taz had stopped that kiss from going further, it proved that he wasn't nearly as into it as I was.

I shook my head, clearing my thoughts. The man was supposed to keep me safe. My body.

"Solo mi cuerpo." I said.

Only my body. I could trust him with that. And that alone. I didn't need him for anything else. Certainly not my heart. I glanced at Mari and César holding hands. Whenever they came within ten feet of one another, it was like a live wire was in the room. Sparks flew. They had been the same when they first met over six months ago. Mari mentioned trying to take things slow. What a laugh. The way he looked at her I didn't think it would be long before he popped the question. As much as he had played the field while working at Club Cuervo, after meeting Mari, something had changed. He was truly committed. I'm so glad it worked out for them, even if it made me wistful for all those would-have-beens in my own life. On my other side, Sofía was nestled into Jac's side trying to stay warm. They were just as bad. All lovey-dovey. Not that I faulted them for cuddling. There was a roof over the train shed. Well, sort of. The huge steel arch trusses might have reduced the impact of wind and weather, but it was still open to the outside. It meant that on a cold winter day like today, the near-freezing temperature kept most people from being out and about. I shivered. Not that I minded the cold. It was another reminder that I was alive. I glanced at Taz. He was scanning the area for threats. I wondered if Taz realized we were in the middle of two couples in heat. He appeared to be dutifully ignoring the obvious pheromones in the air. I sighed. My breath came out in swirling puffs that looked like smoke. It made me crave a cigarette, even though I had quit smoking years ago. But that didn't mean I didn't get the urges now and again.

"I've got the tickets." Taz said picking up his pace, encouraging everyone to move faster.

ST. LOUIS SECRETS

He grabbed my elbow and propelled me forward. I frowned. What was his problem? I didn't mind the warmth of his body so close, but I could do without the shoving. His normal grumbly self was peeking through. Not that I was a ray of sunshine myself most days, especially with the direction my life was headed.

"Slow it down, pendejo. My legs are not as long as yours."

"I could always pick you up," he whispered in my ear.

I pressed my lips together, refusing to admit just how appealing his offer might be. I wanted to scream at him, but his body was so close and distracting. I let him guide me. The guys took their cue from Taz and all six of us walked faster to the main entrance. I only had a few moments to take in the enormous rope course above the aquarium. That would be so much fun to do. I wondered if I could talk the girls into it. Even though I was a little afraid of heights, I wouldn't mind the thrill. I'd be game if they were. I caught Taz staring at me. He shook his head and my shoulders slumped. Of course, he'd be a killjoy. I stuck my tongue out at him as he jostled me inside.

I might have been sore about not getting to play on the ropes, but I was suddenly mesmerized by the projection on the ceiling. It was similar to the incredible light show in the Grand Hall at the hotel, but this time, it looked like we were underwater. I hadn't been scuba diving in years. It took me back to those memories, when the world was quiet, just alone with my thoughts. A gorgeous mix of blues and greens danced above us. The surface bubbled and gently bobbed back and forth with sunlight filtering through. Fish swam all around us. I felt the tension in my shoulders loosen. The soothing music made me relax bit by bit. I felt transported to an oceanic paradise. I stared in wonder watching the show with a smile on my face. This is just what I needed. I leaned against Taz. I could feel the tension in his body at my back, but I didn't care. If he wanted to remain close, then he could be my standing full-body pillow while on guard duty. I watched the show in silence. At one point I closed my eyes soaking in Taz's warmth. I couldn't believe how hot his body ran. After the chill from the outdoors, it was making me drowsy.

"Rosa," Taz said in a gruff voice.

I turned my head lazily, leaning back further. "Yes?"

"You need to move." His voice was strained. I shifted my position and suddenly felt him; his hard shaft pressing against my backside. Oh my. I licked my lips. Maybe Taz was more affected by me than he let on.

"The others are heading to the train," He said.

I frowned glancing around. We were alone, except for a woman in a blue sweatshirt and khaki pants. She stood just behind a roped-off section beneath an archway that said 'Trains'. Being relatively alone with Taz in the semi-darkness touching was making my stomach do cartwheels. Staring into his eyes, I detected no passion, only anger. I frowned. Taz's body may have reacted to mine, but he wasn't happy about it.

I nodded, disappointment flooding me. I would have enjoyed remaining that way a little longer. Touching. Sort of. Dios mío. I was desperate for affection. It made me stand a little taller and force some distance between us. I walked past the ropes and down the short hallway the woman gestured to.

"All aboard." She said as we hustled to join the rest of our group inside the train car.

"What were the two of you doing out there?" César asked with a huge grin.

Mari elbowed him. "Stop making them uncomfortable."

"Oof. Why are you always doing that to me?"

"Because you're acting like a teenager."

"Guilty," he chuckled.

I laughed along with him. Maybe his undercover persona that I had gotten to know while working at Club Cuervo wasn't all that different than his true self. Everyone sat down and the conductor began the tour. The train didn't really move, but it felt like it. The seats vibrated and the projectors cast images on the

ST. LOUIS SECRETS

walls that made it look like we could see through the windows of the train to the outside. We moved from old St. Louis, to what the city looks like today. The conductor then decided to take to the sky so we could see the whole city from above. And then the train plunged into the Mississippi. All around us swam fish that lived locally, and then the train accelerated through the water at warp speed to the Gulf of Mexico. We saw exotic aquatic species that lived in the ocean, ending with a great humpback whale. The train then zoomed back to the aquarium and we ascended back to dry land. All of us cheered. I think we all needed a break from the stress of dealing with the trial. Even Mr. Grumpy Pants chuckled. We were all grinning ear to ear when we left the train. I even hooked arms with Taz when we walked toward the aquarium gallery. It felt comfortable. Just like we were a normal couple taking in the sights. A slight tension thrummed through his body and made me glance around. It was an almost imperceptible change. We were no longer alone. Not that anyone looked threatening. The majority of visitors were parents and small kids. Other than the tanks with various fish to see, there were tons of interactive activities. I didn't mind that one bit. I was suddenly in a playful mood.

"You up for some hands-on?" I asked Taz with raised eyebrows.

His heated stare told me he was thinking dark thoughts that had nothing to do with the educational exhibits around us.

"These here are the red garra." A staff member on the microphone said to the group as we approached. "Also known as doctor fish. They nibble on dead skin, specifically your cuticles, and are used in salons all over the world for manicures and pedicures."

"I dare you to put your hands in the water," César said to Sofía.

She scowled at him.

"Come on girls." Sofía said to Mari and me. "If we don't do it, I'll never hear the end of it. He will call me a gallina."

"Your brother calls you a chicken?" I asked.

"Not if I have anything to say about it."

"But why do we have to do it?" Mari said eyeing the pool with all the fish swimming just beneath the surface. She gave a shiver.

"Girl power." Sofía held up her fist. "Let's show these guys we're not afraid of nunca."

I grinned. Sofía was a riot. "Ready?" I asked as we all lined up along the edge of the tank.

"Tres. Dos. Uno."

We all stuck our hands beneath the surface. The small fish swarmed. It looked like a feeding frenzy. It made me think about how long it had been since I had an actual manicure. We all let out squeals of nervous laughter, but we kept our hands in the water. No one was calling us gallinas.

"This is so freaky. My hands are vibrating," I said.

"Just like the seats on the train." Mari giggled.

"And other things from a hidden drawer in my bedroom," Sofía whispered.

We all chuckled.

"Check it out Taz," I said. "You managed to get me a spa treatment after all."

"I live to serve," he said deadpan.

"Dios mío. The man has a dry sense of humor. No es posible."

A reluctant grin formed on his lips.

After stopping at the washing station, we proceeded to the next tank. A staff member was holding a stick with a red ball over the surface of the water.

"What do you think that man is doing?" I asked the others. "Did they train the fish to jump like dolphins?"

The guy in the blue aquarium shirt chuckled. "These are not jumpers. They are spitters."

ST. LOUIS SECRETS

He had lost me. My English was good. I was bilingual, but some English words and phrases left me baffled.

"Spitters?" I asked.

A few of the fish started shooting water at the red ball, and surprisingly, most managed to hit their target.

"They are called archer fish," he said. "Sharpshooters of the sea."

"That is awesome," Mari said.

"That's nothing. I could hit that easy." César said.

"I bet, I could spit twice that distance." Jac chimed in.

Taz whispered something to the boys that had them both chuckling. It had to be something naughty by the muffled comment.

"I don't understand men." I shook my head.

"You're not alone. I don't get the appeal of half the things they do." Mari said. "Spitting? Why on earth is that something to be proud of?"

"Boys and their competitive nature." Sofía shrugged. "Let's see how long it takes them to figure out we've left."

We snuck away to the next exhibit but didn't get very far. Taz was way too observant.

"No wandering off ladies," he jogged to catch up to us.

It made me realize how difficult it was going to be to sneak off when the time came. I sighed. It was no use worrying about it now. Mari was waving me over to touch a starfish. A few minutes later Sofía dragged me over to another exhibit.

"Come check out the jellyfish touch pool. You only use these two fingers," she explained showing me her middle finger and pointer.

"That sounds like a line from one of those pay-per-view channels up in the hotel room." I chuckled.

"Oh, you are so bad," she said. "Dirty minds think alike. That's why we get along so well."

ZIZI HART

The aquarium staffer cleared his throat. "Um yes, you dip your fingers into the water, just beneath the surface, and wait for the moon jellyfish to float up. They will lightly brush your fingertips. It's super gentle. Of course, you'll want to pay attention to only touch the dome side and not the tentacles."

"So, no touching the stingers," Sofía said. "You got that César?"

"I can follow instructions, sis."

"Hmm," she said. "That's debatable."

I loved the sibling banter. I could tell they loved one another, but they also took every opportunity to give each other shit.

"Have you met Lord Stanley?" A little kid who couldn't be more than six pulled on my scarf like he was ringing a bell in a clock tower.

"Uh. No?" I responded wondering where the kid's mother was. I glanced around, but she was nowhere to be found. No must have been the wrong answer because he grabbed my hand and dragged me to another section of the aquarium. I had no choice but to follow along. I couldn't help but smile. The kid was pretty darn cute. A little redhead with freckles. The rest of the gang trailed me, chuckling at the kid's enthusiasm. He was very passionate about introducing me to this person.

"Meet Lord Stanley." The kid gestured to a tank. "He's famous."

I studied the tank. A dark blue speckled lobster was crawling along the sandy surface. His antennae were wiggling back and forth. It made it look like he was waving.

"Well, introduce yourself," he gestured to me and the tank.

"Hello Stanley," I said.

"He's a Lord." The little kid whispered out of the side of his mouth.

"Oh, sorry. Lord Stanley, it's so nice to meet you. My name is Rosa."

Taz cleared his throat.

ST. LOUIS SECRETS

Oh, shoot. I had a different name. Crap. I had already forgotten my new first name. What was it? I couldn't very well ask Taz.

"I mean Mrs. Connor."

I looked down at the kid who had a huge cheesy grin.

"Lord Stanley is such a pretty blue. I've never seen a lobster that color before. That's kind of rare, huh?"

"Super rare. Like one in a bazillion or something like that."

"You don't say?" Taz asked, kneeling next to the kid.

Even crouched down, Taz still looked enormous.

"Yeah. He's the maso- whatchamacallit for the St. Louis Blues. They're a hockey team, ya know."

"The mascot." Taz nodded. "I think I read something about Lord Stanley online."

He reached out to the little kid. "Well thank you sir for making sure we got to meet him in person."

The boy's tiny hand was about the size of two of Taz's fingers. They shook hands. It was absolutely adorable. I had no idea that Taz was so good with kids. By the looks of it, he'd make a pretty great dad. Not that I had any business exploring that idea further. Taz had told me over Thanksgiving he had never been married or had kids. It seemed like a shame. Not that I had either. I doubted it was ever going to happen for me. Especially in my current predicament. Heading into WITSEC at 39, I most likely missed my chance at having a family. Not that I hadn't purposely chosen that path. Bringing a kid into the Lorenzo family, a life filled with danger was a mistake. Kids had never been a possibility. My hopes and dreams for a family had died long ago.

After we found the boy's frantic mother, who had two other children in tow, we headed over to another large pool. The aquarium staff were feeding sting rays. All of us watched as they swam in formation.

"So graceful," Sofía said. "Almost like it's choreographed."

"Dancing," I sighed. "That reminds me of the good old days. Back in Bogotá, my girlfriends and I would all hit up the clubs on the weekends. You couldn't get me off the dance floor."

"You're not that old," Mari said. "The way you talk, I'd think you were ancient."

Some days I felt that way. I was older than Mari by 13 years, but it had more to do with how I lived. The danger and worry had aged me.

"I remember the first time that César danced with me." Mari closed her eyes and swayed. "He swept me off my feet."

"You know he was a dance instructor back in Albuquerque." Sofía grinned. "He did it to pick up girls."

"Like he needed help with that." Jac jabbed César in the ribs.

"Oof," he grabbed his middle. "It wasn't like that. I enjoy dancing. I always have. Salsa, Tango, Samba, Rumba. It doesn't matter. I love them all."

César started dancing around. "My feet just want to move. I can't control them."

Jac cleared his throat. "I did a little line dancing at a few bars. I'm not like César with his smooth moves, but I can follow the beat and not fall flat on my face.

Taz bit his lip. He almost appeared nervous. Everyone was staring at him. We had all opened up and we were waiting for him to share.

"Alright. My mom made me take tap."

A laugh bubbled up in my throat. "You? Tap dancing?"

The guys were rolling, bent over. Full belly laughs.

"Oh my god," Jac said, wiping tears from his eyes. "Badass Taz is a tap dancer. Nope. I'm picturing a gigantic Gene

ST. LOUIS SECRETS

Kelley with a cowboy hat dancing in one of those old movies. That image will be in my head forever."

"I'm no Gene Kelley but I'm still pretty good." Taz said.

"Dude. That made it worse." César shook his head.

After the rays, we decided to head into shark canyon. It was dark and spooky with light patterns glowing on the floor as we walked through the tanks of sharks and other fish along the path. The couples had all paired off again. It meant I was walking next to Taz. Some tension had loosened between us. Maybe it was all the laughter or the fact that we were sharing a little more of our pasts.

"I think it's cool that you tap," I said. "Didn't mean to laugh."

He smirked. "Sure you did, but I appreciate you trying to make the effort."

"I'm serious. That takes real skill and exercise. I'm sure being a big guy would make it even harder to do."

"Yeah, I had to develop more flexibility early on."

"Sometimes your body type makes it nearly impossible to pursue a passion." I shrugged.

"It sounds like you speak from experience," he said. "Did you ever want something like that?"

I bit my lip. "Maybe. I wanted to be a ballerina." I looked down at my body and scowled. "My body's not really designed for it. A little top heavy." I glanced at my rear. "And bottom heavy too."

"Those things aren't a problem from where I'm standing." Taz eyed my assets with interest and it warmed me from the inside.

I tried to hold in my grin but failed. "Well, the dance studios told me I wasn't a good fit," I shrugged. "So, I found something else. I learned the traditional Latin dances. Nana paid for my lessons. I wasn't half bad. Not that I pursued any competitions. That part didn't interest me. I just wanted to go out to the clubs. Dancing equaled freedom. It was a way to get away from it all. Nobody at the clubs told you what to do or criticized you. There were no demands when you came to a bar. You drank and had fun, and danced until the sun came up. That was the best period of my life, in my early twenties when life was simple."

Chapter 11

Taz

The phone started vibrating and I rubbed my eyes. I was half awake already, but it was early. Checking the clock, it was a little after 5 in the morning. The sun had yet to rise. No one messaged me unless it was important. The message from Huck read, 'Hey Boss man. Feed coming through patchy.'

'Checking.' I replied.

I stretched and glanced around the suite. I peeked in on Rosa. She was sleeping soundly. It had been a late night for everyone. It was good catching up with the guys. I missed them. We didn't have many chances to hang out. César and Jac were a riot. More like brothers to each other, than just old high school buddies. Now that Jac was going to marry César's sister, they would be family; brothers for real. It made me think of my own brother and how I left things back in Houston. I needed to make things right between us, once I got through this trial. Then I could focus on mending fences back home.

I quietly moved about the room, so as not to wake Rosa, checking the power and wires from the cameras. Nothing seemed disconnected. Everything looked fine from my side. I opened my laptop and the browser was spinning. I tried a couple of resets, but it didn't fix the issue. I wasn't able to diagnose the issue from my side. I needed IT to come out and take a look. Other than wiggling some wires and checking my laptop, I didn't have the tools or the experience to be able to tell what was wrong.

My phone pinged.

'You doing funny bus with the witness?'

I chuckled. 'No.' I messaged back. Only Huck would ask something like that. He had a one-track mind.

My phone buzzed again.

'Jus say if you are. No need to lie. I'd cover for you.'

I shook my head. I didn't need Huck to tempt me. Rosa was already doing that enough on her own. She oozed sex appeal with every fiber of her being. Rosa took that moment to throw back the covers and roll over on her stomach. At least she was wearing something. Not that it was doing much good. The nightgown she wore rode up to display sexy panties and an equally sexy ass. Those long golden legs were toned from her workouts. Since I hadn't supplied her with a treadmill, she had found an exercise channel on TV. Watching her work out was distracting as all hell. I reckon the woman knew exactly what it was doing to me. I rubbed a hand down my face.

'No wire issues from my side.' I messaged.

'Is that a metaphor?'

'What's with all the questions?'

'Inquiring minds. Living vicariously. Bored as shit. Take your pick.'

I went back into the living room.

'Contact Sam. Send him out the next chance he has.'

'Roger that.'

I left my computer open in case the network came back online. My browser continued to spin. I wondered if the internet was down for the whole hotel, or if it was just certain sections having an issue. I called down to the front desk, but nobody answered. I left a message. They were probably low on staff at this time in the morning. I could always walk down to the server room, but I didn't want to leave Rosa unguarded. If the camera feed went down, and something happened to her. A chill went up my spine. I don't think I'd ever forgive myself. My choices were simple. Send someone else to guard her, or wait for the IT Security guy to show. Since the cell phones seemed to be working without issue, I called the office wanting to check the other witness locations. I had a bad feeling. Something felt off. Maybe I was just being paranoid, but I wanted to verify that no other locations were experiencing the same issue.

"Hey Sandi," I said.

"Taz. It's so good to hear from you. Is everything all right?"

There was a slight trembling in her voice. I knew she was worried about me, even though she had no reason to be. For one, we weren't an item anymore. For another, I was her boss and more than capable of taking care of myself.

"I need you to patch me into another witness protection detail."

"Is your witness ok?" Sandi asked.

She said witness like the word left a nasty taste in her mouth.

I didn't need this right now. Maybe if I ignored it.

"Fine. She's fine. Patch me into Franklin."

"Do you need someone else to relieve you? What's it been? A week with no break. Didn't you say how dangerous that was out in the field working 24x7? Your physical and mental acuity isn't as sharp."

"Are you trying to piss me off?"

"No, Chief. You know what's best."

The passive-aggressive comment had me shaking my head, even if she did have a point. I was irritable. It was evident by the way I snapped at her. I knew that being on alert for long periods could wear anyone down. Sleeping on an uncomfortable pull-out mattress wasn't helping matters. Not to mention the sexual attraction between Rosa and myself. Sandi was throwing the rule book at me, and I didn't like it. She was telling me how to do my job. It didn't matter if she was correct. I was still the boss, and I'd make the decisions.

"Put me through to Deputy Marshal Franklin," I said again harshly, not wanting to continue the conversation.

"Yes, Chief," Sandi said with a hint of snark. It reminded me of the tone that Rosa often used with me. How did all women have that tone of voice that made you feel like everything was your fault? It made you want to apologize, but I couldn't do that. It would undermine my authority.

Sandi went through the steps on her end and patched me through to the team. We changed the communication channels regularly so no one would be able to join from the outside. It was usually done via a custom internet program with sophisticated encryption software. If I couldn't access the normal way, I'd have to go old school and call them. It required a secure line.

"What's up?" Franklin asked when the call went through.

"You got any internet issues on your side?"

"Hang on."

I heard typing quickly for a few seconds.

"Nope. Bandwidth is good. Signal secure. How about you?"

"Having problems on our side. But there could be an innocent reason."

"Can you check with the others and let me know?"

"Sure thing Chief."

I heard the clicking of keys in the background.

At least Franklin knew the chain of command and respected it. Even though I hadn't been in St. Louis that long.

"No issues with any other teams. We are all good on our side."

That was a relief. It meant no one was targeting all the witnesses at once. It had crossed my mind the moment Huck had reached out. Most people might not assume that, but it was my job to think of worst-case scenarios and then circumvent disaster.

ST. LOUIS SECRETS

"Good work Franklin. Keep me apprised through office reports. I'll call back in later. Just know that I will be offline until IT remedies the situation."

"Will do Chief."

A few hours later Sam showed up with a duffel full of gear.

"I already checked downstairs. There are several conferences right now. The wireless bandwidth is maxed out."

I nodded. I figured it might be something like that. However, that didn't account for it being down at 5 in the morning. What conferences were going on then?

"What can you do?"

"If the hotel knew we were feds, we could have them prioritize the bandwidth to us, but if you want to keep it undercover, then I'll have to go another way. I can add some wifi amplifiers to boost the signal."

"Do it."

"What's going on?" Rosa asked.

She was in her robe and looking adorably rumpled. It made my mind play out circumstances where I was involved in making her look like that. Darn it Huck. Thanks for putting those ideas in my head.

Chapter 12

Rosa

Sam walked past, brushing against me. I felt a slight tug on one side of my robe and realized he dropped something in one of my pockets. I slid my hand inside, feeling the cold metal. I kept it in my hand, so one pocket didn't appear to be lower than the other.

"I'm just going to head to the bathroom."

Taz tilted his head, giving me a puzzled expression.

I closed my eyes. I was being muy estúpida. I wanted to kick myself. Normally I didn't ask for permission. It was far too suspicious.

"Just telling you, so you won't send out a search party thinking I've gone missing," I said it with enough snark that it masked my earlier mistake. I marched to the bathroom with arrogance in every step.

He waved me away and I had to force myself to keep my walk steady and not run. As soon as I was inside, I locked the door and fell against it with a sigh. The item that Sam had dropped in my robe's pocket was a phone. Excitement thrummed through my body. My whole body tingled. This is what I needed. What I had asked him for. Sam had come through. I'd have to figure out a way to thank the guy. I turned on the shower to mask any sounds. I went through the history. Nothing. It was blank. A prepaid burner. Perfect. The battery was full, but I didn't have a charger, so I'd have to use it sparingly. Or I could ask Todd downstairs to check lost and found. People always left chargers at hotels. I could call him from the hotel phone when Taz went to sleep. Or better yet, I could call him from my new cell. I noted the number of minutes available to me as well. I thought about all the people I needed to contact.

I picked up the hotel phone in the bathroom and waited for a dial tone. It only took Taz a few moments to see I was on the line.

"What are you doing on the phone, Rosa?" He asked through the bathroom door.

"Getting some extra bath towels and tampons from concierge." I yelled. "Unless you want to call them."

"Fine. Just make it quick."

I grinned, knowing there was no way he'd want to do that. At least now when he heard me talking on the phone, he wouldn't be overly concerned.

I dialed the concierge. Todd answered.

"Hi, Todd. I was wondering if you could do me a huge favor."

"Of course, Mrs. Connor. What do you need?"

"Can you go over to the gift shop and pick up some tampons and charge it to the room? Send those up along with a few extra bath towels."

"Of course. No problem. Is there anything else?"

I listened at the door. Sam and Taz were talking about something technical to do with wiring. It meant he wasn't listening in on my phone conversation.

"Yeah, could I get your cell phone number?" I asked.

"Uh, Mrs. Connor. Not sure your husband would like that."

"Oh, it's nothing like that. As handsome as you may be, I would never cheat, no matter how tempting."

ST. LOUIS SECRETS

He chuckled. "In that case," He said and rattled off his digits.

"I'll call you right back."

I hung up and dialed from my new burner.

"Mrs. Connor?" He asked.

"Yep, it's me. I wanted to ship something to the hotel. It's a surprise for my husband."

"Oh. Yeah, sure thing. But why did you need my cell?"

"If you haven't noticed, my husband is a bit of a control freak. He tends to listen in on my phone conversations. I can't keep any secrets from the man."

"He does that? Eavesdrops?"

"My husband doesn't trust me." I sighed. "It's complicated."

He cleared his throat. "It's not my place to question."

"The address?" I asked.

"Of course. Just have the package shipped to St. Louis Union Station Hotel at 1820 Market Street, St. Louis, MO 63103. You can have it sent to my attention, and I'll contact you when it arrives."

I gave Todd my new cell phone number and thanked him.

One step of my plan was in place. Now I needed to contact a trusted friend back home in Colombia. I'd start with a text because I didn't know that I could call internationally from the burner.

'Nadia my dear friend. I need my insurance sent. It's time. -RL.'

'Verify.' Came the reply.

I typed over the code, a series of words and dates that meant something only to us, but nothing to anyone else. It was the name of the restaurant where we worked together and our hire dates.

'Where are you? Are you ok?' She asked.

'I'm fine. Just need the item mailed.'

'I miss you.' Nadia replied. 'Not the same here without you.'

I felt the same way.

'Miss you too.'

Nadia was a waitress, and completely outside of the family business. She had held onto a flash drive for me that I needed for a deal. Not a drug deal. It was far more valuable, at least to me. I couldn't risk keeping it at my apartment in Santa Fe, and especially not in my room at the Lorenzo compound.

I messaged Nadia the address that Todd had given me.

'I'll text you again when it's safe to do so.'

'Ten Cuidado.' She messaged.

Yes. I'd be careful. I had to. It was a matter of survival.

'Tú también.' I replied.

I wondered if I was taking too long in the bathroom. Taz wasn't talking with Sam any longer. Had the IT guy left? There was a knock on the bathroom door. I was standing too close and jumped.

"Yes," I said.

"Your towels." Taz cleared his throat. "And other stuff is here. Right outside the door."

"Thanks," I said.

I waited five seconds for him to walk away. Unlocking the door, I snagged the items and slammed the door. I caught a glimpse of him in the living room, but his eyes were averted. I wondered if he thought I might have had a bloody accident. I grinned. It was useful info to know the man was squeamish about my monthly visits. I could use that to my advantage.

I re-locked the door and focused on my next contact. I had been thinking about him since the moment I joined Witness Protection months ago. Nicolas Mendoza. He was the only man I trusted, and even that had limits. We had an unusual relationship. Right now, I needed his help. He was my only connection to Maria's son. Ramón was to contact Nicolas if things went sideways back in Santa Fe. I made arrangements the day Ramón

ST. LOUIS SECRETS

arrived in the U.S. about 7 months ago. I made sure Ramón memorized Nicolas' cellphone number. I tested him frequently so he wouldn't forget. I'm so glad I did. I prayed Ramón made it safely. Nicolas was a good guy, for a Mendoza. The guy worked building security at a pharmaceutical company in Albuquerque. The Mendozas were a major stockholder. While the business appeared legitimate on the surface, the Mendozas were rivals. They were in the same drug trade as the Lorenzos. They had just diversified a little more.

While Ramón was street smart, the kid didn't speak very good English and la policía were looking for him after the drug bust. I just hoped they weren't looking too hard. I told the feds that he barely knew anything, which was true. He had only arrived from Colombia a month before the big drug bust. The extent of Ramón's training involved the legitimate side of the business, getting supplies for the bar. He was just a barback in the club. He was innocent. Not that the feds believed me. They probably assumed the kid was a crook since he was a Lorenzo. My family name was tainted because of Luís and his brothers. The feds didn't realize many of those in the Lorenzo family were just like me, just a pawn in their games. We worked for them because we had no other choice.

I texted Nicolas.

'Checking on my package. Did it arrive?' I asked.

'Who is this?'

'Conejita Morada.'

Purple Rabbit. It was his nickname for me in grade school. I had brought a purple rabbit backpack on my first day of school. It had been a gift from my Nana. Nicolas and Felipe had attended the same school as Maria and myself. Even though the Mendozas and Lorenzos traditionally loathed one another, for some reason the four of us all got along. Maybe it was a way for us to rebel against our families. Or maybe it was because our positions weren't particularly important in the hierarchy. It allowed us just enough freedom to make decisions the family would deem unforgivable. Whatever the reason why we became friends, it had allowed us to rise above the hatred, and form an unbreakable bond. With Maria and Felipe, it evolved into love during high school. Maria got pregnant at seventeen. For Nicolas and I, we never ventured further than friendship. We were smarter and less emotional than our cousins. Unfortunately, we were also cursed with best friends destined to become tragic lovers. Nicolas and I would often quote lines of Shakespeare to one another, a forewarning of the impending doom. We could see the writing on the wall but could do nothing to stop it.

'What delivery are you talking about?'

I frowned. Was his phone being monitored? I didn't want to spell it out just in case. But he was asking for confirmation. I guess that was fair. This was a burner phone. A number he didn't recognize. That made me consider the best way to respond.

'A surprise package. The woe of Maria and her Romeo.'

I was referring to Ramón. Maria and Felipe's son. Their affair had been as tragic as Romeo and Juliet, although for Maria and Felipe it had not ended in death, at least not right away. Nicolas and I spent most of high school hiding our cousin's relationship from our respective families. We knew what would happen if they were found out. Still, they both died at 37, within a few months of one another. Neither had ever married. Nicolas and I had both stayed single as well. For me, I was a cynic about relationships. After witnessing the years my cousin Maria spent pining for Felipe, I believed love to be a fantasy. Despite her son, Ramón, she was still heartbroken that she could not be with the only man she ever loved. It would have been impossible with our families. They had known each other for three decades, two of which they had been lovers. Nicolas and I had helped them see one another. We had arranged for multiple secret rendezvous over the years. Sometimes I wondered if we should have refused. I guess it could have been worse. At least Maria got to see her son grow into a man. She died just after Ramón turned 19. I don't

ST. LOUIS SECRETS

believe Felipe ever got the chance to get to know Ramón. We all decided it was far too dangerous.

'Romeo's package arrived in one piece.'

I let out a deep breath. Ramón was safe, at least for now. Relief flooded me. I had to give Nicolas more information, but I couldn't risk it over text messages. I had to see him in person. There was no other way. He was the only man I ever trusted. We had kept secrets from both our families for 30 years. That's why I had initially asked Nicolas for his help. He was smart and discreet, and we both owed one another. That loyalty had been built and tested throughout the years. It went beyond friendship. He was more like a brother to me.

'Where are you?'

'St. Louis.'

'You with the feds?'

'Yep.'

'Dangerous game you play.'

He was right. By contacting him, I was violating my agreement with the feds. They could easily cancel their agreement with me and prosecute me for my crimes. Although, I knew they needed me for my testimony. That was the only reason I could be such a pain in the ass, and get away with it.

'Need to meet.'

'I want what you promised me.'

I rolled my eyes. Of course, he wouldn't do it for free.

'It's on the way.'

Nadia was shipping the flash drive to the hotel. Todd was expecting it and would contact me when the "surprise" for my husband arrived. Nicolas needed whatever was on that drive. I had stolen it from my cousin, Luís back in Colombia. It had been encrypted so I had no clue what was on it, just that it was muy importante.

'Is it shipping directly to me?'

'No, it's coming here first.'

'That wasn't part of the agreement.'

'Plans change. Deal with it.'

'When do you want to meet?' He asked.

I had thought about this too. I knew that Taz went into the office on Thursdays. He'd have to send someone else to watch me, and I'd figure a way to escape the hotel for a few hours.

'In two days. Thursday, at noon.'

'Where?'

I had pulled up a map of the city and the hotel where I was staying. There were several possibilities. I'd know more when it got closer.

'Not sure. Somewhere downtown. I'll give you a location the day of.'

'I'll make arrangements. But I need you to call me tomorrow night.'

'Ok.' I texted back even though I had no idea how I would do it.

Even with the shower and fan running, Taz with his supersonic hearing would hear me talking. I had to get out of this hotel room. Somehow.

I checked the settings on the phone turning the ringer to silent. There were so many things I needed to tell Nicolas, but I needed to do it in person. I wondered briefly if I should have asked him to keep Ramón in Albuquerque or bring him with to St. Louis. Which location would be safest? I didn't have a clue. Maybe we could discuss that tomorrow evening. I stepped into the shower and let the water wash away my anxiety, or at least I tried. It didn't work. I finally gave up, returning to the bedroom and crawling under the covers still in my robe. Not only did I need to figure a way out of the hotel room tomorrow night, but I also needed to find a hiding place for my phone. This was too important to let Taz find it before I could meet with Nicolas. I wouldn't have another chance. Time was running out for me and Ramón. I just hoped that the same loyalty we shared all these years still existed after our cousins' deaths. If he decided I wasn't worth the risk, he

ST. LOUIS SECRETS

could easily turn over my whereabouts to his father. I'd have another family after me. Like I needed to up the danger in my life.

Chapter 13

Taz

Rosa walked into the living room in jeans and a soft sweater. Both looked painted on. I forced my eyes to concentrate on her face. That twenty pounds of extra weight had gone straight to her curves, even though she didn't need any help in that department. Distraction should be Rosa's middle name.

"Hey, Taz." Rosa blinked her long lashes at me. "Any chance the girls can come over and play?"

I squinted and tilted my head. What was her angle? Her expression gave me nothing but hopeful innocence. It was an act. She had to be up to something. I had guarded thousands of witnesses over my time with the US Marshal Service either in the courtroom or at safe houses, and they all had hidden agendas. Or maybe I had grown jaded over the years. I knew she was bored and stressed. It was typical for witnesses to be jittery before a trial. The three girls had gotten along the other night. What could it hurt if they came over? Everyone was a little on edge. A lot of time and effort had gone into this trial. It needed to go perfectly. We couldn't afford any mistakes. El Lobo Rojo was going down. Failing to send him to jail wasn't an option.

"I'll give them a call." I agreed. As long as they hadn't made plans, I didn't see why not.

I dialed Jac's room number first. Sofía answered.

"Rosa wants to know if you'd like to visit?"

"Is something wrong with her fingers?"

"What do you mean?"

"Why isn't she calling me?"

"Because she's not allowed on the phone."

"Wow. I hope that's just because she's in WITSEC and not because you are one of those men who won't let women do anything on their own."

I sighed. Why couldn't Jac have left his fiancé back in Albuquerque?

"It's a WITSEC rule."

"Oh good. I didn't want to preach feminist doctrine at you."

"Please don't." I winced. My sister did enough of that already. She called both my brother and I Neanderthals.

"Alright. I'll call Mari and be over in a bit."

She hung up.

A half hour later there was a knock on the door. I checked the peephole. Mari and Sofía were standing there giggling. Why did I agree to this again?

Rosa waited behind the separating wall to the bedroom, just as I had instructed her to. As soon as the door closed, she rushed into the room squealing.

"I missed you."

The girls hugged one another, and I scratched my chin watching the encounter. I didn't understand women. Not at all. She had barely met Sofía, and from César's account, Rosa hadn't known Mari all that long either. But they all seemed like old friends.

"Are you talking to me or the tequila?" Mari grinned as she pulled a fifth from the bag she was carrying.

The girls got settled in the dining room. Sofía pulled out a deck of cards and shuffled them like a dealer.

"What should we play?"

ST. LOUIS SECRETS

"Poker." Mari and Rosa said together.

"Just not strip poker." Rosa grinned. "Sorry Taz. We're not your entertainment."

I rolled my eyes and picked up the magazine sitting on the coffee table. As they started playing 5-card stud, their chatter, laughter, and easy camaraderie loosened the tension in my shoulders. I liked hearing Rosa laugh. She didn't do it nearly enough. I shook myself. It wasn't my business. I shouldn't care either way. She was a job. Nothing more. If it got personal, I'd be careless. And that would be dangerous.

"Hey, I've heard The Hill has great Italian food," Rosa said.

"Really?" Mari groaned. "I love Italian."

"Yum," Sofía said. "Sounds delicious. Now I'm starting to get hungry."

"Maybe we can go out somewhere for dinner?" Rosa asked. Her eyes glanced up and met mine.

"Is there a particular restaurant you're interested in?" Mari asked.

"I read about Zia's in the hotel magazine. It looked amazing. It's one of the few things Taz lets me read."

Rosa was always poking fun that I didn't let her do anything. I grumbled while I flipped through the same magazine she was talking about. There were rules against outside media. I had to suffer through re-reading the same stuff she did. It wasn't fun for me either, but it was necessary to keep everyone safe.

"The pictures look amazing and Todd says it's one of the best restaurants in the city. Apparently, the sauce is unbelievable. They sell it at the grocery stores and are always running out of it."

"Who is Todd?"

"He's a concierge. Super nice guy. A total workaholic. You can find him down in the lobby most days."

Rosa walked over and snagged the magazine from my grasp. I scowled at her, but she just shrugged and walked away. I didn't like that she was talking to Todd. She wasn't supposed to use the phone or answer the door. Exactly when had they had the conversation? I knew of only a handful of calls for room service even though I frowned on her doing it. The only other time I could think of was when she had escaped down to the lobby that first night. Although with her, you never could tell. Those dark brown bedroom eyes held too many secrets.

Rosa flipped to the ad for Zia's and showed the girls the menu. I agreed that their food was amazing. I had sampled a variety of restaurants after moving to St. Louis from Houston. My mouth watered as the girls discussed different entrees. My stomach growled. Rosa glanced over at me and smirked. I called Jac's number knowing that César was with him.

'You guys make dinner plans?'

'No. Not yet. We're just finishing up with the AUSA.'

I knew they were discussing the case with the prosecution. The trial should have started already, but Luís' lawyer had filed a motion to suppress evidence.

"How's the trial going?"

"About like you'd think," Jac said.

"It's complete BS." I heard César say in the background.

"Yeah," Jac agreed. "The defense lawyer went on and on that the evidence was obtained illegally. It was inadmissible. Yada. Yada. But we all know the warrants were good."

"You think it's a stall tactic?" I asked.

"Who knows? Maybe the judge is hoping we'll come to an agreement and finally settle."

"No way," I yelled. The girls glanced over at me. I turned away from them and lowered my voice. "Luís needs to get the maximum. No deals."

"I know. The prosecution doesn't want to settle either. I've made it clear there has been too much time and money invested in the drug bust and building the case. It stretches multiple states and law enforcement agencies. I told them the same thing. No plea deals."

ST. LOUIS SECRETS

"Good." I let out a whoosh of breath.

Most federal cases never went to trial. The judicial system was an expensive process. I remember my mentor, a Texas Marshal back home used to always say, "The too's will getcha every time. Too many crimes, and too little time." That about fits the Federal court system. Plea bargains had become the norm with some ninety-five percent of federal cases settling. The other five percent went to trial. Luckily for the prosecution, nearly all resulted in convictions. Our case was solid. Based on the amount of cocaine in the shipment, along with other drugs and guns, he should be going away for a very long time. Not to mention the detailed notes taken by Mari's brother, a CI who had worked the case before his untimely death. That kid had gotten names, dates, and locations of shipments. We would be able to take down more people involved in the drug operation. But taking down someone in Luís' position within the Lorenzo family, a Colombian drug trafficking empire was going to make a mark. It was a huge win for our side. Not only would it reduce the shipments, but it would send a message to others. We were not going to stand by while drug shipments continued to cross the U.S. border unchecked.

"What was the media like at the courthouse?" I asked.

"Insane. They have the camera in Luís' face most of the time. He's playing up the angle that he's an immigrant trying to run his business, and it's all a huge misunderstanding."

"When the witnesses start parading through the courtroom, and all the evidence is presented, he'll be singing a different tune."

"I'm sure."

"What about the El Lobo Rojo angle?" I asked.

"The media loves the name. A journalist for the St. Louis Post-Dispatch said the Red Wolf has a ring to it."

"It's not just the name, but how he got it."

"The rumors surrounding the number of murders committed by El Lobo Rojo had the journalist practically salivating over the story. If we can get Luís to admit to his nickname in court, the papers will crucify him."

"Is he planning on testifying?"

"Right now, no."

"His ego is too big. I bet he wants to tell everyone. Rosa said back in Colombia, no one called him Luís. Everyone called him by his nickname. He loved the fear. Got off on it. She thinks he misses that."

"Well, his slick lawyer doesn't want him on the stand."

"That's a smart play for the defense, not that it will help him."

"I agree."

"What does Luís think of the publicity?"

"He's a smug bastard. You know how he was with the cameras. He should have been a politician. Luís smiles like nothing can touch him. It makes me sick." Jac said.

"Glad I'm not there. I'd want to punch him again."

"Probably best, you're not," he chuckled.

"How much longer do you think it's going to be?"

"The judge mentioned he would hear the rest of the defense's reasoning for evidence suppression over the next two days. He won't allow the defense to de-rail the trial any longer than that. The judge will give his ruling on Friday. After that he's bringing in the jury. The official trial starts on Monday. It could be as early as Tuesday, that witnesses will be brought in to testify."

"Well, wrap it up. The girls are hungry and so am I. They decided on Zia's."

"I'll call to put in a reservation."

"I can meet you there with the girls," I said.

"You got it. I'll text you the time slot I get."

The girls had been listening to my side of the conversation. I was wondering why it had grown so quiet. After hanging up, the girls whispered back and forth.

"We'll be back." Mari and Sofía said heading to the door.

ST. LOUIS SECRETS

"Where are they going?" I asked Rosa.

She shrugged. "They wanted to dress up for dinner. I told them my options were limited."

I felt like I should apologize for her lack of wardrobe, but then I bit my lip. She got the allotted funds like all the other witnesses. It wasn't my fault.

Before long Mari and Sofía were back with bags of outfits, makeup, and jewelry. Apparently, Mari made jewelry for her Etsy store, so she wanted to give Rosa a few matching pieces with whatever outfit she decided on. They all got ready together in our suite. The volume rising in pitch with their animated conversations made me crave some headphones. I went back into the living room and tried to turn the volume of the TV up to drown them out. It wasn't working. I think they were trying to talk over the TV. I finally gave up and stepped outside the hotel suite for a few minutes to stand in the hallway. The silence was blissful. But it only lasted a few minutes. The door opened behind me.

"Come back in. We need a male opinion." Sofía said.

I got shoved onto the couch for an impromptu fashion show.

"Rosa's not sure which outfit looks best, and neither of us can agree. She's trying on borrowed bits and pieces from both Mari and me."

I shook my head and sighed. How did I get roped into this? What did having a Y chromosome do with judging fashion? I had been trying to keep my professional distance, and my eyes locked north of the horizon. Now I was being forced to stare at Rosa's curvy assets. It was going to be the death of me. Every outfit she tried on showed a little more skin. By the end, I was sweating. She looked like a wet dream. My throat dried up. I was going to tell her to take it off. She couldn't wear that last one in public, but I stopped myself. Everything I was about to say, would make me sound like a jealous lover.

"They all look good." I managed to get out. I closed my eyes.

"You don't think this is a little much?" She asked.

I glanced at where Rosa was gesturing. It was the necklace. That must have been one of the pieces that Mari had given her. I wasn't about to insult her. She was another witness in the trial. Mari had been drugged and almost kidnapped by Luís.

The trouble was the piece of metal and stone seemed to draw your eyes to her cleavage. I licked my lips and stared. My mind blanked and only carnal thoughts tumbled around in my brain.

"Taz?" She asked.

"Fine. Fine. Yes." I blew out a breath. "So, is everyone almost ready? We should get a move on if we want to make our reservation?"

The restaurant wasn't far away; only 12 minutes from the hotel and less than 5 miles away. Once we turned on Shaw, it didn't take long for the scents of garlic, basil, and oregano to permeate the air around us. Driving through The Hill at dinner time was an experience of culinary delight. Homes and restaurants alike smelled heavenly. Pots of spicy Italian gravy slow-cooked over stovetops, getting ready to serve the hungry masses. The intoxicating aromas left everyone in the car salivating.

"Dios mío." Rosa inhaled. "Everything smells divine. How can anyone live here and not weigh 500 pounds?"

"Lots of sex." Sofía joked. "That's what Jac's grandmother says. She's part Italian and swears that's how she keeps her figure."

The girls giggled.

"I need to meet that woman." Rosa laughed. "She sounds like a hoot."

ST. LOUIS SECRETS

"You bet. We'll have to plan a trip. She's in her seventies, but you wouldn't know it by the way she acts. I think you and her would get along great." Sofía said.

I knew that was never going to happen, but I didn't want to dampen the mood, so I kept my mouth shut. I should have never allowed her to get so close to Mari and Sofía. Not that I had much of a choice in the matter. Rosa was creating friendships she couldn't keep. Her new life would have to start fresh, with no ties to her old life. It was one more reason for her to hate me when we separated ways.

The Hill was busy and parking was scarce. I had to drive around the neighborhood for a bit. I passed Charlie Gitto's, and Mama's. You couldn't go wrong with any of the Italian restaurants on The Hill. They were all fabulous. After a few minutes of scouring the neighborhood, I scored a parking space right across the street from Zia's on Wilson. The last thing I wanted was for the girls to walk several blocks in heels. I also couldn't drop them off and leave them unguarded while I parked. Even though The Hill was relatively safe, I wouldn't risk the girls' safety. The Italians that lived in the neighborhood were a tight-knit community and took care of their own. Nobody stepped out of line without approval. Supposedly, The Hill had been mafia-free since the 80s, but rumors told a different story. Ties in the families ran deep. If someone from Colombia was after Rosa, they more than likely wouldn't do anything here for fear of reprisal.

Strolling into Zia's with three beautiful women, I felt a little like Bosley escorting Charlie's Angels. Two brunettes and a blonde. Rosa had worn her wig. I thought she looked better with her naturally dark brown hair, but I also didn't want anyone to recognize her. Rosa's natural beauty and vibrant personality stood out in a crowd. Even with the disguise, it was hard to mask her vivacious energy. Pairing that with her thick Colombian accent, no amount of camouflage could really hide her. Several people turned to stare at us. We were dressed up to go out on the town. I had even put on a dark suit. I didn't want to look out of place next to the girl's glammed-up attire. I glared at those around us. I didn't like how much attention we were getting. I didn't have a backup. I should have asked some of my deputies to tag along, but I gave them the night off. With Jac and César, I figured we would be covered, but they weren't here yet. The high-top tables in the bar left little standing room while we waited for our table. Sofía ordered drinks at the bar. I found a few chairs for the girls by mean-mugging some men at the next table. Even on a weekday and with a reservation, we still had to wait. Jac and César arrived slightly after we did.

"Mind if we join you and your harem of hotties?" César asked.

He slid in behind Mari and planted a kiss on her lips. "I think I'll take this one off your hands."

Mari squealed when he picked her up. He stole her seat and planted her on his lap in one smooth move. Jac was a bit more subtle, sliding his arm around Sofía's waist. He started nibbling on her ear and she giggled.

"Did you miss me?" He asked.

Rosa and I stared at one another. I moved closer to her to give the other two couples room. Her eyebrows raised. I didn't quite know what I was doing. I suddenly felt like an awkward teenager on a first date.

"Do you know what you want to eat?" I asked.

"I don't know. Whatever is cooking in the kitchen smells amazing. Have you been here before? Any recommendations?"

"Chicken parm or the toasted ravioli. Both are unbelievable. But really everything here is good. Whatever you're in the mood for?"

Rosa licked her lips. "So many things are tempting."

She wasn't looking at the menu anymore. Rosa was staring at me. Her eyes held heat. The draft from the front door of the restaurant wasn't enough to cool the temperature between us.

"Sir," The hostess said, "Your table is ready."

ST. LOUIS SECRETS

I blew out a breath. I'd take the distraction. Anything to not follow up on what Rosa's eyes were begging for.

Chapter 14

Rosa

The burst of ripe tomatoes in the marinara sauce sent my tastebuds to paradise. The pasta was cooked to perfection and the chicken drenched in a zesty parmesan coating made me moan with every bite. I was in heaven. If there was such a place on earth, it was here in St. Louis at Zia's on the Hill. The chicken parm was literally to die for. That thought made me pause, and reflect on my cousin Ramón. I needed to make sure he was ok. The meal was nearly over. I couldn't eat another bite of my entrée, not because it wasn't muy deliciosa, but because worry had stolen my appetite. Sneaking away from the table to make a call hadn't been as easy as I thought it would be. I knew I was running out of time.

"Order some dessert for me," I said to Mari as I slid out of my seat.

I waved the waiter over.

"Where's the bathroom?" I asked.

He pointed about twenty feet away. I refused to look at Taz for fear he would be able to read my mind. He always seemed to know exactly what I was about to do. Taz was perceptive. Way too perceptive for my taste. I could usually lie with ease. Growing up in Bogatá, that was a life skill acquired out of necessity. My heart was in my throat. He knew where I was going and could stop me if he wanted to. Walk. Don't run. I told myself, forcing my steps to be unhurried. I could feel his gaze burning into me. Reaching the door to the bathroom, I glanced back at the table. Our eyes met briefly. I quickly opened the door and slammed it shut, locking it behind me.

The stall was private. With all the noise from the restaurant, even if Taz did wander over, he wouldn't be able to hear a thing. I dialed Nicolas and started pacing back and forth in the small space. By the third ring, I was nervous. By the fourth, I was nearly in a panic. I might not get another shot at calling him tonight. What would Nicolas do if he didn't get a call? Would he not show up tomorrow at noon, like I asked him to? What did the Mendozas think about the whole situation? I'm sure they were celebrating Luís' downfall, but what moves were they making? They might seek to expand their territory. They could have decided I was a liability. Not that I knew the inner workings of their family, but the Lorenzos and Mendozas worked in the same business. Our shipments took similar routes. If I gave information to the feds, more than likely it would affect the Mendozas as well.

He answered on the fifth ring, and relief flooded me.

"Buenas noches Conejita Morada."

I gulped in breaths of air. "Nicolas. It's so good to hear your voice."

"Apuestas al caballo perdedor."

"I did not bet on the losing horse. I got stuck with him. I had no choice."

"There is always a choice."

"Like Maria and Felipe had options?"

"Good point," he said. "But they were driven by their emotions. I thought you were smarter. Used your head and not your heart."

I sighed. At one time maybe.

"You know I made a promise to Maria."

It was his turn to sigh.

"I know. And that's why I'm bound to honor your request. Otherwise, I'd be tempted to let you deal with the consequences alone."

"No, you wouldn't." I gave a harsh laugh. "The guilt would eat you alive."

"It already does," he mumbled.

"I don't have long. I'm holed up in a bathroom at a restaurant. The others will hunt me down soon."

"You mean Chief Deputy Marshal Bennett."

I frowned. "How did you know he was the one watching me?"

"We have eyes and ears everywhere. My father is most interested in the case, especially in your testimony."

Having the attention of Mario Mendoza was not something I wanted. The Lorenzo brothers were bad enough.

"Did you hear about José?" I asked.

"Yeah," he laughed. "What a dumbass."

I shrugged. "He wasn't too bright, but someone got to him. Did you hear who might have done the hit?"

"I don't know."

I wasn't sure I believed him. There was a slight hesitation in his voice like he might know something and didn't want to tell me.

"Would you tell me if it was someone in your family that ordered it?"

"No," he said.

At least he was honest.

"But it wasn't a Mendoza hit. We'd have no reason to kill off a witness. My father would probably buy him a cerveza for testifying against Luís."

"Do you have any ideas?"

"There are rumors. The immediate suspect is Luís. It makes the most sense. Plus he's made inquiries. The older Lorenzo brothers are a possibility, but I doubt they would waste time or money on Luís. They sent him away for a reason. However, people have been known to do stupid things for family."

"Ouch."

I knew he meant me and what I was willing to do for Ramón and Maria. But I couldn't help how I felt. Maria was the first one in the family who was nice to me. I owed everything to her. Maria's son, Ramón was more like a nephew than a cousin to me, especially due to our age difference. He was 21 and I was 39.

"Of course, there is a third possibility," Nicolas said. "Revenge. Since José was a sicario. It could have been a family member of one of his hits wanting to even the score," he gave a harsh laugh. "I rather like the irony of that."

"It couldn't have just been an accident?" I asked. "Wrong place. Wrong time."

"I don't believe in coincidences."

"Yeah. Me neither." I agreed.

"How are you going to escape the watchful eyes of the Marshal tomorrow?"

"I have a plan. You remember how well I played hide and seek when we were little?"

He chuckled. "But you always cheated at that game. You went outside the boundaries."

"I didn't cheat. I was creative."

A knock sounded on the door. I wondered if there was a line forming on the other side.

"I gotta go." I bit my lip. "Did you bring Ramón with you?"

"How do you know I'm in St. Louis already?"

I didn't. But I also knew Nicolas wouldn't fail to show up. He always kept his promises and wouldn't be late. To make the meeting, he'd either have flown in today or first thing tomorrow morning.

"Yeah. I brought the kid. He wouldn't take no for an answer. Said he had to see you again."

ST. LOUIS SECRETS

My eyes started tearing up. I'd get to see him one more time.

"Thank you." I sniffed.

"Don't start bawling. I never know what to do in those situations."

"I'll see you tomorrow at noon. I've been considering different places. I think the St. Louis Zoo will probably work out best. Once I'm there, I'll message you where I'm at."

"Sounds good. And be careful."

"Don't let your dad hear you talk like that." I scoffed. "Caring about a Lorenzo? He'll have you shot as a traitor."

"What my father doesn't know," he said. "Will keep us both alive."

Ain't that the truth? After Nicolas hung up, I freshened up quickly, knowing the call had taken longer than I wanted it to. I stared at the mirror, schooling my expression, getting ready to face my crew. Because that's what they were. Mari, César, Sofía, Jac, and even Taz had become mine in a way most of the Lorenzo family had never been. Even though we didn't share blood ties, we were all in this together. We had a common goal, taking down Luís Lorenzo. El Lobo Rojo. The bane of my existence. Did I feel bad lying to them? Sure. But it was necessary, even if it meant ruining the trust I had built. I just hoped I'd live long enough to ask for their forgiveness.

Chapter 15

Taz

My phone rang at 9. It was the office.

"Bennett here."

"Hi Taz," Sandi said. "Can you come in a little before the team meeting today?"

"Sure. What's going on?" I asked.

"Just some internal issues that need your attention."

"Can you be more specific?"

"Not over the phone."

What the hell did that mean? This line was secure. Or it should be.

"I need someone to watch my witness. Who's available?"

"Deputy Weber was scheduled to relieve you. I can send him over early."

"Yeah. That'll work. As soon as he gets here, I'll head in."

"Thanks," she said and hung up.

I wondered what that could be about. I hadn't been with the Missouri branch that long and I wasn't up to speed on the many nuances of running the district office. I'm sure several of the deputies had been disappointed not getting the position, even if it was only temporary.

ZIZI HART

Thirty minutes later Frank showed up.

"This here is Deputy Marshal Frank Weber." I introduced the man to Rosa.

She lounged on the couch in her robe flipping through a fashion magazine. Her eyes rose giving him a brief glare before returning to her magazine.

"Ah. My new babysitter. Lovely."

"Rosa's a handful. Don't let her give you any sass?"

She took the opportunity to show me how fluent she was in obscene sign language. I couldn't help but smirk. I actually liked her sass, even if I complained about it. The woman still had spirit, despite all she had been through.

I was anxious to get to the office. As soon as the meeting was over, I could get back here. I didn't like leaving Rosa with anyone else. Especially after spending some additional time together, I rather liked her willful attitude. It kept me on my toes. I didn't want to admit it, but I also enjoyed her company. Maybe a little too much.

The office was busy, but I didn't mind the chaos. That's probably why I enjoyed Rosa so much. I smiled as I walked into my corner office and started flipping through a pile of paperwork and mail that had accumulated while I had been what was the word Rosa used? Oh yeah, babysittin'.

Sandi walked in and closed the door.

"What is it that needs doing?" I asked.

She took a seat and crossed her legs. Sandi took time smoothing out the wrinkles from her skirt. I wanted to give her time to say whatever she needed, but I was also impatient. A habit I had never outgrown.

ST. LOUIS SECRETS

Sandi licked her lips. "I need to know why you broke up with me."

"What?" I shook my head. That's what this whole thing was about.

"This is highly inappropriate."

"Just like it was highly inappropriate for you to fuck me on your desk." Sandi shrilled.

I didn't like that harsh language. If it had come from a man, I would have put him in his place.

"That was fifteen years ago." I lowered my voice, hoping she'd do the same.

The walls were thick, but there was still a chance someone could overhear our conversation, especially with Sandi's high-pitched voice.

She shrugged. "I want to know why."

I rubbed a hand down my face, not believing this was happening. How long would I have to pay for my transgressions? This is why I didn't get serious with anyone. I was happy being a bachelor. Relationships brought drama. I didn't need that in my life.

"We were young. It was a mistake. Co-worker romances don't work. Especially in our field."

"So, it's just because we're working together?"

Sandi looked hopeful. I didn't want her to quit the job, thinking that would somehow fix what had gone wrong between us. The co-worker thing didn't help, but it was more complex. We just didn't want the same things.

"What did I do wrong?" She asked.

"Nothing," I said honestly. "What's with all these questions?"

Sandi slumped in her seat. She sighed. "I don't mean to sound all wounded, but my self-esteem is shot after the divorce. My ex cheating on me was just the beginning. Lately, it just seems like, I don't know. No one wants me."

I sighed. When did therapy become part of my job duties? I wasn't good at this sort of thing. Didn't we have HR to discuss warm and fuzzy feelings with? Not that I'd want Sandi to discuss this with them, especially in regards to what we did, even if it was fifteen years ago, and mutual. They would still frown on the situation. I already had the Attorney General breathing down my neck. The man always had it in for me. I hardly needed to give him more ammunition.

"Are you hitting on guys here at work?"

She bit her lip. "Yes."

I shook my head. "That's your problem. If they're smart, they'll say no."

She jumped to her feet, her face flushing.

"Sit down," I commanded.

She did take a seat but clearly wasn't happy about it. Sandi sat with crossed arms and a frown.

"Us breaking up had nothing to do with you. You're beautiful and smart. There is nothing wrong with you and you didn't do anything wrong when we dated." I flinched at the word dating. That wasn't really what we did back then. It was more athletic hookups to erase bad memories of the job. At the time, I thought she felt the same way. But when she got too serious, I had ended it. Apparently, quite badly. Over the years we lost touch since we worked in separate states. I had heard from a mutual friend that Sandi got married years ago. I hadn't realized she had divorced before taking the job in St. Louis. Not that it would have stopped me from accepting the job, but at least I wouldn't have been blindsided. We had worked together for 6 months at this office, fifteen years ago. I tried to recall how she took the breakup. I don't remember her being that upset. She knew my assignment in St. Louis was temporary back then, just like it was now.

"You need to look outside the office for your needs." This was so embarrassing. "You're barking up the wrong tree with me. It will never happen again. I'm older and wiser now. You should know better too."

ST. LOUIS SECRETS

Sandi blinked up at the ceiling. "I know you're right. I appreciate you talking with me. My ex really did a number on me," she smoothed out her skirt and stood. "I'll go man the phones," she smiled, although it didn't reach her eyes.

Huck came running in and almost knocked Sandi down.

"Sorry," he panted. "Chief, we got a call. Another witness. Pablo. He's missing."

"Oh, geez." I slammed my fists on the desk and stood. "Sandi, go. Huck, details."

Huck rattled off the information. I wondered if we would find Pablo dead too. Who was doing this? What a crappy day this was turning out to be. The Attorney General was going to blame me for this. He said it was a mistake that I was ever given this position, even if it was only temporary. Now this would just prove him right.

My phone rang and I noticed it was my brother Blake. He rarely ever called me. Last year when my sister had been hospitalized, we had differing opinions on how to handle the situation. Harsh words were said, and there was still bad blood between us.

"I don't have time to talk," I said.

"Dad is in the hospital."

"What?" I asked, collapsing into my chair.

"Heart attack."

I pictured my dad, a huge man, taken down by some medical issue. It didn't seem possible. The man was larger than life. I squeezed my eyes shut.

"Is he going to be ok?"

"He's yelling at the doctors. So yeah. I think so."

"I'm in the middle of something. But once things are sorted, I'll come home."

"Dad didn't want me to call, but I thought you should know."

"Thank you for that. Can you keep me informed?"

"Sure thing," he hung up.

I shook my head. Could anything else go wrong today?

"Sir I need to speak to you," Sandi said running over to me.

I was rushing around the outer offices. I was not going to go through this with her again. How many times did I have to tell her? We were never going to happen.

"What?" I barked out.

She hesitated for a second then blurted, "Deputy Weber called in. Rosa's gone."

The room just dropped twenty degrees. The blood in my veins felt like ice. My mind swirled with a frenzy. If she died, there would be no place on earth the man responsible could hide. I shouldn't have left her. I still would have been there at the hotel if it hadn't been for Sandi.

"You," I said with a growl, pointing at her. Was she the leak? Had she set Rosa up? And all the others?

She grabbed her chest and started backing away from me. I knew when I got like this, my face froze into an expressionless mask that made hardened criminals run in fear. I gripped the desk I was leaning against in an effort not to reach out and do something unforgivable. I forced myself to hang onto a shred of my control.

Sandi finally found her voice. "It's not my fault," she whined. "I didn't know Rosa would take off the moment you left. You should be blaming her, not me."

I knew this. In my head, I did. But reason had flown the coop. The rest of the office was watching me closely. I inhaled

ST. LOUIS SECRETS

sharply and closed my eyes. My breaths were ragged. I forced them to even out. Losing it wasn't going to help the situation. We needed answers. Right now, I had no idea if Rosa was dead. I had to assume she was alive. Right now, she was only missing. I wouldn't allow her to be killed on my watch.

Sandi punched the blinking button on the phone in front of me.

"I'm handing you over to the Chief."

She gave me the receiver.

"I'll give notice sir." Deputy Weber said. His voice shook with emotion. He cleared his throat. "You'll have it before my shift ends."

He was a good man. I had read his history, like I had for everyone at the office. Their credentials were astounding. I had an amazing group of people working under me. I didn't know if I would have a job after this fiasco. Three missing witnesses. The last thing St. Louis needed was to lose manpower on top of everything else.

"No, you won't." I spit out. "You'll help me find her."

Huck's eyebrows rose. He was watching me closely, ready to reel me in if I lost it. It might have been my tone of voice or the fact I was nearly screaming. I never lost my temper. Or almost never. There was a reason I had gotten my nickname. I was usually like ice in tough situations. I could compartmentalize my feelings and deal with issues logically. But if things got too personal, I went off the rails. Just like I was doing now. I reacted like the Tasmanian devil in those cartoons, a swirling hurricane of destruction in my path. I nodded to Huck to let him know I was controlling it. He nodded back.

"Stay at the hotel," I said to Weber. "Send updates through Huck."

I let out a breath and stormed into my office, slamming the door.

My fists were tight. White knuckles and heavy breathing. I tried to focus on that. Breathing. What information did we have about her whereabouts? What reason did she have for leaving? The whole thing didn't make sense. Unless someone had gotten to her. But how? Did I really think someone had managed to kidnap my witness? No. It made more sense that she left on her own, which meant there was still time to get to her. We also needed to figure out where Pablo was. But that took second priority. I needed to divide my team and search for both.

There was a knock on the door. I cleared my throat.

"Enter."

It was Huck.

"You won't be throwing stuff at me, will you boss?"

I shook my head.

"Close the door."

"Not sure if I should be in here alone with you. Might be dangerous."

"Eff You."

"There you are." Huck grinned. "You had me worried there for a minute."

I cracked my neck, loosening my shoulders. He closed the door.

"I got the video of Rosa walking west on Market toward 22nd. It shows her getting into a cab heading south."

"Probably toward I-64." My mind spun. "Did you get a cab number?"

"Sure thing. Sandi's calling the cab company now."

Another knock on the door. This one was soft and hesitant.

"Come in."

Sandi walked in slowly. Her shoulders were slouched and she rubbed her hands together like she could feel the chill in the air.

"Um," She licked her lips. "We have a drop-off point for the cab," she sighed. "Forest Park Visitor's Center."

ST. LOUIS SECRETS

I pinched my temples. Could Rosa have picked a tougher location? Forest Park had 1300 acres of lakes, athletic fields, and walking paths, including museums, a skating rink, an outdoor theater, and a zoo. Most of the places were free to the public, so she could literally be anywhere. The place was massive. It was going to take forever to canvas. If she was escaping federal custody, why hadn't she gone to the airport, bus, or even the train station? Why Forest Park? She knew someone was targeting witnesses. Rosa had read the article about José. Why would she jeopardize her safety like this? She wasn't stupid. Rosa had been brought up by a ruthless family and managed to survive all these years. I shook my head. It was no use trying to come up with reasons. They didn't really matter in the scheme of things. I had to prioritize. I just wanted to get her back in one piece. There was a threat against her and she was out there all alone. I thought of all the things I knew about Forest Park. They had implemented new security measures, installing video cameras. Although I didn't know how much of the park they covered. Security patrols were handled by a limited number of Mounted Police and a few Park Rangers. I knew the basic layout of the park, but I'd have to rely on their expertise once we got there.

"I want someone at the visitor's center, even though she's more than likely gone. Check with the staff, and search the building." I said to Huck. "Fan out on the walking paths. I'll head to the Mounted Patrol Unit. We need someone checking feeds on the park's video surveillance. There is a lot of ground to cover. She is more than likely on foot, but she could have taken another cab somewhere else. At this point, we don't know anything."

"What about Pablo?" Sandi asked.

"We need to split the teams to search for both."

Huck was on his radio calling out names and getting the teams rolling. I didn't need to give him any more direction. This is what he excelled at.

Sandi stood there looking down at my desk. I followed her line of sight and noticed my fists were still tight. I forced them to relax.

"I'm sorry," she blinked back tears. "I didn't realize how important she was to you."

What did she mean by that?

"You swear you weren't involved in this?"

"Her escape?" She asked. "No, of course not."

I wasn't sure I believed her but I didn't have time to question her. I also didn't like that she could read me so easily. It meant I wasn't masking my emotions.

"Focus on the tasks at hand," I said to Sandi. "Call all the out-of-town people from the Lorenzo case. Make sure everyone is on high alert. Our resources will be spread thin."

Sandi stood taller. "Yes, Chief."

"Let's roll," I said to Huck.

One witness dead and two more in the wind all from a single case. This was not good. If all three ended up dead-. No. I couldn't go there. Thinking along those lines was dangerous. Did I believe Sandi was the leak? That she had somehow orchestrated this? No. But someone at the Marshal's office was involved. And right now, everyone was a suspect. Unfortunately, I needed all the manpower I could get to find the witnesses. After that, I'd have to relocate everyone. We were running out of safe houses. I'd have to get creative. Rosa was our key witness. She knew the most secrets. Without her testimony, Luís could walk. Rosa had negotiated her protection agreement and had just violated it. Not that it would matter to the prosecution. We still needed her. I needed her. I'd find her a place that no one else knew about. That was the only way to keep her safe. Then I'd handle the traitor.

Chapter 16

Rosa

The walk down to the boathouse from the visitor's center took longer than I estimated. The path was slippery in part due to a recent snowstorm. The snow had melted just enough to form ice patches. I wasn't wearing the proper shoes. The feds didn't provide me with snow boots, but then again, they hadn't expected me to be outside very much. I walked faster. There was a main street just ahead. I was almost at Government Drive, finally. I had mapped out my walking path. Just a little further down was the zoo. I should be there in no time. A cop car rolled past. I ducked behind a tree. He was moving slowly like he was looking for someone. Mierda. Could they be looking for me already? I knew it wouldn't take the Marshal Service long before they discovered I was gone. I just figured I would have a little more time. At least I had the forethought to be dropped off at the opposite side of the park. The police car stopped. He wasn't moving. Doble Mierda. I'd have to go another way.

Backtracking, I followed the path around the lake. It had plenty of trees for cover. I checked the map on my phone. The internet was painfully slow. I shook the cheap prepaid phone like a magic 8 ball, thinking it might help with the signal. I was no good with electronics. I should have grabbed a map from the visitor's center. Would have. Should have. Ugh. My heart rate sped as I jogged down the path. I hadn't been exercising much lately. The amount of effort it took and my lack of speed were discouraging. Or it could have been the extra twenty pounds of weight. Curse St. Louis and their delicious food. I stopped for a moment and looked at my phone. The map had finally loaded. I could cut across the park through Picnic Island. That would take me over Art Hill, and from there I could turn down Fine Arts Drive to Government. The zoo was just on the other side of the Art Museum.

"Rosa."

I heard someone yelling behind me. OMG. It was Taz. He was on a quarter horse. What the hell? Where did the guy get a horse from? I glanced around looking for some place to hide, but he had already seen me. I noticed a bike leaning up against a tree. Who was out here in this weather biking? People in St. Louis were nuts. I hopped on the bike and a tall guy circled the tree zipping up his pants. He must have been taking a whiz.

"Hey, lady. Get off that bike. It's mine."

"Lo siento mucho. Emergencia." I yelled over my shoulder as I rode away.

Taz was gaining on me.

I peddled as fast as I could around the windy turns and came to a suspension bridge. It looked icy, but I didn't have a choice. I sped across, saying a little prayer that I wouldn't slip and slide my way off the bridge into the water below. My bike skidded, but I managed to keep control.

"Aaagh." I heard behind me.

I turned in time to see Taz splashing about in the lake. His horse stood on the other side of the bridge neighing. The horse must have known better than to cross the bridge. I didn't blame him for bucking Taz off. I hadn't wanted to cross either. Taz was yelling up a storm, which meant he must be ok; just soaking wet and mad as hell. I picked up my pace across another suspension bridge and onto the other side of the island. I'd have to ditch the

ST. LOUIS SECRETS

bike somewhere. I was too conspicuous. After the third bridge, I dropped the bike at the tree line and joined a group of kids and parents heading up the snow-covered hill. They were sledding on the snow leading down to the lake.

When I got to the top of the hill, I veered off from the group and crossed the street. There was another police car. Maldita policía. I went the only way I could, which was straight into the Art Museum. Taz was talking with the officer. How had he gotten here so quickly? I thought I had lost him. Taz spotted me, but I was already at the top of the stairs. Luckily, there was no line. I got in, snagged a map, and veered to the left. Running through the exhibits, I made my way to another exit on the opposite side of the building. I had noticed a sculpture garden on the map. While the museum had plenty of places to hide, I couldn't risk staying here for very long. I found a coat check room and was able to ditch my white coat for a black one. It was cute, but not very warm. I regretted the exchange almost immediately. I also stopped in the bathroom to take off the blonde wig. Someone had left a scarf and hat on one of the hooks in the stall. Another prayer was answered. Gracias, Saint Dismas, the patron saint of thieves. I slid the pink hat over my ears and wrapped the green scarf around my neck, covering my mouth.

The south entrance of the museum was fairly quiet. I strolled through the sculpture garden at a leisurely pace, trying not to look suspicious. What I wanted to do was sprint, but I controlled the urge. Crossing Valley Drive, I stayed close to the trees. There wasn't a path, so I had to stomp through patches of snow and ice. My shoes and socks were soaked by the time I reached Government Drive. At least I had made it difficult for la policía to track me. My discomfort wasn't important. I had to get to the meeting point. That was the only thing that mattered. Taz had left earlier for the office, which was a good thing because it had taken me longer to get through the park. A quick glance left and right. No policía. I let out a long breath of relief. I was able to walk straight across the street to the north entrance of the zoo. I picked up a map finding the spot where I would meet up with Nicolas. He had texted me three pictures. I was to meet him at the third one. It was on the South side of the zoo. At the River's Edge. It was a heavily forested area and the perfect spot to stay hidden.

"Were you followed?" A man in the shadows asked me.

It was Nicolas. I recognized his voice immediately. I wanted to tell him no, but that wasn't exactly the truth, and he'd know I was lying.

"I was, but I lost him."

"Are you sure?"

"Yes."

I thought about how angry Taz would be after the chase I led him on. Would he ever forgive me? Or did it even matter? It's not like I'd know him much longer. One way or the other I was leaving after my testimony. Either in a new city, with another life, or in a body bag.

Nicolas stepped from the shadows. I knew the drill. He searched me for wires and weapons. It was quick and efficient. All business.

"I've kept up my part of the bargain," he said. "Have you?"

I pressed my lips together. "You know I don't have it with me." I licked my lips. "It's on the way. Maybe a couple more days."

"How are you going to get it to me?"

"Once I get confirmation of the arrival, I'll send you a message."

"You better come through," he warned.

Nicolas stuck his hands in his pockets as he watched a family walk past, searching for the animal in the exhibit.

ST. LOUIS SECRETS

"How is Ramón?" I asked.

"The kid's fine. He's staying low. I left him back at the hotel."

"I thought he wanted to see me," I said. "Why didn't you bring him to the zoo?"

"Because I'm careful. That's why. I don't take risks. He stays under the radar. For now."

"Have you told him everything?"

"Just the essentials. How he's related to the Mendoza family," he chuckled. "He wasn't keen on meeting the family. Said he just wanted to work, so I got him a job."

My eyes went wide. I hadn't done all this, saving him from the Lorenzos only to have him wind up working for the Mendozas.

He chuckled. "Not with the family. There's no connection. He works at a warehouse under a fake I.D."

"Once the trial is over, it should be safe for him to go back home."

"I think he might be sweet on some girl he met at a bar in Albuquerque," he shrugged. "Might be hard to get him back on the boat."

I hadn't thought that he might be happy here. That hadn't occurred to me as a possibility. I always thought of him safe back in Colombia, but I never asked Ramón what he wanted. Not that I had the chance after the drug bust. My initial thoughts were around his safety. I didn't want him to go to jail. I thought WITSEC was the only option. It was selfish of me to want to do that to the kid. He shouldn't have his options stolen from him. I wouldn't force him to go back to Colombia. I knew how much I hated being tossed from relative to relative growing up. Having no stability. No choice. I wasn't going to do the same thing to Ramón. How could I stop the cops looking for him? Maybe I could talk to Taz. That is if he listened to a word I'd have to say after leading him on this merry chase through Forest Park.

"I need to tell him about his uncle," I said.

"You mean Luís. The kid has quite a few more uncles now."

"Yeah, I guess so."

"He looks just like his dad." Nicholas looked off in the distance. His voice had gone soft. There was silence for a few moments, then he shook his head. "Good thing he doesn't act like him though."

"He got good manners from his mamá." I agreed.

"You aren't going to tell me where you're staying?"

"Not on your life pendejo."

Nicholas grinned. "Such a mouth on you Rosa."

"Don't get me started." I laughed.

"We'll be here for a week."

"Where are you staying?" I asked.

"Union Station Hotel."

My spine stiffened. Of all the rotten luck.

Did he know where I was staying and was just toying with me? Or was this just a coincidence?

He was watching me far too closely The cabrón must know.

"Where's that?" I asked, concentrating on keeping my expression neutral. "Midtown?"

Nicolas scrutinized my face for a few moments. "It's just west of downtown. Not far from the arch."

"Do you have the address?"

He rattled it off.

I nodded. "I can have the package sent to your hotel's front desk or directly to your room when it arrives."

"What you don't find my company to your liking?"

I grinned. "It's just so hard to get away."

"That Marshal is persistent," Nicholas whispered. "I'll be in touch," he faded into the shadows and disappeared into a crowd of people walking through the exhibit. I frowned. I didn't get to talk to him more about Rámon. That's the reason I escaped in the first place. Why was he leaving? The crowd cleared, and Taz stood there looking like he was ready to kill. My eyes must have been as big as saucers. He had finally caught up to me.

"Jueputa."

I hadn't lost him like I thought. He stalked toward me. His coat and pants were soaked. It didn't look like he had even bothered to dry off. Ice dusted his hair.

"Rosa," he said my name like a curse. I could swear I saw steam coming off his body. Or maybe I was just imagining things. The closer he got, the more frightened I became. Taz seemed completely unhinged. I knew the man had a temper. He kept it hidden, but I had seen the signs. Repressed rage. I knew men who had similar issues with anger. They bottled it up until it exploded. I didn't want to be around something like that. Not again. I knew what they were capable of. I gulped. What was he going to do to me? I should run, at least until he cooled down. Glancing left and right, I searched for options. I shifted my stance, getting ready to sprint.

Chapter 17

Taz

I was vibrating with anger. The fear in her eyes was palpable. I didn't like it, especially knowing I was the cause. Rosa looked ready to bolt, and I wasn't about to let her slip away.

"Don't you dare move a muscle," I said through gritted teeth.

Water still dripped down my hair onto my shirt. I had chased this woman across the park, been thrown into the lake, lost her in the art museum, and tracked her through the zoo. I was fed up. I should have been cold, standing there soaking wet on a freezing December afternoon in St. Louis, but instead, I was on fire. My blood was boiling.

"You don't understand," she said, her voice trembling.

"Not a word." My voice came out like a hoarse growl.

I didn't want to hear her excuses. I grabbed her arm roughly and spun her around. Frisking her body, I found a phone.

"What's this?" I asked, shaking it in her face.

She turned her head away. Rosa knew she had been caught. She blew out a breath in frustration.

"You're all wet."

My eyes opened wide.

"And whose fault is that?"

She crossed her arms in front of her.

"Yours for following me."

"It's my job to protect you."

"Stellar job right now. You're dripping all over me. Do you want me to catch a cold?"

For the love of-. That's what she was mad at. I shook my hair out, sending droplets of water all over her. She screeched.

"We're leaving. Now."

She finally stopped her grumbling complaints and let me lead her back through the zoo in silence. After exiting the zoo, we still had quite a walk to where I parked the car. Rosa stumbled on the sidewalk, but I wasn't slowing down, not until we were safely back at the hotel. I picked her up and threw her over my shoulder. She gave a little high-pitched yip, but I kept walking. A few people stared, but no one approached us. I think they all knew better.

The car ride back to Union Station took forever. Traffic was horrid. It matched my mood. My shoes sloshed as I shifted gears and my seat was soaked. I hadn't packed a towel. I mentally added that to a list of supplies I wanted to keep in the trunk from here on out. Rosa kept fussing with the heater, trying to turn it warmer but it was already on the highest setting.

"Why doesn't this thing work any better?" She slammed her fist on the dashboard. Rosa rubbed her hands together and blew on them.

"Maybe you can pack a warmer coat next time you escape."

"Is that what you think? That I was running away?"

"What else could it be?" I asked. "You violated your agreement."

Rosa slumped back into the seat.

"I was coming back, you know," she muttered.

My eyebrows rose. Did she expect me to believe that nonsense? That she was planning to come back and testify?

"I'm good at tracking fugitives. No one gets away."

Her mouth scrunched into a frown.

"Is that all you think of me as? Someone you have to hunt down and arrest?"

Her voice sounded hurt, and I glanced over. It looked like she might have tears welling in the corners of her eyes. It took a lot to make the woman cry. I knew this.

No. Hell no. It was all an act. She was just trying to get my sympathy. Rosa was a con artist. Her ploys wouldn't work. I forced myself not to give in, even though it was killing me to see that lost look in her eyes.

When we got back to the hotel, I stormed in with Mrs. Connor in tow. Todd's eyebrows rose when he saw us. It could have been the trailing water I was dripping across the lobby floor or my stormy expression. He opened his mouth briefly then closed it. Todd must have thought better. He didn't utter a word. The kid was finally learning how to handle me. Shut up and get the hell out of my way.

Rosa didn't say anything the whole elevator ride up. We got into the suite and I checked to make sure we were alone. Only after bolting the door, did I release my hold on her. The hotel phone rang and I answered.

"Hey Chief, I saw you got her back."

"Affirmative." My voice was gruff.

"I've been messaging you."

"My phone took a dip."

"It looks like that's not all that did."

"We'll debrief in an hour." I glanced over at Rosa. "Make that two."

"You got it, boss. I'll inform the team."

I hung up and Rosa just stared at me. She had already taken off her coat and tossed it on the back of the couch along with her hat and scarf. Rosa unbuttoned her sweater and added it to the pile. She took a tentative step toward me, and then another. Rosa was wearing a short-sleeved T-shirt. I glanced at the marks on her arms where I must have grabbed her. I didn't realize that I had been holding her quite that tight. She didn't rub at the marks, but I knew they must have hurt.

I sneezed.

"You have to get out of those clothes," she grabbed my hand and pulled me into the bathroom.

I stood there as she started undressing me, unbuttoning my shirt. I didn't want to move fearing that I might do something crazy. She was right, with the cold weather and the lake water from the park, if I didn't get changed into something warm soon, I'd run the risk of catching something. She looked confused when she came to my gunbelt. I took over and removed all my weapons, setting them on the counter.

Rosa turned on the shower. She was taking care of me and I realized I wanted her to. It was a novel concept someone taking care of me for once. Protecting me. Even if it was from something as simple as a cold. I noticed that Rosa was wet too. In her effort to help get me out of my wet clothes, hers had gotten damp as well. Not as soaked as I was, but she was still shivering. I held the edge of her T-shirt and stared into her eyes. She gave a sharp intake of breath. I gave her time to say no, but she finally nodded. I pulled the shirt over her head. Her bra was that sexy black number. I traced the edges with my fingertips, pushing down the straps on her shoulders. I reached around her to unclasp the back, and let it fall to the floor. I licked my lips. Beautiful full breasts, with taught nipples. I wanted to worship them for hours, but she turned away from me, pulling off her shoes. Rosa peeled off her wet socks and skimmed out of her jeans and underwear. She stood in front of me in all her glory. While I had watched her undress, I had removed the rest of my clothing as well. It was hurried movements that reminded me more of the days when I was an awkward teenager. In fact, I felt more like a teen than a middle-aged man of 45. Once relieved of our clothes, we both took our time looking at one another. She was built with curves that I wanted to explore for days. Steam from the shower was smoking up the bathroom. I led her to the shower and the first warm spray of water felt like a balm to my skin, but I hardly needed it. Inside my body felt like an inferno. Suddenly nothing could keep me from Rosa's lips. They were so soft and inviting. I couldn't help myself. I pressed her back against the shower wall and kissed her like I was starving. It was brutal and demanding. My body molded into hers, and I stoked that fire inside. She moved against me rocking and moaning, her breasts rubbing against my chest. One hand stroked that sexy ass of hers, while the other thrummed her nipple like plucking guitar strings. And the sounds that she made. God Almighty. Her sexy moans were my undoing. I got down on one knee and parted her folds. She looked down at me, her lashes wet with the spray of the shower. Her pussy was hot to the touch. I wanted a taste. Not just wanted. Craved.

"Taz," She said watching me. The hungry look in her eyes surely matched my own. We had both been fighting this urge inside for what seemed like an eternity. The moment my lips touched her pussy, her head leaned back against the tile and she wrapped her legs around my head. My hands gripped her ass. Rosa gave me complete access and trust that I would keep her from falling and make this good for her. She said my name over and over as she rocked her hips back and forth. I smiled at the way she said my name. I wanted to keep hearing that, so I twirled my tongue, licking and sucking, avoiding her clit, making her as crazy as I felt. She undulated for me. Rocking into me, as I took what I wanted. What I had wanted since the moment I met her. She cried out my name so many times as she rode my mouth like a cowgirl at a rodeo. Bucking and writhing, and moaning. I finally focused on her clit, and her cries got louder and louder. I gave a soft bite to her mons and she came with a surge so powerful she was shaking. I kept up the ministrations getting every last whimper until her legs loosened and went limp. She blinked lazily down at me.

"Wow. I needed that." I said as I climbed to my feet.

She laughed.

"That should be my line."

"Mmm. Just a taste." I licked my lips savoring the flavor of Rosa, "but I need more."

Her grin got huge. She glanced at the shower. I think she was trying to figure out the logistics, but I knew it wouldn't be comfortable, and I didn't want our first time to test the limits of my flexibility or hers. She huffed, clearly not sure what to do.

"You're too damn big."

"That's not a complaint I hear often."

"I didn't mean it that way," she stared at my cock. "I meant your whole body is huge."

"Let me worry about the details. Are you warm enough?"

"I'm on fire," Rosa said.

"Me too."

I dried her off, and she enjoyed drying me off a little too much. I finally had to stop her, or I'd be taking her right here on the cold bathroom tile.

"I can't believe how muscular you are," she said. "You could be a bodybuilder."

"It's genetics."

"Bullshit. You must work out constantly."

I did hit the gym in between my work schedule. But you needed to stay in shape if you wanted to work cases. I might have let myself go soft if I worked behind a desk all day, but that wasn't my way. So workouts were more of a necessity.

I bundled both of us up in robes before opening the door.

"What about the cameras?"

I grinned. "I feel another internet glitch coming on."

I yanked the cord to the camera pointing at the bed.

She laughed. "How devious of you Marshal Bennett?"

"That's Chief Deputy Marshal."

"Oh, I forgot you are el jefe."

I liked her calling me the boss.

"I'll show you just how devious I can be."

ST. LOUIS SECRETS

Rosa stripped off her robe and leaped on the bed. She threw the robe at me and it bounced off my chest, landing on the floor.

"Prove it," she demanded.

And I did. Multiple times. At least up until the phone rang two hours later.

"Did I give you enough time?" Huck asked.

"Yep."

"Not gonna share any details?"

"Nope."

He sighed. "Was it good?"

Huck knew that I didn't kiss and tell, but he never stopped pushing.

"You have no idea," I said glancing at Rosa. She was curled up in the covers, fast asleep.

"Figured she would be a hot tamale in the sack."

"I can neither confirm nor deny."

"You don't have to," Huck said. "Your smug attitude speaks volumes."

I slipped on a T-shirt and jeans and walked into the living room.

"Not worried about what the AG will say if he finds out you're sleeping with the witness?"

"Who's going to tell them?" I asked.

"Not me. That's for damn sure." Huck chuckled. "You've let me slide in the past. As long as there are no recordings, as far as I'm concerned, it never happened."

I grinned. Huck had my back, and I had his. He would protect my secret, but I needed to be careful what I did with Rosa in front of the cameras. If someone else was watching, the rumors would spread. Not that I planned on a repeat performance. I needed to maintain control of the situation. I hadn't even discussed the fact that Rosa had broken her signed agreement with us. Testifying was a requirement, but she also couldn't escape custody. I'd have to talk with the AUSA on the implications.

"Now that you got that out of your system, you ready to work?"

"Shut up," I said.

"Alright. I get it. Enough chit-chat." Huck chuckled. "I'll put you through to the rest of the team if you're ready."

He conferenced me in.

"Any news on the team searching for Pablo?" I asked.

I had a bad feeling. It was taking too long to find him. Everyone gave updates, but then we switched over to Rosa. I had confiscated her cell phone, but it didn't provide me with much information. I gave the digits over to an investigator. They would research to see if they could figure out who she was communicating with.

"Did you get anything else from your interrogation with the witness?" Sandi asked.

Huck morphed a chuckle into a cough.

"Sandi, what are you doing on the call?" I asked.

"Taking notes," she said.

"We don't need admin on this one," I said. "Sandi, I need you to concentrate on calls, bringing in more resources. Everyone else knows what to do. Report into Huck for those searching for Pablo. He's running point. Pablo's not as critical of a witness. If he's gone, let's not waste much time on it. Two days max. After the trial, we can hunt him down. We need to prioritize. Rosa's testimony can send El Lobo Rojo away for good. Now that we have the witness back, this job is almost done. Less than a week before she testifies, then we can get her squared away in her new life, so we can get on with ours."

Chapter 18

Rosa

I blinked my eyes open. I heard Taz talking on the phone. He did that quite a bit, checking in with his team. That last part left me cold, despite the warm blankets cocooning my body. He wanted to get on with his life. I mean I didn't expect that he would be promising me his undying love after a few rolls in the hay, but it felt harsh right after we had been intimate. This was just a stop on the train for him. Nothing more. And I knew he was telling the truth. That's one thing I learned since getting to know him. He didn't lie. Oh, he might sugarcoat a situation, or refuse to talk about something. The man still had secrets, but he never outright lied. At least not to me. It might have been easier if he had.

I was still glad we had gotten that out of our system. We needed to. The unresolved lust had been building until it became almost unbearable. The problem was now that I realized just how fabulous sex could be with him, I wanted more. It sounded from Taz's point of view, that he felt the exact opposite. I should have figured. Typical man. He got what he wanted. I needed to figure out my next steps. There were a lot of unknowns in my future. I wondered where my new life would be. What state would they set me up in? They surely wouldn't have me stay here in St. Louis. So that meant, whatever we had between the two of us, would end in a week. My heart gave a little flutter. I didn't know what to think about that. Not just the uncertainty of a life with no ties, but losing the only connection I had made. As much as our wills battled against one another, I'd miss him. He mattered to me. I closed my eyes when I felt the mattress dip.

"I know you're awake," he said, "Your breathing is different."

I forced myself to grin. I guess there was no use faking being asleep around him. It wasn't going to do me any good. Taz kissed me. It was a quick peck on the lips, but I wanted more. So much more.

"I have to turn the cameras back on, so behave."

"Make me."

"Honey I would love to, but I have work to do. You gotta get ready for this trial, and I have other cases to review."

I forgot I wasn't his only job. He was the big wig controlling the whole East District of Missouri. I rolled over not liking how it made me feel. I was just a piece of his job. A checkmark on his list.

"Hey. Don't be like that."

"I don't know what you mean," I said. I hated being petty like this. I wasn't a needy person, at least not usually.

He slid his hand down my back and squeezed my ass. I turned to see his expression, but he had already walked away. I heard the click of the wire back into the camera and my excitement fizzled like a wet firecracker. It was a bit like watching an R-rated movie and realizing it was on a regular TV channel. All the swear words and sexy stuff had been edited out. My life had just gotten censored, just when things were finally getting good. I shoved the pillow over my face and screamed.

ST. LOUIS SECRETS

Breakfast came and went. It was uneventful despite my best efforts to get a rise out of Taz. I wore my sexiest Marshal-acquired clothing, and it wasn't doing the trick. By lunchtime, I came up with a plan, but Taz was back on another call.

"I want to talk to you about why you left. You say it wasn't an escape. If not, then what was it?"

I knew this was coming. I wasn't willing to talk to him about my reasons, but I also knew he wouldn't let it go, and I wanted him again, so I'd have to give him something.

"I had to get a message to someone."

"Back home? Do you mean Colombia?"

I snorted.

"No. That would violate the agreement. Plus, I'm not stupid."

"So, you did read the agreement," he nodded. "Who did you go see?"

"I can't tell you."

"Why not?"

"Because it's none of your business." I shrugged.

"What does that mean?" Taz asked. "If you need to make a call, I can make arrangements."

I scoffed.

"Why can't you trust me?" He asked.

I gave him direct eye contact and shook my head. "You just don't get it."

He frowned. I knew he was trying to understand me, but growing up the way I did, trust was almost impossible. Everyone was out for themselves. If you believed any differently you were naïve. I had lost that innocence long ago. Hope was just a four-letter word you used to tell yourself lies. Hope was for suckers.

"I've discussed the incident with AUSA."

"Who is that again?" I asked.

"The Assistant US Attorney." Taz said, "The lawyer prosecuting the case against Luís."

"Why is he involved?"

"Mr. Chambers has your agreement. If you violate the terms, we have the right to prosecute you for your crimes."

My shoulders tensed.

"What about my testimony?" I asked. "Isn't that my get-out-of-jail-free card?"

Taz shook his head. "Life isn't a game."

Chills traveled up my arms, causing me to shiver. Did I just screw myself by meeting with Nicolas? I didn't know that the US Marshal Service would follow through on their threat. Would they really put me in jail even after I testified?

"I want another deal or no testimony," I said.

"Don't be difficult Rosa."

I shrugged. "No comprende."

Taz blew out a breath. "I'll work it out with the AUSA. You won't go to jail. I promise."

After dinner, we finally had some free time. He was done with conferences, and I wanted more of everything Taz had to offer. If I could only get one week with him, I was going to take every second I could. I went to the bathroom and got everything in place.

I screamed.

Taz came running. Just like I planned.

"Help," I said grinning. My heart was pounding. I was naked sitting on the countertop, legs spread, playing with myself.

"What's wrong?"

Taz came up short. He glanced around looking for threats, then his eyes settled on me and what I was doing. His pupils dilated, and he watched with hungry eyes.

ST. LOUIS SECRETS

"I'm in distress," I said making my words all breathy, rubbing the moisture up and around, circling my clit. His eyes were focused on my movements. I had his full attention. I could see the bulge outlining the zipper on his jeans. Taz licked his lips.

"That's what you do, right?" I asked leaning back against the mirror. "Help damsels in distress?"

His mouth twisted into a smirk.

"Is that what's happening?"

"Don't I look to be in distress?"

I rolled my hips, dipping my fingers inside and out of my core, pumping my fingers while making soft mewling sounds.

"Mmm. Mmmmm."

"Looks like you don't need my help. Seems like you have everything under control."

"That's where you're wrong."

"Am I now?" He said rocking back on his feet.

I threw a wrapped condom at him and he caught it.

"I need an extra hand. Or two. Perhaps something else?" My eyes locked with his. "Are you up for it, el jefe?" I kept stroking myself, rocking back and forth, keeping myself on the edge, not letting myself go over. It was sweet torture. Taz's face was flushed. His arousal was clear by his stance. He liked what he saw.

"You wouldn't turn someone away, would you? Someone in need?"

"That wouldn't be very gentlemanly of me at'all."

His Texan accent was getting thicker by the second.

"Well don't keep a girl waiting. I'm in need of a ride, cowboy."

"Are you now? Well, I reckon I could accommodate."

I grinned, loving when we bantered back and forth like this. Taz got within inches of me and stopped. My blood was pounding in my veins. I could hear it in my ears. I wanted to scream. Beg.

Please. Touch me. I repeated in my head over, and over.

I forced myself to be patient. The anticipation built until it felt like torture. Sweet, sweet torture.

A whimper slipped from my lips. That must have been what he was waiting for because Taz took over where I had left off. In minutes, I was coming hard, clenched around his calloused fingers. Taz didn't have the hands of an executive. He had the hands of a man who worked the fields. He slipped those thick fingers between his lips sucking off my juices. I watched through heavy lids. Taz slid on the condom and in one smooth thrust inside me. At this angle, it was difficult to take him completely. I slid my hands under his t-shirt and whipped it over his head. The man was stunning. Even though he was in his mid-forties, you couldn't tell by his physique. Sculpted abs. Chiseled pecs. Powerful biceps that flexed as he thrust harder. Faster. I bit his shoulder. The pain drove both of us on. Another wave swirled through me. The pressure built and built until I couldn't take it anymore. My nails scored scratch marks down his back as I came, moaning his name like a prayer.

Sweat dripped down his face and splashed onto my chest. Not that I minded in the least.

"How was that for a ride?" He asked panting.

"Yee haw, cowboy," I said in my thick Colombian accent.

It had us both laughing until tears rolled down our cheeks. I wrapped my arms around Taz hugging him to me. I know we needed to separate and clean up, but I didn't want this moment to end. He pulled back first. I bit my lip, staring up at him. Taz rubbed his thumb over my bottom lip and kissed me so tenderly. Nothing like what the fast and furious sexcapades warranted. It had me puzzled. Taz's expression was just as stunned for a moment, then he walked to the shower leaving me sprawled on the counter alone and confused. When he came to collect me and escort me to the shower, his features were back to normal. Stern and in charge. No questions in his eyes like he had a minute before. I reluctantly let him guide me under the stream of warm water, but Taz didn't stay with me. He washed up in the sink.

I wanted to tell him to join me, but I experienced something I rarely ever felt. Uncertainty. That expression was burned in my brain. What did it mean? Was I starting to crave something more? Was he? I lost hold of the bar of soap and swore up a storm trying to retrieve the darn thing. I peeked out the curtain to see if Taz heard me, but he was already gone, along with his clothes. My shoulders slumped. The wave of endorphins was wearing off from my climax. So much for another round. Not that I was about to give up. Sex was way more fun than worrying about the upcoming trial. I'd just have to use my imagination. I smiled. Taz needed the distraction too. After all, who knew him better than his wife? I laughed glancing at the ring on my finger. Maybe I could use this fake marriage to my advantage somehow. Devious plans were spinning in my brain. I'd recruit Todd for assistance. I just needed to figure out how to get a message to him. Taz would be watching me more closely.

Chapter 19

Taz

What was I thinking? It was one thing to have sex with Rosa last night, but today after things had settled down? I should have more self-control. I might be willing to give myself a pass after tracking her down. I had been furious with Rosa. Lust had mixed with anger, and I had taken out all my frustration on her. All the pent-up heat between us had exploded, leaving all my good intentions floating in the wind. My anger was still on simmer. She never had told me the reason for her escape. Rosa had to get a message to someone. That's all she had said. I didn't like her having secrets. Right before she had screamed this afternoon, I had gotten a message from the team. Pablo still hadn't been found. Didn't she realize the danger she was in? Rosa took little regard for her safety. I was afraid of what might happen to her if she tried to escape again.

All those feelings I swore I didn't possess came rushing forward until I couldn't think clearly. Rosa made me crazy. It was as simple as that. I was compromised. In the front of my head, I realized I had to pull myself off guard duty. It was the right call. The trouble was, I didn't trust anyone enough to take over. Now that we slept together, would Rosa start expecting things? Things I couldn't give her. I watched her march out of the bathroom in a soft, fluffy white robe. I wondered if she had anything on underneath. I tried not to stare, but it was impossible. Rosa glided into the living room with sexy hip swishes. She flipped through the meager magazine offerings and selected one with a sigh.

"Maybe we could ask the concierge to send up some books," Rosa said as she settled onto the couch, curling her legs beneath her and flashing me in the process. It answered the question of what she was wearing under the robe. Nothing.

"We can ask Todd for some steamy romances," she said with a twinkle in her eye.

"I don't think you need any more ideas."

She shrugged. "True. I'm extremely creative. I don't need books for that."

I just bet. It had me blowing out a breath. Was it getting hotter in here? I went to the thermostat and turned it down a degree.

"We can't do that again," I said.

"You mean have sex?" She asked. "Got a problem with your stamina?"

"That's not what I meant."

"Then ethics is a problem," she grinned. "Are you suddenly the poster child for morality?"

"Hardly." I glared at her. It was unnerving how easily the woman pushed my buttons.

"Then you're worried about the relationship dynamic. Perhaps concerned that I might tell on you?" Rosa flipped a page. "Probably a big no-no in your world. Sleeping with a witness."

My jaw ticked. I didn't like that she had pinpointed the issue so precisely. Yeah, I was worried about that, but there was more to it. If I got into trouble with the brass, I'd deal with it. I wasn't asking her to hide anything.

"I'm not concerned you'll tell."

Rosa looked up from the magazine. "You think I won't?"

"I know you won't. It's not your style."

ST. LOUIS SECRETS

"Hmm," Rosa said as she got up to drop the magazine down on the coffee table.

She walked in front of me, forcing me to back up. Rosa pressed her palm to my sternum. I allowed her to push me down into the chair. Rosa leaned over me. She was far too close. I could smell the herbal shampoo and the lilac-scented soap she used.

"You think you know me, but you don't."

Rosa stalked away to the bedroom. I was ready to go after her, but I heard a ping from my phone. A text message. I hoped it was from Huck or the office. We needed to find the missing witness. While my retrieval team had been successful, the other had not.

'Team B checked in. It's not good news, boss. Call me.'

I dialed Huck's number.

"What's the update on Pablo?"

"Stabbed at Fairground Park. He was taken to SLU Hospital."

"Is he conscious?" I asked.

"I don't think so. Hang on," he said. "I'm messaging Jules for an update."

"Who is Jules?"

"My contact at the hospital."

"Can you trust her to not talk?"

Huck chuckled. "Yeah. Jules is cool. She works in the ER. I've always been a sucker for the Florence Nightingale types."

Figured he would have a girlfriend at the hospital.

"Who found him?" I asked.

"Local PD."

"Did they know it was Pablo?"

"No. He's still considered a John Doe. They'll run his prints once he's out of ICU, but he's not wanted in the U.S., so they won't get a hit right away.

"What did the officer call it in as?"

"A mugging. Fairground Park is pretty rough. It probably just looked like another random act of violence in the city."

"How did we find out it was Pablo without prints?"

"We got lucky. I've been monitoring police chatter. Sam tapped into the hospital camera feeds and was able to run facial recognition when he came in. That guy is a tech genius."

Thank goodness for IT. At least we'd be able to circumvent the media. The last thing I needed was for this to come out. A witness from a high-profile case going missing was bad enough, but to have one of them hurt? We couldn't have that kind of publicity.

"Sh-iit," Huck said stretching out the i.

"What happened?"

"Pablo is dead. Must have died in ICU."

"Damn. Can we interview the medical staff and the paramedics to get details? We need to see if anyone heard anything. Any clue to figure out who did this to him?"

"I've already sent a deputy to the hospital. I can see if Jules can catch the paramedics before they head back on call. Hang on."

I waited for a few minutes, pacing back and forth in the living room.

Huck came back on the line.

"She said the victim had lost too much blood by the time the paramedics arrived. He was unconscious when he got to the hospital. There was nothing the doctors could do to save him."

"Did Pablo say anything in the ambulance?"

"She doesn't know. But she can give the names of the paramedics to the deputy to track them down for an interview. It doesn't look good, boss."

Way to state the obvious Huck.

I couldn't believe another witness was dead. At least it wasn't while he was in custody. The US Marshal Service took pride in its 100% success rate. No witness in WITSEC had ever been killed while in protective custody. The caveat was that they followed the program rules. Pablo had escaped custody. It

ST. LOUIS SECRETS

wouldn't tarnish the US Marshal Service's record, but if the Attorney General had anything to say, it would sure as hell tarnish mine.

"Deputy is on the scene," Huck said. "He's getting the body sent over to the ME. We've got a friendly over there that can slow-roll the autopsy if we need her to."

"I'll make some calls and get the case moved to Federal. You got a case number?"

If the local PD didn't have any leads, that might make it easier for us to take over the case. We didn't need the press catching wind of this.

"Sure thing. I'll have Sandi email the paperwork."

"If I haven't told you already, you're a godsend."

"Make sure that reflects on my next pay raise, Chief," Huck said.

I chuckled.

"Will do."

I hung up. If we could get through this, I'd recommend everyone a pay raise. We were all working overtime on this case. Even though it came with the job, this one was different. More than just high-profile. It was personal.

I went in search of Rosa after the call. She wasn't in the bathroom or bedroom. Her robe was on the bed. Rosa stood naked in the walk-in closet with her hands on her hips. I stared at her golden skin and the graceful curve of her backside for far too long before heading back to the living room.

"I thought you wanted a show," she said.

Damn. Rosa had heard me sneak away. Or had she known the whole time? It was like the woman had eyes in the back of her head.

"Maybe later," I replied, grinning.

I pulled my emails up on the laptop and went through my reports. They provided me with the park location and other details surrounding Pablo's death, but they didn't tell me why.

Discovering the exact steps he took to escape protective custody and how Pablo got from the safe house to the park wouldn't take long to figure out. My team was hunting down leads now. I just hoped it led to some clue on who had killed him. We needed proof that it was Luís. A mugging. I shook my head. That was a joke. Although we could use that assumption to our advantage and spin it that way for the media. It would keep the heat off the investigation. But I knew the truth. Someone was targeting and killing off witnesses. It meant Rosa might be next.

    I went into the folder with shared legal files and pulled up the agreement Pablo had with the prosecution. He wasn't as essential as some of our other witnesses. He had been given immunity from any crimes committed on U.S. soil for his cooperation, but Pablo wasn't going into the witness protection program like a majority of the witnesses. He would testify and then be deported back to Colombia. What would happen when he returned home as a rat to the Lorenzos? I didn't care at the time what legal agreement each of the witnesses had signed, but I needed to review them more thoroughly. Is that why he had risked an escape? From the preliminary ME's report, Pablo had no defensive wounds. That meant he trusted whoever had attacked him. That's why a mugging made no sense. Not that I had believed that for a second. I knew I would have to tell Rosa. I couldn't keep something like this from her. I just didn't want to see that look on her face. Fear. She tried to hide it, but I could see through her mask. Rosa put on a brave face. Now and again, her vulnerability would peek through the mask when no one was looking. Or maybe she only revealed that to me. It was probably for the best to get this over with. Maybe a healthy dose of fear would be a good thing, and she'd finally show a little caution. The woman was far too cavalier with her safety. I needed to change that. Maybe shaking the fear of God into her, would finally make the woman realize the danger and let me do my job. I couldn't do a thing if she ran.

Chapter 20

Rosa

Taz sat at the dining room table with a serious frown on his face. He had been working on his laptop. As I walked in, he watched me with such intensity that I couldn't help but smile. My hips swayed as I strutted around the room. His gaze didn't waver. His perusal of my body sent tingles to my extremities. I shivered. How could he have such an effect on me with barely a glance? I never had that sort of reaction with anyone else. Not in my entire life. There was something about the man that just sparked something deep inside. I tried to nonchalantly peek at what he was reading, but he shut his laptop before I got the chance. I shrugged, sauntering to the chair on his left side. I wanted to put my feet up. While I could have easily used the empty chair to my left, I decided Taz's lap would do just as nicely. Plus, he was far too serious right now. I wanted to see him crack a grin or yell. Anything was preferable to the silence between us. I propped my feet on his lap. His expression was priceless. Equal parts frustration and awe at my daring. I wiggled my toes.

"I remember the other day you saying to Todd on the phone that no one but you would be giving your wife a massage. Was that a lie?"

"No."

"Then put up or shut up," I said, pressing my toes against his crotch.

His reaction was immediate. He grabbed both my feet, preventing me from doing any damage. Not that I had been planning to do anything. Much. I mostly wanted to tease. It didn't appear that Taz knew what he wanted by his confused expression.

"My feet hurt," I complained. "Too much walking from the other day."

Taz tilted his head.

"And whose fault is that?"

"Yours. For chasing me."

"About that," he said.

I wiggled my toes. Taz started massaging my feet. He dug calloused fingers into my arch and heel, stroking and kneading. My body started to feel like Jell-O in no time. I slouched in my chair. Dios mio. This guy was good. Tension left my body, and my eyes rolled back in my head. Goosebumps formed on my bare legs. I was in my pajamas. Tiny shorts and a fitted T-shirt with a Looney Tune character print, small spinning Tasmanian Devils. Whoever shopped for WITSEC had a sense of humor. It was a soft cotton and one of my favorites. Not just for the comfy feel, but because of how Taz stared at me whenever I wore it.

"Who were you going to see?" He asked.

I blinked. Of course, he'd keep asking about it.

"No one you need to worry about."

Taz dug his knuckles in deeper, working the muscles. It felt fabulous.

Senseless sounds came from my lips as he worked his magic fingers over my aching feet.

"I'll be the judge of that," he stopped massaging. "I want a name."

I licked my lips, trying to concentrate. It was a mistake to give him information. I couldn't trust him.

"Is this some new interrogation technique?" I asked.

"Darn it, Rosa. You're in danger. Don't you know that?"

ST. LOUIS SECRETS

He stood, and my feet fell to the floor. Why did I have to keep so many secrets? I wanted to tell him. I really did. And that was an unusual thing for me. I didn't trust. I couldn't afford it. It was a strange concept. I bit my lip. He was staring at me. Frustration was clear in his stance.

"Pablo's dead."

My eyes went wide, and my jaw dropped. That wasn't what I was expecting to hear. I swallowed thickly. No wonder Taz was upset. They had lost another witness.

"When did this happen?"

"He went missing the same time you did."

The impact of what happened hit me. I put my head in my hands. I couldn't believe this. Pablo had been a friend. Sort of. He didn't deserve to die. Sure, he was a bit of a lech and a criminal, but he wasn't all bad. Even though he held a gun on me at the big drug bust months ago, it's not like he had wanted to do it. He never would have pulled the trigger. Given the chance, he would have let me escape even though he worked for Luís. He was one of the few in the organization I could tolerate.

"Why didn't you tell me?" I asked.

"I just found out myself."

"How did he die?"

"A mugging?"

"What?" I asked, astonished.

Pablo would not have been mugged. He was a fighter. I just couldn't see it happening. I guess someone could have gotten lucky with a gun.

"Was he shot?" I asked.

"Stabbed."

That was ridiculous.

"Can I read the report?"

I figured he would say no. He certainly didn't need to show me, but he surprised me by opening his laptop and sliding it in front of me.

My eyes must have widened.

"Just the report, Rosa. Don't think I'm giving you internet access."

"Of course," I said with a grin. A thrill ran through me. He trusted me. At least with this. He had been reading the police report when I walked in. It was still up on his screen.

Pablo had been stabbed 5 times. He had no marks on his arms. No defensive wounds. I frowned. He didn't put up a fight? The officer who wrote the report noted that the victim reeked of alcohol. A tequila bottle was found not far from the body under a park bench.

"This doesn't make any sense. Pablo wouldn't let someone kill him. At least not like this."

"Even if he was passed out drunk?"

I scanned the rest of the document but couldn't find much more information.

"Have they done a tox screen?"

"Not yet. The body is heading to the ME's office for an autopsy. The police may not show this as a priority, but the feds are taking over the case."

I let out a sigh. It was a relief that Taz was taking this seriously and listening to my thoughts on the matter.

"This is not what it seems. Check for some sort of poison or maybe an anesthetic or paralytic."

"Why do you think that?"

"There are two problems with the theory that Pablo was too drunk to defend himself. First, Pablo gave up alcohol quite a few years ago. He's had his ups and downs throughout his life, but Pablo stayed clean through it all. Getting arrested by the feds wouldn't have pushed him over that edge. Second, there is no way someone stabbed him five times without him defending against it. They might have gotten one cut maybe, but not five. No way." I blinked up at Taz. "You have to believe me. This was staged. Whoever killed him wanted to make the police think it was a mugging. At least initially."

He grinned. "I like how your mind works."

"I'm not an idiot," I said, scanning the document one more time.

"And Pablo had to have known whoever did this to him, otherwise there would have been blood on his knuckles. He was a street brawler, with a surly attitude." I sniffed. "He was such a pendejo, but Pablo was ok." I shrugged. A tear rolled down my cheek. I closed my eyes not liking the emotion roiling inside me. The guy had been a friend or at least an ally. Since I didn't have that many, to lose even one was heartbreaking.

"I'm sorry," Taz said. "I didn't realize you and he were close."

I shrugged. "We weren't. Not really." I groaned. "Ignore the waterworks."

Taz wiped away the single tear.

"Come here," he stood, pulling me into his arms. It felt so warm and safe. I let him rub my back and comfort me. Having someone hold me was rare enough that I melted for him. The trouble was it made the tears flow freely, and I hated that. Still, I didn't pull away.

"Don't worry."

I laughed. Turning off worry wasn't something anyone could do. He must have known that and chuckled too. I wanted to see his expression, but holding him felt too good. Once my laughter died down, I sighed. My head rested against his chest. I never wanted to leave this embrace. I know it was stupid. We'd eventually have to move from the position we were in. I heard his phone go off, but he didn't get it. He just continued to hold me. I bet he'd give me as much time as I needed. I finally pulled back enough to look him in the eyes. The sympathy that filled them almost brought me to tears again. I forced myself to straighten my spine.

"Thank you," I said. It was the first time I had uttered those words to him. I did appreciate everything he did. It felt like we had crossed some threshold. Some bridge between us. I wasn't quite sure what it meant, but it filled me with something close to hope.

"We need to relocate again."

My stomach plummeted, and my body tensed.

Taz reacted by gentling his hold on me.

"Everything will be fine," he said.

I finally stepped back. Rubbing my arms, and avoiding eye contact, I gave a self-deprecating laugh. Everything was not fine, and it never would be. It was too easy to lose myself in the moment with Taz. I needed to hold myself apart. I couldn't risk my heart with this man. I knew better. Relocating was going to make things difficult for my plans. The flash drive was being shipped here to the St. Louis Union Station Hotel, not to wherever we were going. That meant that whatever plans I had in the works, I needed to finalize. Getting a hold of Todd was more important.

"When will we be leaving?" I asked.

"I'm making the arrangements. Maybe a day or two at most. Surveillance will be doubled. And I need you to behave."

I grinned. "Now that is asking too much, and you know better."

"Do it for me," Taz said.

He kissed me. It was tame by our standards, but still, my eyelashes fluttered and butterflies filled my stomach. When he pulled away, I realized we were still on camera. What was that all about? Every time I thought I had him figured out, he surprised me. I shook my head, hoping it might jump-start my brain. I couldn't think clearly with Taz's warm touch still so recent. My body was still covered in goosebumps. I cleared my throat.

"I, uh. Well, maybe I should start packing." I said, and dove into the bedroom. Once I was out of Taz's direct line of sight, I let out a deep breath. Concentrate. I chided myself. I still need to get my hands on the flash drive. The one I had promised to Nicolas for services already rendered. What would he do if I failed in my mission? Friend, or not, we had struck a deal. Now that we

ST. LOUIS SECRETS

were leaving the hotel, it just became more difficult, not to mention that there would be more people watching my every move. Double surveillance, Taz? Thanks a lot.

Chapter 21

Taz

I knew Rosa was plotting something, I just didn't know what. She was being far too cooperative. Well, most of the time. She still wouldn't give up who she had met with and why she was at Forest Park. And no matter how persuasive I was in and out of bed, she refused to give up the information.

"It doesn't matter how many times you ask me, I'm not going to tell you why I was at the park. I didn't meet with anyone involved with the Lorenzos. It was a personal matter and it has nothing to do with the case. Taz, please. Just let it go," she sighed.

"You're lying."

Rosa rolled her eyes. "I am not."

I huffed. This was getting us nowhere. "I have to make some arrangements downstairs. Can you stay put?"

She crossed her arms.

"Maybe," her eyes lit up. "Although I do get bored easily."

I shook my head. Her mischievous nature was going to be the death of me.

"Bolt the door behind me and don't let anyone in but me," I said. "And don't open the blinds."

She saluted me with her middle finger.

ZIZI HART

I heard the bolt slide into place before I started walking to the elevator. I thought about how I was going to explain this to the director. I couldn't tell the office where I was going. The director was going to tear me a new one, but he had given me latitude in the past. I was hoping he'd do it again because I wouldn't be taking no for an answer. I might be tanking my career, but I was doing my job. Keeping the witness safe and getting her to the courthouse for the trial was my priority. My reasons were both personal and professional. While those lines often blurred, in this case, they weren't in conflict with one another. I needed to call Jac and César as well, hoping they would be willing to back my play. Not that I'd tell them where I was stashing Rosa either. It might be paranoia, but I couldn't trust anyone right now.

I went to the concierge. Todd was on the phone. As much as I complained about the guy, he was discreet and could get things done quickly and efficiently. He was good at his job and I appreciated that. He held up his finger as I approached. I waited with my arms crossed.

"Yes, I have it. I can do that. No problem, Mrs. Connor. I will take care of everything." Todd said hanging up the phone.

My eyes must have been bulging out of my head by his reaction. Todd took a step back. He cleared his throat and brushed non-existent lint off his jacket. It hadn't taken me long to get downstairs. Rosa must have jumped on the phone the second I left.

"What was my wife asking for?" I said through gritted teeth.

Todd's face turned purple.

He cleared his throat again. "A gift for you."

Why did the guy seem embarrassed? Or maybe he was just nervous. My temper did tend to get the better of me. At first, I thought Todd might be spying on us, but it turned out he was genuinely good at his job. The guy was just observant and had been nothing but helpful. I should feel bad about how I had treated him during our stay. My mother always told me my social skills were lacking.

ST. LOUIS SECRETS

"Mrs. Connor was checking on your birthday presents. She wanted to surprise you. Happy early Birthday, by the way."

I blinked slowly. How did Rosa know it was almost my birthday? My actual one, not the fake one from my ID. And what exactly was she getting from Todd?

"I don't need anything. I'll just tell her you can't get whatever she wanted."

"She actually asked a few days back. It's sort of too late to return," he shrugged. "I'm afraid it will still be charged to your bill."

"I won't contest the charges. I just don't need any darn gift."

"If I might be bold sir," Todd said, "Trust me. You're going to like this one."

Todd didn't know me. I didn't like gifts, and I sure as heck didn't like birthdays. But I wasn't about to argue with him. I would be having words with Rosa when I got back upstairs.

"We will be checking out tomorrow. I'd like to get my bill finalized so I can get everything paid ahead of time. I'll need an itemized receipt so I can submit for business expenses."

"Just give me a moment," Todd said going behind the check-in desk.

I glanced around the lobby. It was getting busy. I wanted to get back upstairs, but I still needed to make a few calls, and I didn't want Rosa listening in. Huck was monitoring Rosa on the cameras. He would let me know if there were any issues.

When Todd came back with the bill, I asked to use one of the small conference rooms for some calls.

I called the Director first and got his secretary.

"It's Chief Deputy US Marshal Taz Bennett. I need to speak with the Director. It's urgent."

"Of course. I'll patch you through."

A few minutes later, I heard the voice of my friend. Jim Walsh. He had been Director of the US Marshals Service for a few years now. I had known him for twenty years working with him a few times on various task forces. He knew my abilities and we respected one another.

"Taz. How the hell are you?"

I chuckled. "This case will be the death of me."

"Yeah. I got a few reports sent over. Fisher keeps calling."

I shook my head. It figures that the AG would have already alerted him of my mistakes.

I swallowed hard. "What has the AG been telling you?"

"That you lost a few witnesses."

I rubbed my eyes. "Yeah. They escaped custody. We think they got outside help. Maybe even within the US Marshal Service."

"Damn. That's a serious accusation."

"You know me. I don't jump to those sorts of conclusions without reason."

"Do you have the source of the threat?" He asked.

"No."

"Well then, what is your proposal?"

"The witnesses all need new safehouses. We'll have to get creative with the locations."

"Transferring them is always a risk. Whoever is targeting your witnesses is smart and well-informed. It could be exactly what they want."

I did think about that possibility, but if their current locations were compromised, we had no choice but to move them.

"I won't let another witness die on my watch. I can't just do nothing."

"You're invested in this case," he said, pausing like there was something else he wanted to say.

I tilted my head. The vague statement left me second-guessing what he was leaving out. What had he heard? Should I ask? Or leave it alone?

The silence grew between us until it was uncomfortable. He knew my sister and why I wanted to take Luís down, but was there something more he wanted to ask?

"How is the job as Chief? Any problems?"

I cracked my neck. I didn't like where the conversation was headed.

"It's fine. No issues. Other than the witnesses."

"How about managing the other cases, prisoner transports, tracking down fugitives, and so forth?"

I didn't want to admit that I hadn't been focused as much on my other responsibilities. I had let the team handle the other cases while I put my energy into this one.

"The office is a well-oiled machine. We are dividing and conquering. I have a great group of deputies."

He sighed. Jim knew I was dancing around the subject.

"Are you watching a witness personally?"

"Yes," I admitted. "She's critical to the case. Ms. Lorenzo is a cousin of El Lobo Rojo. I'm ensuring her safety. You know how important this case is to me."

"I do. That's the only reason I'm not reaming you a new one right now."

"I appreciate it."

"The AG has been breathing down my neck about this case. At least the media hasn't gotten wind of things. Otherwise, I might not have a choice in the matter. You understand what I'm saying."

I let out a breath. I knew what he was implying and was grateful for the heads up. The AG didn't like me, or maybe it was just my attitude. As soon as the news realized that witnesses from the case were dead, I'd be in big trouble. Hopefully, by then, we'd have a conviction.

"I have a trap set to help me find the leak." Erroneous information was put into several witness files. I hoped whoever it was took the bait.

"Keep me informed," he said with a sigh and hung up.
That went better than I imagined.
I dialed Jac.
"What's up?"
"We are ready to relocate everyone. I'm sending you a text with your new hotel. It's a suite with two rooms. I've assigned a deputy to follow you. Do you have security covered between you and César?"
"We are good except if we have to go to court without the girls."
"Ok. I'll text the number to call if you need a security detail in the room. I'm limiting those in the rooms until I figure out who I can trust. Also, I'm not going to one of the normal safehouse locations with Rosa. The address is not tied to the US Marshal Service."
"That's a dangerous play. You won't have backup." Jac said.
"I know. That's why it's going to be harder to reach me."
"You think it's El Lobo Rojo?"
"We have people watching him, but we can't be certain. Nothing links back to him at this point."
Jac swore softly. "Damn, this sucks. I can't wait until this trial is over and that man is finally behind bars."
"I feel the same. Just watch your back." I said and hung up.

Chapter 22

Rosa

Todd handed me the steamy romance novel I had asked him to hunt down. It was by my favorite author.

"You found it. Gracias Todd. You are the best." I hugged him.

Taz rolled his eyes at my need to show affection. I not so discretely flicked him off. Taz shook his head and turned away.

I slipped an envelope with cash into Todd's pocket. It was almost all I had left, but the guy had certainly earned it.

"In appreciation for all your help during our stay."

"Look for the bookmark," he whispered in my ear.

I'd have to look for it later. Taz was watching too closely. I nodded.

"Did you give your husband his birthday present?" He asked.

"Not yet. I'm saving it for tomorrow." I wiggled my eyebrows.

Todd chuckled.

Taz crossed his arms, expression all surly. Even if he had overheard the conversation, he would only think it was the cake I planned on baking. I had told him that Todd had gathered ingredients for a homemade cake I was making him. Taz didn't know that I asked for other items as well. A certain piece of silk and lace I'd be wearing when I served Taz the cake was going to be a surprise. If he didn't appreciate that, I'd be tempted to smash the thing in his face. Taz had complained about me doing anything for his birthday, but I had put my foot down. He had finally given in. I didn't realize celebrating his birthday would be such a battle.

Why couldn't he enjoy the moments life held? Didn't he realize how precious they were? Taz was far too serious for his own good. He needed to lighten up. I wondered if he even had a life outside of his work. My life was in shambles, and I pitied him. I found that incredibly sad. Not that I'd tell him any of this. It would only lead to another fight.

Taz pointed at my hat, and I pulled it down low on my forehead. My dark locks must have come loose. I had to shove my hair into the slouchy beret Taz had gotten for me. It was my punishment for tossing the blonde wig at the art museum. Taz hadn't offered to replace it. Not that I wanted another. I hoped I wouldn't have to wear a wig ever again. The thing was hot, and the pins were a pain. Plus, my real hair would get all smooshed and go every which way, the moment I took the wig off. I wondered briefly if we would continue with our aliases, Mr. and Mrs. Connor. I kind of liked pretending to be his wife. The car was brought around while Taz scanned the street. He was on high alert, talking with someone on his earpiece, ensuring everything was clear. I waited for something to happen as he opened the door. Panic took a grip on my lungs. I couldn't seem to pull in enough oxygen. A sniper could be anywhere. If I was in the crosshairs now, could Taz really do anything to save me? Even a big badass like Taz couldn't stop a bullet with my name on it. I finally pulled in a ragged breath and blew it out. I could see my breath from the cold. It came out in puffs of smoke like one of those old

ST. LOUIS SECRETS

locomotives. I felt the tension in his palm as he escorted me into the passenger seat.

He quickly rounded the car and got in.

"I set your bag in the back seat," Taz said while putting the car in drive. "When we get onto the highway, I need you to grab it and put it in your lap."

I frowned. "Why?"

Taz groaned. "Always with the questions. Can you just do as I ask for once?"

I shrugged. "I guess. Since it's almost your birthday."

Once on the highway, he drove with erratic lane switches. Taz watched the rear-view mirror and pulled off onto an exit. Any turns we made were abrupt and last-minute. There were so many turns, that I felt almost dizzy. I knew why he was doing it. Taz was trying to lose a tail.

"I didn't realize we would be on a carnival ride."

"Silencio," he said.

"Ah the man does speak a little Spanish. That is good to know. I can swear at you more often."

"As soon as we get into the parking garage, be ready. We're ditching this car."

I nodded.

Taz pulled into the garage and we went deeper underground. We circled a few times until no one was behind us, he pulled into a space and shut off the car.

"Duck down," he said.

I slid down in the seat easily, but Taz was much larger. I worried for a moment that he would be visible, but I should have known better. Somehow, he managed to lower the seat back and squish his body down. He used a mirror to track a car that screeched tires as it blew past our parking space. My heart was pounding. Taz had his bag in his lap.

"When I give the signal, run across to the tan car behind us. I want to make sure there wasn't a second tail."

I swallowed hard and nodded.

We waited what seemed like several minutes, but was probably a lot less. Time seemed to slow down while I was waiting.

"Now," he said.

I opened my door and slid out, closing the door as silently as I could. I raced back to the tan sedan. Taz already had it unlocked. We waited another minute before pulling out. I wasn't sure what vehicle had been following us, but Taz seemed to relax once we were back on the highway.

"Where are we going?"

"Do you know how to shoot?"

I stared at him, wide-eyed. "Um. I guess. But it's been a while."

"That's what I thought," he said. "We're going to stop at a gun range and BBQ place called Sharp Shooters on our way to the safe house."

"You're taking me shooting?"

"Yeah. And I'm giving you a weapon just in case I have to leave the house."

"Isn't that a big no-no?" I asked.

"The weapon or leaving you unguarded?"

Honestly both, but I didn't want to pressure him about leaving. That might give me the opportunity I needed. I just didn't think we had developed that level of trust.

"The gun."

"I doubt you'd turn it on me."

He was right. I wouldn't. But I was surprised that Taz realized it.

"First, I need to know you're proficient. I don't want an accidental trip to the hospital."

I grinned. This was going to be fun.

"I'll try not to aim for your corazón."

"You've already hit that," he mumbled.

ST. LOUIS SECRETS

The brick building was nondescript except for posts in the shape of bullets just outside the front door. Instead of going inside right away, we walked over to a side courtyard with picnic tables.

"Hey Joe," Taz said to the guy at the grill. "What's good tonight?"

Joe opened the lid of the grill, and a sweet and smoky cloud of deliciousness wafted in our direction. My stomach growled. I hadn't been that hungry until now. After a quick conversation with Joe, Taz directed me inside the building to check out the range. Since the lanes were full, we ate first much to my delight. We ordered BBQ ribs, baked beans, and fries. The spicy BBQ sauce tasted as good as the aroma. In fact, everything was amazing. After eating, I wanted nothing more than to curl up and take a nap, but our lane became available. Taz rented a variety of guns for me to try. He also included his own firearms in the mix. Taz went through the specs of the various guns. I was familiar with most, but listened and nodded like it was all new to me. When I picked up the 9mm Sig Sauer and went through my first clip, he whistled low.

"I had no idea you were this good."

I grinned glancing at my shot grouping on the target.

"Does that make you nervous?"

He shook his head.

"On the contrary, it makes me breathe a little easier, as long as it's not me in your sights."

I tried the rest of the guns, but I liked the 9mm semi-automatic Sig Sauer best.

"I'm partial to the 9 mil Córdova back home." I grinned holding the 9 Sig in my hands. "This has a similar grip. But I'm not opposed to the Galil Córdova."

He shook his head. "As much as I want you protected. Giving you an assault rifle was not what I had in mind."

"No one would mess with me with one of those in my arms."

"If you need something like that, then things have gone to heck in a handbasket and there'd be a lot more to worry about than simple personal protection."

We left the range, and Taz did similar twists and turns going to the safehouse, checking for tails. He drove down a street called Hartford and pointed out a cute little brick house with white shutters.

"That's the safe house," he said as we circled the block.

"Why aren't we going in? Is there a problem?"

"I want to check out the surrounding area first."

I noticed a building with a sign that said Hideaway a street away from the house. It looked like a bar, or maybe a restaurant for all I knew. Not that I was hungry after the meal we just had. Driving down an alley, Taz pressed a few buttons on his phone and the door to a detached garage opened. I noticed the house he had pointed out was on the other side of a yard that had seen better days. I wasn't looking forward to the trek through the backyard.

"Where are we?" I asked.

"South City."

I shrugged. That didn't mean much to me, but hopefully, it would to Nicolas once I reached out to him. Right now, I had to play it cool. I still needed to meet with Ramón. A new location made things more difficult, but not impossible.

"Am I going to get my gun soon?"

Taz rolled his eyes.

"Let's get inside first."

We exited from a side door in the garage. Our footsteps were loud as we crunched through the snow and dead weeds as we walked up to the house. I tried to avoid the mud where the snow had melted, but couldn't miss it all. My shoes were a mess when we got to the back stoop. While I had concentrated on my footing, Taz was watching the surroundings.

After he unlocked the door and got us safely into the kitchen I breathed a sigh of relief. Taz still thrummed with tension. I worked at getting the mud off my shoes while Taz checked all the rooms before he was satisfied.

"All clear," he said.

I went into the living room and collapsed back into the couch with a sigh. I thought Taz was going to join me but he sat down at the kitchen table with his computer and started making phone calls. As tired as I was, I didn't want to sit still. I couldn't. My body was filled with adrenaline after the gun range. Or it could have been the tension from relocating. That tended to leave me antsy. I wandered around the house investigating the space. The window coverings were simple, either black-out curtains or blinds. I doubt much of any light would show through from the outside. The décor was very masculine in browns and blues, but it didn't fit Taz. Somehow, I knew this place wasn't his. I saw a few security cameras and frowned. I wondered who would be watching the cameras. I'd have to ask him about it later. I returned to the living room. Taz was just finishing up and joined me on the couch. He handed me the 9 Sig. My eyes widened and he chuckled.

"Don't be so surprised. I took you to the gun range for a reason."

"I thought it was your idea of a date. Or maybe foreplay?" I grinned.

He touched my cheek tenderly and turned away.

"There's a problem."

I gulped not liking the tone of his voice.

"What is it now?" I asked, hating that my voice cracked.

He turned back toward me, smile gone.

"I need to go to the office. It's nothing to worry about."

"Who will watch your star witness?" I gestured at myself trying to lighten the mood. He was far too serious and despite his reassurance, it was making me nervous.

"Only me. No one knows about this place. I borrowed it from a distant relative's friend. That way it can't connect back to me."

"What does this friend do?" I asked.

I didn't really care. I just wanted to keep Taz talking. I didn't want him to leave. Even though I needed to make contact with my cousin. I felt safe when Taz was around. As grateful as I was for the gun, it was still no substitute for the man in front of me.

"He's in the military, overseas at the moment, and won't be back for another month."

He rubbed my arms up and down. I hadn't noticed that I was shivering. "Keep the gun holstered in your purse, but close at hand."

Taz forced me to look him in the eyes, lifting my chin with his finger.

"Everything is fine. I wouldn't leave if I didn't think this place wasn't safe."

I nodded and forced my shoulders to relax.

"I trust you," I said.

"I won't be gone long. Can you stay put?"

"Sure," I said, knowing it was a lie.

"I mean it. No running off."

I bit my lip. "I'll be here when you get back. I promise."

He shook his head. "I shouldn't believe you. But I don't have much of a choice."

Taz kissed me and I melted for him. It didn't last as long as I wanted and I felt cold the moment he left the house. I couldn't sit still. Being alone was making me even more nervous than before. I went through my bag, searching for the ingredients Todd had gathered for me. I put everything away in the kitchen. I'd bake tomorrow. I went back through the bag, searching through the inner pockets until I found the other item Todd had gotten me; another burner phone since my first one had been confiscated. I told Todd my other phone had broken and I didn't want my husband to find out. It would ruin his birthday.

I called Nicolas from the bathroom, careful to avoid being seen by the security cameras. I knew Taz didn't trust me, regardless of him giving me a gun. I was going to violate his trust once more, but I couldn't figure a way around it.

"It's Rosa," I said.

"New number?" Nicolas asked.

"Something like that. The old one is burned."

"Hmm. The Marshal?"

"Good guess." I laughed.

"Can you meet me somewhere with Ramón?"

"When?"

"Now. If possible. I doubt I'll get another chance, and I don't have much time."

"What's the address?"

"Can you get to a place called the Hideaway? It's in South City."

I heard typing in the background. "It's a piano bar. Not too far away."

"How long until you can get there?"

"We can be there in fifteen."

"Did you get the flash drive?"

"It was delivered this evening. You upheld your part of the deal."

I let out a deep breath.

"That's why I'm willing to drop everything and meet you. Well, that and Ramón is being a pain. He's just as desperate to see you."

Leaving a note on the refrigerator, I told Taz I was going to the Hideaway for a drink. I hoped he would forgive me. I kept the Sig Sauer in my purse and walked through the alley and down one block to the bar.

ZIZI HART

The moment I stepped in the front door I grinned. This was the perfect place to meet my cousin. It felt warm and cozy with red walls trimmed in black. Intricately carved baroque mirrors, sconces, and vintage paintings created an old-world feel among real people. I bet most of them were locals. None of them gave me a passing glance. I'm so glad this wasn't some posh, pretentious club with flashing lights and loud music. If it was, we'd end up yelling our conversation over techno dance music. Here the only competition would be the soft music from the piano. I chose a table in the second room, furthest away from the bar.

Ten minutes after I arrived, I saw Ramón walk in. It had only been half a year since I had seen him, but he looked so much older. He had even grown a beard. Nicolas wasn't with him, but that didn't matter. It was Ramón I wanted to see. It was like a long-lost reunion. I hugged him like I would never let him go.

"I missed you so much."

"Yo también," he said.

I pulled back from the hug checking him over, making sure he was ok. These last few months had been torture not knowing if he was still alive.

"Were you hurt at the warehouse?" I asked, worrying what Luís might have done to him.

Not that I had seen him hit, but the whole drug bust was a blur. I'd often have nightmares of what transpired. My imagination would play tricks on me in my dreams and warp what really happened that night. I did remember with crystal clarity Ramón pleading for his life. As far as I knew his Uncle Luís had never threatened the kid like that before.

"No," he said. "Physically. I was fine. Just confused. I got sick." Ramón blushed. "I ran to the corner. No one wanted to be near me. Everyone was so busy, so I ran."

"You're the only one that escaped," I said. "It's impressive. Especially with the number of law enforcement officers at the scene. They are still looking for you."

ST. LOUIS SECRETS

"I know. That's why I've been lying low. I think that's the phrase. Nicolas has been helping."

"How has that been going?" I asked.

Ramón shrugged. "Ok. I guess. There's a whole family I never knew about. Kind of strange. Not that I've met them yet."

I nodded. "It's probably for the best. You don't need that kind of drama right now. One thing at a time, huh?"

"Yeah. I guess."

"Your mother didn't want you in the life. You know what I mean by that, right?"

"Yeah. No drogas."

"Not just taking drugs. No selling either."

"No hay problema."

"Listen, I needed to tell you more about your Uncle Luís. You know I'm testifying against him, right?"

"Nicolas explained things to me. He said you were a rat. It made me mad at first. That you would betray the family like that."

I sighed. Nicolas was a straight shooter. It figures he'd put it like that. I didn't want to waste time defending my actions. I had to get back to the house before Taz returned from the office and found me missing. I left the note for him just in case, but I wanted to avoid the fight if I could.

"Uncle Luís killed your father."

There was no sugarcoating the situation.

Ramón's face paled.

"Your father's name was Felipe Mendoza. Did Nicolas tell you that?"

"Yeah, he did. He also told me that Felipe loved mi mamá, but the families wouldn't allow them to be together.

"That's true. The Mendozas and Lorenzos have fought each other for as long as I can remember. The relationship was doomed from the start. I'm sorry you couldn't get to know him growing up."

"But I did."

It was my turn to be shocked. "When was this?" I asked.

"Felipe would often stop by and walk with mi mamá at the park or the flea market. He took us to the movies and museums. I always thought he was one of her guards. He was fiercely protective of mi mamá. Other men would try to talk to her and he would scare them away. He told me jokes and made me laugh, but he never mentioned in all those years that he was my father."

"I'm not sure he knew for certain. Your mother told him she had another lover. It made him angry at first, but I think it was her way to prevent him from pursuing a marriage proposal, or his rights to you. If the birth certificate said the father was unknown, she didn't have to worry about anyone challenging custody."

"I remember Uncle Luís and Mamá arguing over a name that she refused to give up. I didn't know what they were discussing at the time."

"What you might not remember is that those discussions usually resulted in bruises. He made sure that María didn't have marks on her face, but I saw the purple marks on her back and her stomach."

Ramón swallowed hard. "I know. I saw them as well. But I didn't know he was responsible. I would be sent to my room after he arrived. Mamá would walk hunched over after his visits. I never understood why."

"Luís is not a good man. I need you to know that. Don't reach out to him. You can't trust him. I need to make sure you won't do anything estúpido. Comprende?"

"Don't you think I would have learned my lesson after having him stick a gun in my face?"

I shrugged. "Your mother never did. I had to be certain. You're a good kid."

I squeezed his hand.

"I'm a man. Not a kid. I'm almost 22 now."

"Eres tan viejo." I chuckled. "I forgot you are so old."

ST. LOUIS SECRETS

I blew out a breath. "The other reason why I needed to see you was to tell you goodbye. I won't be able to see you again. I had hoped to get you into protective custody with me. It would mean never seeing any of your family anymore. Nicolas told me you didn't want that."

"I don't. But I understand why you do."

"Your mother wasn't the only one hurt by Luís."

"Did he hit you?"

I looked away not wanting to meet his eyes. I nodded. I felt a few tears fall down my cheeks. Ramón squeezed my hand. Giving me support without forcing me to look in his direction. I let out a deep breath. When I was finally brave enough to turn around I saw Taz standing behind him. I inhaled sharply and my eyes widened. The shock and fear made Ramón jump up from his chair. He bumped into Taz's chest.

"Disculpe," he said.

Taz was staring at me. Ramón must have recognized him because he scurried out of the bar. Taz could have chased him. It looked like he wanted to. I wiped the tears from my eyes with a cocktail napkin and waited for him to say something. Anything. The silence grew until I couldn't take it any longer.

"You got my note," I said.

He sat down in the empty chair. "Yeah."

"You're not mad?" I asked.

"I was."

"But not anymore?"

Taz shrugged. "I overheard the conversation."

I let out a huge breath.

All my secrets were out in the open.

"So, you know who that was and why I needed to talk to him?"

"Why didn't you come to me with this?"

"Would you have really listened?" I asked.

"We need to have trust between us."

I chuckled. "How is that possible?" I asked.

Taz held my hand. The same one that Ramón held minutes ago.

"I'm going to make you a promise. I'll get the warrant for Ramón quashed if you give me everything. Any question I ask, you answer. No more secrets between us. Is it a deal?"

I swallowed. To be an open book with this man. Anything he wanted to know. I had wanted Ramón's freedom. He was offering that.

I signaled for the bartender to get us shots of Patrón. When the drinks were delivered, we clinked glasses.

"It's a deal," I said before slamming the tequila down.

My eyes closed and I prayed this decision wouldn't put me in the ground. Even if it did, I'd say it was worth it. I'd do anything to save Ramón and keep my promise to his mother.

Chapter 23

Taz

I woke to my phone buzzing on the bedside table. I had always been a light sleeper, not that last night I had gotten much sleep. Rosa and I had gotten into an argument after leaving the Hideaway. I might have yelled at her for leaving the house, even though I realized why she did it. Rosa needed closure with her cousin. But reason be damned. It was stupid for her to risk her own life like that. I couldn't help but bring that up during our heated discussion. That had been the wrong thing to say to her. Both our tempers ran hot. The battle had ended in the bedroom. Angry sex had never felt quite so satisfying. I still hadn't asked her all the questions I wanted to. Her emotions seemed so raw. I can't believe that she had been on the receiving end of Luís' beatings. I should have assumed from his file. But when I learned of that, I buried my emotions. In that moment, I wanted to hunt the guy down and kill him for causing her pain.

    I leaned over Rosa to reach for my phone. It was on her side table. We must have switched sides during one of our athletic debates. She stretched awake, pressing her naked breasts into my chest, temporarily distracting me from my goal.

    "Give a chica some rest, pendejo. I'm sorry I made that crack about your age. No need to prove me wrong. Again."

I grinned. "I'm not up for another roll. My phone's ringing."

"Is that what that noise is?" She shrugged.

All it did was make more of her body press into mine, causing me to lose focus once again.

"If you aren't up," she said with eyebrows raised. "You could have fooled me."

I shook my head. My erection was poking Rosa in the stomach. "It's morning wood, sweetheart. Nothing else."

"Well, keep your nada to yourself. Some of us need our beauty rest."

She rolled over, and I was able to reach the phone finally.

"You need to come into the office." A haggard voice said over the line.

I sat up in bed rubbing a hand over my face. I gave myself two slaps on my cheek trying to wake up fully. I recognized the voice on the line.

"Sandi, is that you?"

"Yes, it's me. Have you been drinking?"

I had been last night. Rosa could drink like a sailor, and I had tried to keep up with her. Big mistake. Even though I was a big guy, and it took a lot to get me drunk, I had gotten way too buzzed. But it had felt good to let go. No one knew where we were. It was safe to let down my guard. My college drinking days were long ago, and I could no longer drink like that and still function at full capacity the day after. My head was pounding.

"What's so important?" I asked, avoiding the question of alcohol.

"The AG wants to meet with you."

"What?"

Sandi sighed. "The director has been leaving you numerous messages. You haven't returned his calls. I think he may want you off the case," she said. "I had to tell him about your erratic behavior."

My jaw ticked. "Did you now?"

ST. LOUIS SECRETS

"I'm sorry."

"I doubt you are."

"Just get here by noon. If you don't show, I don't want to deal with the Attorney General's temper. He's as surly as you are."

"Oh honey, no one else is that bad," I said and hung up.

I grumbled and got out of bed, searching for my bag. I hadn't unpacked anything yet. I glanced at the time on the phone. It was after 11. I needed to shower, shave and get to the office in less than an hour. What to do about Rosa? I couldn't trust anyone to watch her. Not until I found the leak in the agency. It wasn't just about the case, or the trial. It was her. I had fallen for her. It didn't matter that it wasn't allowed. It had happened, and I couldn't change that. Nor would I want to. I didn't know what that meant for our future, but I'd deal with it when the time came. Right now, her safety was all I was concerned about.

After getting ready in the bathroom, I followed the scent of roasted peppers and garlic into the kitchen. Rosa was at the stove. I snuck up behind her, giving her a quick kiss on the shoulder. She yipped and dropped her spatula.

"Don't you know better than to sneak up on someone when hot grease is involved?" She scolded me. Rosa picked up the utensil that had fallen to the floor, providing me with a good view of her backside. She was wearing those adorable PJs, and I wanted nothing more than to tear them off her and drag her back to bed.

The toaster popped and she swatted me out of the way, pulling out a toasted English muffin. Rosa slid the spicy egg and cheese into the muffin and wrapped it in foil.

"It's fast and easy, but I don't want you leaving here on an empty stomach."

She handed me the breakfast sandwich and a coffee in a to-go cup.

I set both on the kitchen counter.

"Fast and easy. Two words I would never use to describe you."

Whatever she was going to say in response got muffled by my kiss. I pulled her into my arms and kissed whatever complaint was on the tip of that wicked tongue. It lasted until we were both dizzy.

"I gotta head into the office. So, no wandering off today, ok."

"I overheard your conversation," she grinned. "Don't worry. All my errands are done."

I tilted my head. "Errands. Not escapes?"

"Toh-may-to. Toh-mah-tey," she shrugged. "I've met with my cousin, Ramón. Said my peace. I'm all yours. No running. I promise. I made you a deal. Anything you want to know."

"You have the gun still. Just in case."

"It's in my purse. Don't worry."

After one more quick kiss, I took the sandwich and coffee and headed out the back door. The cold wind whipped the lapel of my jacket open. It stole my breath as I walked to the garage. There was still snow on the ground in patches. It was supposed to be warming up in St. Louis today, but it sure didn't feel that way. I sipped the hot coffee as I checked my phone app. I had set up wireless cameras in the front of the house and around the garage so I could monitor the property for potential threats. Everything was working and looked secure, so I backed the car out of the driveway and into the alley.

On my way into the office, I thought about the ass-chewing I was about to receive. Meeting with the AG was always a pain. The guy didn't like me, no matter what I did. My best guess was that he was still holding a grudge over what I said at a D.C. party a few years ago. I had been complaining that there wasn't enough focus on building out task force initiatives to combat our drug trafficking problem. The DOJ was spending far too much time and money on other matters. I may have also added that I thought the AG had his head up his rear end at some point during

ST. LOUIS SECRETS

the conversation. But that was more or less the scotch talking. The AG had overheard and had walked away angry. If the man had confronted me at the time I might have apologized. Not that I usually pulled my punches. A problem of mine that my brother Blake pointed out to me regularly.

Sandi was there to greet me at the office.

"He's here already," she said directing me to the correct conference room.

I was glad I had the coffee on the car ride over. Dealing with the AG without caffeine would have been unbearable.

"Finally, you're here," he said when I walked in.

I glanced at the clock. It was 12:01. I was a whole sixty seconds late for this last-minute meeting.

I sighed and sat down.

"Where the hell have you been?" He asked.

"I'm guarding one of the witnesses for the Lorenzo case. The one you told me was a high priority. Pulling me away is putting the witness at risk."

"You shouldn't be involved in the day-to-day security detail. The Chief is supposed to oversee that sort of thing. Didn't you learn anything in those leadership training courses?"

"I'm more of a hands-on Chief Deputy," I said.

He grinned a feral smile, all pearly white teeth. Henry Fisher had the perfect teeth of a politician.

"I've heard all about your hands-on activities with your witness."

My face froze. Who talked? Was it Sandi?

"I'm not sure what you're talking about?" Evading the subject was going to be the only way I'd make it through the day with my job intact.

"Are you sleeping with your witness?"

I cringed. It was a direct question. I couldn't lie about it. Based on the AG's reaction, he must have proof. Otherwise, he wouldn't be here. Could I get around not answering the question?

"Henry," I sighed. "I'm not sure what you've been told."

"That's Mister Attorney General to the likes of you."

"Who I sleep with is none of your business."

He laughed. It was a harsh bark. "It is my business when it involves the US Marshal Service. Are you going to deny sleeping with Rosa Lorenzo, or are we going to continue to play games?"

I rubbed a hand over my face. This was not going as planned.

"I'll take your silence as admission. I want your resignation immediately."

"You don't have the authority."

His jaw dropped. It was true. Legally he couldn't force me to resign. It had to go through the US Marshal Service Headquarters. Of course, they would be influenced by the Director and the Attorney General. But firing someone took time. It was a process. An investigation would take place before the hearing. I'd be allowed to respond to any allegations before a decision was made. I planned to fight the AG's accusations. I just needed for this case to close first. I refused to leave Rosa without any protection. No one but I knew where she was staying at the moment. I wanted to see this through to the end.

"Bringing Ms. Lorenzo to the courthouse for her testimony is my responsibility. I'm not about to hand that off to someone else. This case is too important. Do what you will to me."

He grumbled. "You've lost two witnesses already. You better not lose a third." The AG marched out of the conference room and slammed the door.

Chapter 24

Rosa

"You have to come with me."

    I blinked my eyes open to see Sam standing over the bed. When did he get here? My muscles were sore, and it was hard to move. I felt far older than my age. I had pushed myself on the treadmill after Taz had left this afternoon. Exploring the house, I found a room filled with gym equipment. I had been so excited by the discovery, that I went a little overboard on exercising. Or it might have been the workout Taz had given me last night. Although I wouldn't complain about that in the least. While exercising, I had gone over all the major decisions I had made throughout my life. My choices led me to the here and now. My world had been filled with drama, not unlike my favorite soap operas. While I enjoyed watching it on TV, I had grown tired of living the drama. After making dinner and baking Taz's birthday cake, the exhaustion hit me hard. I decided to lie down for a quick nap.

    I cleared my throat. "Where's Taz?" I asked, rubbing the sleep from my eyes.

    The house was dark. It must be late. Taz should be home from work soon. I must have turned most of the lights off before I went to bed. Sam hadn't bothered to turn any back on. It seemed strange to me for a moment, but then I shook it off. He must have really good night vision. The only light I could see was coming from the bathroom.

"There's no time," he said glancing over his shoulder. "Chief Bennett sent me to come get you."

I blinked faster and forced myself to sit upright. "What happened?"

"Get dressed."

Sam thrust a pair of jeans, a sweater, and sneakers at me. From his expression in the semi-darkness, he looked worried.

"El Lobo Rojo knows where you are. I have to bring you to a different safe house. You have to hurry."

I nodded. "Ok."

If Taz sent Sam, it must be serious.

Sam shoved me in the bathroom to change. It took me less than a minute. When I got out, Sam already had my stuff in a bag. He handed me my coat and I grabbed my purse. Sam hurried me down to the basement. I was puzzled as to why we weren't heading out the front or back door. After making it down the steps, he led me over to a metal tool rack. My eyebrows rose.

"It's an underground tunnel," he yanked on the rack, and the wall moved behind it creating an opening. "They are all over the city. Quite a few of them were used during prohibition."

"We're escaping through old liquor tunnels?" I asked. "Is there a sniper outside the house?" My heart started pounding harder and my breath grew shallow. I wouldn't put it past Luís to put a hit out on me. Who did I know that might do the job? "How did they find me?"

"I don't know," he said.

"This place was supposed to be secret," I complained.

"Again. Don't know." Sam said, clearly frustrated that I had stopped moving to interrogate him. "We have to hurry. The Chief didn't give me much time."

What did that mean? I frowned.

ST. LOUIS SECRETS

Sam held my hand and led me through the tunnel like he had traveled through it before. I couldn't see much from the small flashlight he held in his hand. We quickly walked for what seemed like several blocks making a few turns before coming to another door. The tunnel was damp, with a musty smell, plus it was a lot cooler than in the house. I pulled the lapel on my jacket closed trying to warm myself.

"Where are we?" I asked.

He put a finger over his lips. I could hear talking and clanging on the other side of the metal door he stood in front of.

"Do exactly what I do," Sam said.

I rolled my eyes. Taz and I were going to have words after this. He should have called me himself. It was another one of his bossy moves that made me want to strangle him. Taz was probably being overly paranoid. I'm sure I wasn't in any real danger. Or maybe I was just trying to convince myself, so I wouldn't freak out. Either way, I couldn't be one hundred percent positive there was no threat, so I was willing to go along. At least for now.

Sam opened the door to another basement. We went down a hallway and through another door. This room held supplies for a kitchen. I could smell baking bread. We were in the basement of some restaurant. My stomach took the opportunity to growl. Sam put on an apron and handed one to me. He scowled at the sound from my tummy.

"Lo siento."

I hadn't eaten lunch. I was waiting to have dinner with Taz and had made quite a feast for his birthday celebration. The main dish was sitting wrapped in foil in the refrigerator waiting to be reheated back at the house. I was disappointed that Taz wouldn't get to taste the food I had made him. I donned the apron Sam handed me, wondering if we had time to pick up some of that delicious-smelling bread they were baking in the kitchen. He grabbed a covered basket and headed upstairs, ensuring I followed right behind him.

"Grab my belt, and hold on," he said.

I held on with one hand and let him lead me through the packed kitchen. No one seemed to pay us much notice. The kitchen staff were all busy at their stations. The large basket covered both our faces from view. I didn't understand how Sam could even see where he was going. We stopped at a counter. Warm cinnamon buns were just sitting on a tray fresh from the oven. It was too tempting to pass up. I glanced around and stole one off the tray, shoving it in my mouth. The cinnamon and sugar melted on my tongue. It was warm and gooey with a cream cheese frosting I could just die for. I gulped. Die. I was running for my life. Why was I still hungry? Weren't you supposed to lose your appetite in these types of situations? Maybe, I should focus instead.

"Hey, what are you doing?" Someone asked in front of us.

Sam whispered something in the man's ear. I didn't hear the words, but the man grew silent and let us pass. The man's eyes were wide with fear. What had Sam told him?

At the door to the exit, Sam held me back with an arm. He set down the basket he had been holding and punched in some digits on his phone.

"We're good," he said, leading me out of the restaurant to what looked to be an employee parking lot.

"Almost there," he panted. "Everything will be ok."

I didn't need the reassurance, but I was grateful all the same. What I wanted were answers to the millions of questions floating around in my brain. The first of which, where was Taz? Why hadn't he sent a deputy? As far as I knew, Sam didn't even carry a weapon. He was IT for Dios's sake. What was the Marshal Service up against if they couldn't spare someone with field experience? I wasn't stupid. This wasn't normal. But then again, what did I know? I wanted to ask, but I could tell by his urgency,

ST. LOUIS SECRETS

this wasn't the time. I bit my lip. Once we were safely tucked away wherever that was, then I'd grill him for answers.

Sam led me to a white van. It said Arch Tech Repair on the side in blue letters. I only just noticed what Sam was wearing. He was in khaki slacks and a dark blue jacket with a logo matching the van. Maybe Sam did fieldwork after all.

He opened up the side door in the back of the van. "Get under the tarp. And don't move or come out unless I tell you to."

I climbed in on all fours. The tarp was in the middle folded up neatly in between several boxes of loose cables. I crawled between the boxes while Sam walked around to the driver's door. He bucked his seatbelt and put on a baseball cap, sliding it low over his eyes. He gave me a minute to get settled under the tarp and then I felt the van backing up. The metal floor was freezing, but at least I had my coat on.

I was jostled around at a speed bump, then we picked up speed. We must have turned onto the highway because he accelerated even faster. The shocks were horrible. I could feel every bump in the road. I shivered from the cold and my nerves. When would Sam allow me to sit up? Surely, we should be out of danger by now.

"Can I get up?" I asked.

"Not yet," he said. "Wait until we get out of the downtown area."

The ride felt like forever.

"You're clear now. Come on up." Sam said as he pulled into a parking garage.

I stretched my back and warmed up my hands on the heater. He left the van running for a few minutes while he checked his phone. Once he was done, we were off again, running through the building. Sam kept checking his phone making sure no one saw us as we traveled the hallways. The apartment building was rundown, but how did that saying go? Beggars can't be choosers. We had gone through quite a few locations in St. Louis since I had arrived. They were probably running out of places to put all the witnesses by this point. When was this all going to be over? Sam unlocked the door to the apartment. There wasn't much in the way of furniture. An old couch with a gold paisley print had stuffing coming out of a few rips in the fabric. The recliner sitting next to it was a faded brown corduroy with stains.

"Take a seat." Sam gestured to the living room.

I set down my purse and bag on the floor. I wasn't willing to sit on the couch or the chair. They both looked like health hazards.

Sam walked over to the folding card table where a laptop was sitting. He started typing. There was only one folding chair that I could see, so I wouldn't be joining him. Not that he seemed to be in a chatty mood.

"Four Seasons, it's not," I said as I walked into the kitchen with peeling wallpaper. The refrigerator held a few bottles of water and a 2 liter of orange soda. The cabinets didn't look any more promising. Saltines, Cheerios, and broken dishes were all I could find.

"Are you sure we're in the right place?" I asked.

"Yep." I heard from the living room.

The windows were all covered in newspaper.

"I take it looking outside isn't an option."

"I wouldn't if I were you."

I shrugged, wandering further into the apartment. The bedroom had a single twin bed with no frame. It didn't even have sheets, and there was a stain on the mattress. No. This was not going to do. They couldn't expect me to sleep there. I opened up the closet hoping to find some fresh linens but I wasn't hopeful. One of the wheels had come off the sliding door, so it took effort to shove it open. A few black duffel bags rested on the floor along with an old pair of sneakers. A few flannel shirts dangled from wire hangers. There was a thin set of sheets, and a threadbare blanket folded on the shelf. A pillow sat next to them. It was the only thing that looked new so far. I decided to check out the bathroom. I crossed myself before going in. I didn't have high hopes. What I found surprised me. The bathroom was clean. Super clean. Eat off the floor clean. Did the cleaning woman start and end in the bathroom? Maybe she got pulled away from the job before she could finish. I glanced through the drawers and cabinets, but other than a first aid kit and toilet paper rolls, they were empty. On top of the sink was a bar of soap and a small hand towel. No bath towels? Maybe Sam had packed some essentials in the duffel bags. I glanced into the living room, but he was still playing around on the computer. I went back into the closet and unzipped the first one. I found sheets of plastic and duct tape. A chill ran up my spine. This was not what I meant by essentials. This was something I'd find at my cousin's house when he wanted to get rid of a problem. I needed to get to my purse. It had my phone and gun. This was wrong. All wrong.

I felt a pinprick on my neck and the world went all wavy. My body plummeted to the carpet.

"You shouldn't touch other people's stuff," Sam said.

My eyes were getting sleepy, but I fought it, forcing my limbs to move. The jerky spasms told me my reflexes weren't working, no matter how much I tried. My heart pounded in my chest, but the beats were slowing down.

"Relax, sweetheart," he said grinning.

I would have punched or scratched that smile off his face if I could have. Sam swiped a lock of hair from my forehead.

"It will all be over soon. I'm just waiting for the final payment."

"Leww-isss." I managed to say. It was slurred but Sam understood what I was asking.

He nodded. "Yes. Your cousin. Luís Lorenzo. You messed with the man's business. Without you, the case will fall apart. It's a shame it came to this. I liked you. But I like money more. And your cousin made me quite the offer."

ZIZI HART

I couldn't believe that cabrón had won again. Where was the justice in this world? That made me think of Taz and what he'd do to Sam once he figured out what happened. I had to believe that he would track the man down and deliver justice. I imagined a bloody demise for the deceiver standing in front of me.

"Why are you smiling?" He asked just before I passed out.

Chapter 25

Taz

I got back to the house later than I wanted to. Coordinating the relocation of witnesses for the trial took up more time than I had planned. Well, that, and being reamed a new one by the AG. At least I didn't have to worry about Rosa. The security surveillance app on my phone was set to alert me if anyone went in or out of the house. It had stayed silent the entire day. I checked the cameras earlier to find Rosa in the exercise room, and then later making dinner in the kitchen. Watching her frost my birthday cake had filled me with an emotion I couldn't quite label. It was sweet that she had done such a thing despite all my complaints. I walked in the back door and into the kitchen.

"Rosa, you up?" I asked.

She didn't answer, and the house was dark. I had seen her lie down and figured she was still sleeping. I knew she was exhausted from the stress. But despite all that, she had made me dinner and a cake. Rosa was pretty darn special, despite her sordid past. I peeked in the refrigerator at the dinner she had prepared. A casserole dish was wrapped with foil, probably ready to heat in the oven once I got home. I felt bad that I had made her wait for dinner. The cake was on the counter. I hadn't been able to see the details on my phone. Rosa could be a professional baker. She had talent. Rosa had sculpted little tornados out of frosting along the edge of the cake. In the center, she had created a 3D depiction of the Looney Tune character himself. It looked like Taz was taking a bite out of the cake. I silently walked through the house not wanting to wake her. The lights were out except for the bathroom. I saw her sleeping, buried under the covers. I kept the temperature in the house on the cool side. I should have told her to adjust the thermostat. There was no reason for her to be uncomfortable.

"You want me to turn on the oven and heat up dinner?" I asked gently touching her shoulder.

Immediately I realized something was wrong. Stripping the blanket from the bed, it revealed wadded-up sheets and pillows to make it appear like someone was bundled under the covers. What the hell? No. Not again. She had promised. No more secrets. I shook my head. Like a fool, I had believed her. I should have tied the woman to the bed, or never left her side. We only had a few more days before the trial. She had met with her cousin Ramón. Rosa said she was done with that life. She had said her goodbyes. This afternoon, I talked with an attorney about quashing the warrant against Ramón. It was already in the works. I was fulfilling my promise to Rosa, and she had broken hers to me. No more running. That's all I had asked. I was only trying to keep her safe. Why couldn't that woman sit still?

I turned on the lights going about the house, searching it from top to bottom. Her duffel with jewelry and cash was missing along with her purse. She had taken the gun with her. My gun. I ended my search of the house back in the bedroom. I sat on the unmade bed, holding my face in my hands. I thought I had been in trouble before. The AG was going to kill me. Forget losing my job, he was going to crucify me for this.

My phone rang. It better be Rosa with some explanation. The caller ID said it was Jac.

"What's up?" I asked.

ST. LOUIS SECRETS

"Someone tried to take out Mari in transit to the new hotel," he said. "César and I were there, but the sniper escaped. The girls are fine. I just wanted to let you know."

"Did you inform the office yet?"

"No. We wanted to call you first. To see if Rosa is ok."

I swallowed hard. "She's gone."

"What happened?"

"I had to go into the office."

"Oh hell," he said. "Did you have someone watching her?"

"No one knew where we were staying. I didn't inform anyone. She should have been safe. I had cameras and alarms. I don't understand how it happened. I have to call the rest of my team."

"If you need anything call. We are going to bunker down at a different hotel. We aren't using the safehouse you gave us. No offense."

"None taken. I'd do the same. In fact, I thought I had with Rosa. Just be careful. I'll let you know once I have her back."

I had to assume I'd get to Rosa in time. I refused to believe anything else.

Even though it would make me look completely incompetent; I had to call my team. Right now, I didn't have any leads on Rosa's whereabouts. Whenever I was out of options, I'd call Huck.

"Can't you guys do anything on your own?" Huck asked. "A half-hour break. That's all I'm asking for."

"It's Taz," I said. "My witness is gone."

"Sorry Chief. I thought it was one of the other deputies calling. Wait. She escaped again?"

"Yep."

I heard typing in the background.

"I don't have your whereabouts. The address for Rosa's new safehouse is not in the files."

I groaned low. "I wanted to protect her myself. I didn't trust anyone to look after her but me."

"How's that working out?"

"Obviously not well," I said. "Also, someone took a shot at Mari. Jac and César are going to a different hotel than what we have in the books. Address unknown. If you haven't noticed, this is a cluster. We have a major issue in the department."

"You mean the leak?" Huck said.

I grimaced. It figured that Huck would come to the same conclusion I had. Internal Affairs was already investigating. Although I hated getting them involved, it's not like I had much of a choice.

"I have surveillance video recordings that I haven't gone through yet. Hopefully that might give us a timeframe of when she left. The house was wired to signal me if any doors or windows were opened, but I didn't get any alerts."

"Does Rosa know how to circumvent the security alarms?"

"She didn't even know they were there. I just told her to stay put."

"That woman needs a leash."

"When I find her, I'll tell her you said so."

"Woah man, don't put me in the crosshairs. Not cool. That woman has a temper."

I chuckled, glad to be able to laugh about something.

"Is Sam there?"

"No. He logged off a few hours ago. Taking some personal time."

"That's news to me. Isn't he supposed to clear that with me?"

"Check with Sandi. Don't put me in the middle. I just work here."

"Ok. I'll send you the link to the video. Send it to only those you absolutely trust."

"In other words, just review it myself and save myself an aneurysm. Not trusting other team members is bad for morale."

"So are dead witnesses."

"Touché," he said and hung up.

I clicked the link to the video recording and sent it to Huck via an encrypted email.

I called Sandi next. "I thought you were off the clock," she said.

"Are you still at the office?"

"Yeah, just shutting down now. But I can log back on."

"Did Sam talk to you about taking some personal time?"

"Oh shoot. I was supposed to tell you. Yeah. It was his mom. She's in the hospital. There was just so much going on today what with the AG coming into the office. I got sidetracked. I meant to tell you in between your phone calls."

I swallowed hard, recalling details from his personnel file. Both his parents had passed away. "Are you sure he said his mom?"

I heard Sandi flip through her notebook.

"Yep, it's right here. His mom is at Mercy Hospital South. He was heading there right after work. I asked him which hospital in case we wanted to send flowers."

"His records said his mother is deceased."

"Really?" Sandi asked. "Why would Sam lie about that? That's not like him."

"Go home. I'll follow up with him later and get to the bottom of it."

Sam had been an exemplary employee for the past five years. I had read his work file. I thought I knew the man. Why would he do anything to jeopardize his job? I guess the why didn't matter. We needed to track him down. My instincts said he was involved, but I didn't have proof. At least not yet. All I had was suspicion. He had been chummy with Rosa, giving her little gifts. At the time, it just seemed like innocent flirting. Sam was shy. Not very good with women. A bit of a geek. Not that I faulted him for any of those things. It was obvious he had a crush on her. I mean who wouldn't with Rosa's body and her natural charisma?

The real problem was Sam had access to everything. All the witnesses, and all the safe houses. It was Sam's job to install the surveillance cameras and set up the secure network. I was hesitant to sick Internal Affairs on him in case I was wrong, but I didn't have a choice, and right now his behavior was suspicious. Not that I pictured him as a killer. Sam didn't fit the profile, but I was betting he was involved somehow. If nothing else, he knew something. Maybe he was being blackmailed, or paid off? Either way, I needed more information.

I called Paul Cohen in IA. He was a decent guy and fair, not like some of the others who went on a witch hunt the moment they got a name to investigate.

"Chief Deputy Bennett? A little late for a call," he said. "I'm surprised to hear from you. The AG called me earlier today to give me an earful. You ready to make a statement?"

I sighed. It figured that the Attorney General wouldn't even give it 24 hours before investigating the matter. He was determined to derail my career.

"Not at this time. Once the Lorenzo trial is over, we can set up a meeting and go over all the details. It shouldn't take more than a week to wrap up the court case. Right now, I need to call in a favor."

"I can slow roll our meeting to give you time to take care of things on your end."

"I appreciate that, but I need something else."

"What's that?"

"Sam Owens. I need to have your guys run a background check on him. The whole gambit. Check his bank accounts and flag anything out of the ordinary. I need the most recent stuff first. The last few months. And I need it all done ASAP."

"Does this have anything to do with your witnesses turning up dead?"

"It sure does, and I don't want Sam to know you're investigating him. He's in IT, so he'll see any search logs through our system. It will have to be done old school."

"Paper files? Geez. You do like a challenge," he groaned. "I'll head back to the office. I've got a key to the records room. I'll ping you what I find."

"I owe you," I said.

"A bottle of scotch," he laughed. "And no cheap stuff. Aged Twenty years or older. That's my price for working overtime."

"You got it."

He hung up.

My phone rang. It was Huck.

"I found something on the video. Although the image was pretty grainy after Rosa went to bed. The lack of light in the house made it difficult to get a clear view of the visitor. Whoever it was, they stuck to the shadows and were aware of the cameras. And Rosa knew who it was. She sat up and talked to them for a few minutes before getting out of bed. The bathroom light was the only reason I could see her expression. I think it was a guy by how he moved. He carried her bag and escorted her through the house. She didn't escape on her own. As far as I can tell though, they never left the house. They went into a door off the hallway kitchen and never came out."

"That's the basement."

I hadn't checked the basement earlier when searching the house. The door was deadbolted shut from the inside.

"How did he get in?"

Huck sighed. "That's the strange part. The first I show of someone else in the house was when he was standing over Rosa asleep in her bed."

I shivered. Someone who wished her harm could have taken her out then. That gave me hope that he had other motives.

"Thanks, Huck. Let me know if you find out anything more."

I went over to the hallway door leading to the basement. There was a slight fan of dirt marks on the hallway tile where the rubber on the bottom of the door had scraped. I hadn't noticed it before. I held my Glock with my right hand and turned the door knob with my left. It was unlocked. With my back to the wall, I flipped on the light switch and listened for movement. I heard nothing but the wind rattling the shutters and the normal sounds of the house settling. The chill from the basement crawled up my spine as I made my way down the creaky wooden steps. Would I find Rosa's body down there? Was I already too late?

I crouched down as I walked as silently as I could. Scanning the damp basement, I detected no movement. Racks of boxes, old paint cans, and various tools filled the space. The washer and dryer hookup had been moved upstairs years ago, but there was still an old rusty utility sink in the corner. When I was satisfied no one was there, I searched for an exit. There were no windows, only another set of rickety steps that led up to a cellar door hatch. It had been concealed behind a tall bush in the backyard. I had wired it with a security camera and alarm from the outside. If someone had left that way, I would have known. The alarm was still on. No alert had been triggered.

There had to be another exit down here. Unless the video feed had been tampered with. That could be a real possibility if Sam had been the one to get Rosa out. He was a genius with technology. We only hired the best. I glanced around the basement looking for anything out of place. Dust covered almost every surface. One wall had a rack filled with gardening supplies. The opposite wall held a rack with tools. Various size mason jars were filled with nuts, bolts, screws, and nails. One of the jars had overturned. Several screws had fallen to the floor. I pointed my flashlight at that section of the room. The screws were far too shiny to have been that way for long. They left an odd pattern, a large arc. It appeared like the screws had been thrown with some force.

I tugged the metal rack that was bolted to the brick wall. Both the rack and brick wall moved as one. A hidden doorway opened quietly on oiled hinges. A few more screws fell to the cement floor in the process. A dark tunnel was revealed. I now knew their escape route. I had read about these old supply tunnels running under the city. They weren't on any map that I was aware of, so it was going to be difficult to figure out where it led. I climbed into the tunnel and checked my cell phone. No signal. As much as I wanted to start searching, I needed to call this in first. Huck answered on the first ring.

"I need a team sent out."

I rattled off my friend's address.

"Rosa escaped through an underground tunnel."

"No way. Like one of those built during prohibition times?"

"Exactly. And I don't have any idea where it leads."

"Rosa has to make things interesting, doesn't she?"

I shook my head. "You have no idea."

Chapter 26

Rosa

I woke with blurry vision and a headache from hell. My body was strapped to a recliner with duct tape. I had a moment of disgust remembering the stains on the fabric. Although sitting on a dirty chair was the least of my worries right now. Sam was back typing on the computer. I could see his face glowing from the backlit screen.

"I know you're awake," he said.

Sam must have heard a change in my breathing.

"Do I need to tape your mouth shut, or do you intend to be good?"

I chuckled. It came out harsh. "Good is not a word anyone would use to describe me, Sam."

He stood and walked toward me. "Call me Ground Zero."

"I won't yell, Ground Zero." I tried to shrug, but my shoulders didn't move. The tape made movement impossible.

I doubted screaming for help would do any good. My guess was the apartment building was abandoned or due to be demolished. I should have recognized the signs when we had entered earlier. I wanted to kick myself for being so stupid. I tried to figure out how long I had been out. The windows didn't offer any clues. Covered with newspaper, they offered no sunlight or landmark I could use as a reference. Knowing exactly where I was at wouldn't be much help in my current situation. Unless I somehow found a way to reach someone. Only then would it be helpful. My gaze drifted to my purse. It was peeking beneath my coat and shoes, in a pile on the floor near the couch. If only I could reach it. I still had my second burner phone and Taz's gun. Maybe I could somehow convince Sam to remove my restraints.

I turned my body in the chair scooting my feet on the floor. The chair both reclined and swiveled. I gave a quick test tug on my restraints while turning to see how secure the tape was. Juepucha. It didn't give. Other than my ability to move my ankle and wrists, I had little mobility. My hands were positioned palms down on the armrests, and the chair was comfortable considering my circumstances. I had been in worse situations in the past. The fact that I had been tied to chairs multiple times in my lifetime might have been a red flag that I had made poor choices.

I heard an email ping noise from Sam's computer. My heart rate increased. How long did I have? Sam said he was waiting for Luís to pay him. My only hope was that my cousin was either too cheap to pay, or was having trouble coming up with the funds. The feds had frozen his accounts. While I knew he had money stashed, they would be limited. I focused on my breathing, trying to calm myself. Panic would do me no good. I closed my eyes and concentrated on what I could do. If I could keep Sam talking, I might be able to distract him long enough to figure things out.

"Did you kill José and Pablo?" I asked cringing on the blunt way I asked the question.

True, I wanted to know the answer, but that wasn't the best way to start.

"Yes," he replied.

I blinked rapidly. I hadn't expected him to answer honestly.

"How?"

He tilted his head. "You're genuinely curious?"

ST. LOUIS SECRETS

Sam walked closer to me. He swiped a hair out of my eyes so I could meet his gaze. I forced my expression to go neutral. I didn't want him to see my disgust. Having Sam this close made me nauseous. I can't believe I had trusted the man. He was working for my cousin. A man I loathed. Of course, there was that other little detail. Sam was going to kill me. I could see it in his eyes.

I licked my lips. "Sure. It couldn't have been an easy task. How did you get them away from protective custody?"

"I thought it might be difficult at first," He grinned. "But not with my skills. José was easily manipulated. I told him Luís had hired me to rescue him. At first, he had laughed. A full-belly, roll-on-the-floor type of laugh. He was bent over double." Sam stared at me wide-eyed and deadly serious. "I don't like people laughing at me."

I didn't respond. What could I say that wouldn't get me killed? "When his laughter subsided, José said there was no way a scrawny guy like me could physically knock out the Deputy Marshal guarding him. I wanted to kill him then, but it would have ruined my plans."

I cleared my throat. "What happened next?"

"I gave him a phone. He was to contact me when he was in the bathroom. I turned off the alarm to the window, allowing him to climb down the fire escape. I met him just outside a convenience store with cash. He was supposed to get a fake passport from the cashier."

"Wasn't he killed in a robbery?"

An evil gleam brightened Sam's eyes. "I put on a ski mask and robbed the store. I made it look like an accident."

"If you wanted to shoot him, why make him go to the store first? You could have done that in an alley or even on the fire escape."

"It needed to be in the papers. Something bloody, but it couldn't link back to him or the case. I couldn't be creative like I wanted to. El Lobo Rojo had specific instructions."

I shivered at what my cousin had in store for me.

"What about Pablo?"

"Pablo was more of a challenge. Not that he was any smarter. But the man didn't trust as easily." Sam walked about the room staring at the computer, and then back in my direction. "Your cousin had to pay more for him, even though his testimony was less vital to the case. El Lobo Rojo didn't like that." Sam smiled at me. "He said I was trying to extort money from him."

"My cousin is cheap."

I heard another ping on Sam's computer. I wondered if my cousin's funds came through. He took a step toward his laptop.

"How did you get Pablo?" I asked, my voice high-pitched.

He faced me with a smile. Sam strolled over to the couch turning my chair in the process. We faced one another, him lounging on the couch and me in my recliner. It could have been a normal conversation if it weren't for the duct tape and the threat of death hanging in the air. I wondered how long I could continue this dialogue before he would grow bored and do whatever it was that Luís had requested.

"You were instrumental in Pablo's demise."

"I was?"

Sam grinned.

I knew that he had been stabbed and found in the park, so I wasn't entirely sure how that connected to me. I knew it would be bad, but I had to keep Sam talking. The moment he stopped, was the moment I was dead.

"I'm intrigued," I said, even though I wasn't remotely interested in hearing horror stories about the death, especially a friend.

"It seems he wanted to meet with you. He was quite desperate to do so. Pablo needed to explain things." Sam shrugged. "It was quite fascinating. He was a thug, and yet he wanted you to know he had no choice when he held you at gunpoint. One of Luís' men had Pablo's sister back in Bogatá. If Pablo hadn't come to Santa Fe and didn't do whatever Luís asked, his sister would have an accident."

I closed my eyes and sighed. "I figured it might have been something like that."

"The man was your friend," Sam said.

My eyes flashed open. It was a statement. Not a question. He already knew.

Sam licked his lips and sat up straight, arms to his knees leaning toward me.

"Did you know that he wanted more? A lot more."

I had flirted with Pablo over the years, and I might have played it up, not that it had gone anywhere. I wasn't estúpida. He was one of Luís' men.

Sam wanted a reaction. I could tell by the excitement in his eyes.

"I had no idea," I said.

He slapped his knees. "Ha. I thought so." Sam chuckled. "Pablo wanted to make it up to you. Rescue you from WITSEC. He was going back to Colombia, but he had devised a plan to take you with him."

My jaw dropped. What in the world? Why would he think that would have worked?

Sam roared with laughter. "I know. The guy was so stupid. But he had a contact. When I tried to give him a burner phone like I had with José, I found out that he already had one. I cloned his phone so I could get his messages. I did them both. That's why Luís had to pay extra."

"I don't remember there being another body found in the newspaper."

Sam shrugged. "Normally I don't leave bodies to be found, but," He sighed. "Luís had his checklist, and I aim to serve."

ZIZI HART

Sam described how he had drugged Pablo and stabbed him multiple times. The friend who had tried to help him was drugged as well. Sam got to play with that one before he killed him. I tried not to gag or show emotion to the details surrounding his friend's torture.

Sam went over to the computer to check his messages. Was this it? Had the funds come through?

Sam sighed dramatically.

"What happened?" I asked, desperate to delay the inevitable.

"Luís hired a sniper to take out Mari. He failed."

Sam walked back to the couch. "Another loose end to deal with." He shrugged. "But not until the funds come through."

I let out a deep breath.

My phone vibrated in my purse. It made a buzzing rattle sound that was hard to miss. Still, I tried to mask the sound with a cough, but it was too late. Sam had found my purse on the floor and pulled out the burner.

"Hmm. Who could be calling you?" Sam asked.

He glanced at the phone and read off the digits.

"I recognize the number. The Chief is calling you. Probably wondering where you ran off to. Shh," he said. "We're not going to tell him. Let it be a surprise."

Sam rummaged through the contents of my purse. "What goodies are you hiding in here? Cash. Lipstick. Your nana's necklace. And what's this, a gun? How unexpected? Did you borrow that from the Chief?"

I shook my head.

"You don't know, or won't say?" Sam said. "No matter, I can find out from the serial number."

He took the gun to his computer and typed on the keyboard. "Yep, it's the boss' gun. I can definitely find something fun to do with that. Thanks, Rosa."

"De nada," I mumbled.

ST. LOUIS SECRETS

Sam had found the two things that had given me hope. The gun and my phone. Now freeing myself from the chair wasn't going to do me a bit of good. He had them both next to him on the table. I slumped in the recliner, depression dragging me down to a pitiful place I called defeat. This was it. I couldn't believe that the final hours or minutes of my life would be spent with a madman who could rival my cousin for psycho of the year. How did I ever get so lucky?

Chapter 27

Taz

Huck managed to find a map of the tunnels. He sent over a group of five men he trusted to track Rosa down. None of them were with the US Marshal Service, which was fine by me. Until we found the leak, I wasn't sure who to trust. Going outside the agency might be the safest bet. The men Huck sent were a mix of military and local law enforcement. I received a call from Paul Cohen at Internal Affairs as we were heading down to the basement.

"What have you got?" I asked.

"No hello?" He chuckled.

"No time for pleasantries. We are heading underground where there's no signal."

"I'm not sure I should ask," he said. "I'll make it quick. I found the file on Sam Owens. Everything looked in order, but the background check sheet was missing. It's standard for all applicants. Even if everything is done online, there is usually a hard copy in the paper files. Or at the very least a reference code, so we can look it up electronically."

"I take it there's no code."

"No," he said. "I'm betting his employment history is fake. The recommendation letter in his file was signed by a Chief

Deputy I knew personally. The date was wrong. He died the year before."

"Can you get Accounting to check out his bank accounts?"

"As soon as they get into the office, I'll turn this over to them. But even if there are irregularities, it's going to take time to dig through. Time I'm sure you don't have. Plus, everything is online. If he's as good as you say with technology, he will notice us poking around," he sighed. "There's something else. I searched a database that's not linked to the internet. One that he shouldn't have access to. I just wanted to check if he came up on any lists."

"What did you find?"

"Nothing. And that's strange. I should have pulled some kind of background. The guy doesn't appear to exist even though he had all the right paperwork when he was hired. I think you know what that means."

It sounded more and more like Sam was the leak. And if he had infiltrated the US Marshal Service, and bypassed all the federal security checks, then he could get away with anything. Was he the shadowed figure in the video? The more I thought about it, the more the clues started to add up. If Sam had shown up at the house, Rosa would have trusted him completely and gone with him without question. The only other choice was someone from her past. Would she have shared the address with Ramón? Did she have other contacts in the city? I still had the burner I had taken from her after the zoo. Maybe one of those numbers could help me find her. Whoever it was on the camera had to know about the tunnel. It must be someone who lived here.

I picked up the burner phone and dialed the most recent phone number. No one answered. I wasn't sure if I should leave a message. In the end, I texted 'Call me back ASAP'. Vague, yet urgent. I had no guarantee the person I was calling was an ally, but I didn't believe she would waste her time calling enemies. My hunch was that Sam and Rosa were together right now. All I cared about was getting her back. I realized somewhere along the way I had fallen for her hard. The testimony and the trial were no longer nearly as important. Even my revenge paled compared to having her safe in my arms once again.

The team and I searched the tunnels for blocks leading in multiple directions. We regrouped at a bakery. All of the other doorways were either rusted shut or hadn't looked used in quite some time. Only two of the doors had oiled hinges. The door in my friend's basement, and the basement to a bakery two blocks away. I checked with the bakery's owner. He didn't know anything about it. But he could have been lying. The owner was sweating during the interrogation. Huck was watching the video from the surveillance cameras pointed around the building. We narrowed down the timeframe when Rosa went missing.

"I've got it," he said pulling me into a small office with piles of paperwork. The video equipment looked old, but I could see two figures walking out of the bakery into the employee parking lot. It looked like Sam and Rosa. I recognized Rosa's coat and beret. Sam was wearing some sort of uniform. He opened up the back of the van and gestured for Rosa to get in. My stomach plummeted when she got in without a fuss. I wanted her to fight back, but she had gone willingly.

"Run the plates," I said to Huck.

He nodded his head, confirming he was already on it. Now we had a starting location, we could start a timeline.

"We need to check if Sam was offline or unavailable during all the witness disappearances."

"You got it, Chief."

I still wasn't willing to automatically assume Sam was involved with their deaths. At least not yet. But none of this information would tell us where they were right now.

Rosa's phone rang.

"Who is this?" I asked.

The person on the line hung up.

I could kick myself. I knew better than to respond. Maybe if I provided some information, they would share.

I sent a text message to the number that just called.

'I need your help. Rosa is in danger. I don't care what your arrangement was with her. I need her new cell phone number.'

Whoever it was, might not want me to know his name. I was fine with that. My best bet was he was a criminal, but I doubt he meant her harm if she reached out to him for help. A minute later he responded.

'Who are you?'

'This is Chief Deputy US Marshal Taz Bennett.'

He pinged me with the phone number.

I called the number. It rang and rang with no answer. I had no idea if the person who responded gave me the wrong number on purpose, or if she just wasn't answering.

I'd keep calling the number regardless. We were running out of time. I drove into the office. Dan Howard was the man I needed to find. He had worked as an IT field technician for the US Marshal Service for only six months. If I had to suspect anyone of being the leak, he would be at the top of my list. The timeframe of his hiring coincided with St. Louis taking over the Lorenzo trial. But Paul Cohen in IA assured me that Dan's background was clean when I asked him for a list of trustworthy individuals to help me track down my missing witness.

I walked down to the IT floor in the US Marshal building. I was meeting with Dan Howard this morning. I had been up all night and my eyes were bloodshot. I sipped stale cold coffee, but the caffeine wasn't having much of an effect.

"Rough night?" He asked.

"I need answers." I barked at him.

Dan slid back in his office chair, the wheels sliding across the linoleum tile.

I explained what we were up against.

"I need to find Sam Owens. We think he might be involved in a witness disappearance."

"Woah," he said, "All right. Your best bet is to do a trace and track his IP address. Trouble is it only works if he's online,"

ST. LOUIS SECRETS

Dan said. "We can activate the GPS coordinates and get a fix. But he could have spoofed it."

"You're not giving me a whole lot of hope here."

"Don't worry. Sam thinks he's a genius. He's not. I'm a much better hacker than he is."

"I don't care about your competition. I just need him found."

"Yes, Chief," he said with a little salute.

Dan had three monitors in front of him. I couldn't keep track of what the man was doing. He jumped from screen to screen with such speed, I could barely keep track. Windows opened and closed. Browsers swished right and then another program swished left as he searched and dug through the network, searching for the man holding Rosa. I grew impatient watching and started tapping my foot.

"He's not online at the moment," Dan said. "I can call you when he is."

"Fine." I blew out a breath. "Let me know when you have something." I stormed off leaving Dan to his computer world. I couldn't just sit there. I was liable to smash something.

I decided to call the hospital just to make sure I wasn't overreacting. The hospital staff verified that Sam's mother wasn't there. They had no record of her or Sam coming by to visit. I coordinated with a deputy that I sent to search Sam's apartment. There was no sign of him. He found files on Luís Lorenzo and all the witnesses' names and their safehouse addresses. Since he was in charge of setting up the surveillance cameras, Sam having that information was not a problem, but he shouldn't have had that information written down in his home. The deputy also found a list of names with numbers next to them. Each one was a witness. I wondered if the numbers corresponded to payoffs.

My phone rang. It was Dan from IT.

"We've got him."

"Finally," I said, "Address?"

He rattled off the numbers, and I shot out of my office calling out to Huck and his team. We all piled into a conference room, and one of the deputies pulled up the address. The abandoned apartment building was on the north side of the city. It was a rough neighborhood. The LCRA, Land Clearance for Redevelopment Authority had already put in an offer to buy the property, but the owner hadn't accepted. It was now going through legal filings, and the property would be seized under an eminent domain order. We called St. Louis PD North Patrol to meet us onsite. The Captain of the District offered me all the resources I needed.

"Do we have eyes inside?" I asked.

"Negative," Huck said. "I've already checked and even if there were cameras inside, they wouldn't be recording."

"Does the building even have power?"

"It's been turned off, but people still live in sections of the property."

"We talked to one homeless man who said he noticed someone enter the parking garage. His description matched Sam and Rosa's. He had seen the man here before but tended to avoid him, saying he had crazy eyes. They went up to the third floor. He said no one goes up there on account of the noise."

"What do you think he's talking about?" I asked.

"From the man's description, I'd bet it was a generator."

"Then Sam could have cameras. He might see us coming."

"Do we have blueprints of the property?"

Another Deputy pulled up the copy on his computer. It was hard to see the details on his laptop, but we didn't have time to pull the hard copy records from the city's building division. It felt like we were running out of time.

ST. LOUIS SECRETS

After discussing our options, we decided on a handful of people dressing as homeless to infiltrate the building. I was one of them. Communication earbuds were distributed to those of us going in. I had argued with the District Captain, but in the end, I had gotten my way. I borrowed some clothes from the homeless man who had witnessed Sam and Rosa entering the building. He took me inside, and up to the second floor. I paid him $200 for his troubles. I was on coms, but Huck was running the show. I waited for everyone to get into place. We tracked down the apartment they were holed up in. Sam must have seen us arrive. When we busted down the door, I found Rosa strapped to a recliner. She had tears in her eyes.

"He's in the back," she gestured, nodding her head toward the bedroom.

I stayed in front of Rosa while one of my deputies searched the bedroom and bathroom.

"Sam's not here," he called out.

"What do you mean?" I asked.

"Taz?" Rosa asked, her voice had gone soft.

One look at her, and I decided to let the team worry about Sam. I needed to see to her first. Nothing else mattered. I flipped open my utility knife and cut her from the chair. Rosa stood on wobbly legs. Duct tape clung to her clothes in patches like some low-budget mummy costume. She hugged me despite the grease on my face, or my grubby clothing.

"He was going to kill me."

"Sam?"

She nodded.

"Luís was paying him to do it. Sam was waiting for the transfer of funds."

I hugged her tighter. To think how little time we had. We had gotten to her in the nick of time.

"I knew you'd come for me."

With her snuggled into my side, I checked in with the team. "Huck, report."

"Nothing yet."

"Sam's not in custody?"

"We're still searching."

Since the elevator wasn't working, we had the stairs covered. Sam wouldn't be able to escape. We'd have a team scour the building. I just needed to get Rosa to safety. I didn't know if Sam would try to take another shot. A patrol officer led me down the stairs and over to our makeshift command center, an old rusty Ford van. I set Rosa in the passenger seat and handed her a coffee. One of the officers pulled a blanket from his trunk and handed it to her. She gave a small smile and wrapped it around herself. The next few hours yielded nothing. Sam had somehow escaped. Officers would still patrol the area, but we had searched every inch of the building. I needed to get Rosa somewhere to warm up. The woman still shivered but she hadn't said a word since we rescued her. Rosa seemed to be in shock.

With Rosa back safe, and Sam in the wind, I gave Paul Cohen the green light to use all his resources in IA to unravel what happened. It was going to be one heck of an investigation and no one would be happy about it, especially the Attorney General. I didn't have much of a choice. We still didn't know if Sam had a partner. The forensic accountants were already going through his financials, but so far had turned up nothing, and by nothing I meant zip. The man the US Marshals had hired, Sam Owens, didn't appear to exist before five years ago. It puzzled everyone just how he pulled it off. Even if the investigation of Sam Owens was supposed to be secret, I knew word would eventually get out that we had a breach in our security. Someone was going to take the fall, and I had a feeling it would be me. The AG had been gunning for me since he took office, and I knew my days as Chief were numbered.

Chapter 28

Rosa

I couldn't stop shivering. Taz had put me in the tub and then left to talk to the guards. They were stationed around the house. We had gone back to his friend's house even though Sam had somehow discovered the address. Now that Sam was on the run, Taz didn't think it was a risk. I shared what Sam told me. He had been working alone, with the exception of the sniper hired to take out Mari. When I mentioned Sam's code name, Ground Zero, Taz's face had turned to stone. He recognized the name but refused to talk about it. I slipped under the bubbles and forced my body to relax. Grabbing the loofa, I scrubbed the sticky residue from my forearms. The duct tape had left a reminder of the incident, and I wanted it all gone.

"You all right?" Taz asked.
I blinked up at him. I hadn't heard him come in.
"Yeah. Fine." I said, knowing I was anything but fine.
I blew out a breath.
"Are you ready to come out?"
I shrugged, feeling numb all over.
"I guess so."
He held out a towel and dried me off. Taz wrapped me in a soft terrycloth robe and picked me up.

"I can walk you know," I said.

"You are mine to protect."

He said the same thing when we first met. I snuggled into his arms enjoying the warmth. Not that it lasted long. Taz bundled me under the blankets and left me to my tumultuous thoughts. I wanted him to stay with me, but I didn't want to admit out loud how much I needed him. Plus, the fact that we had chaperones. I'm not sure how I felt about that. Protected. Yes. But there was a part of me that would risk safety for it to be just the two of us once again. I missed that dynamic. I wasn't sure we'd get that kind of alone time before the trial. After that, I'd be gone, squirreled away in some part of the U.S., safe but alone. I heard the clock tick, focusing on the sound trying to fall asleep. My mind wouldn't let me. Eventually, I got up and put my casserole in the oven. The least I could do was feed my protectors. There was no use for it going to waste. Everyone loved my arroz al horno. I had made a baked Spanish rice dish with chorizo, tomatoes, onion, and garlic. It had been one of my Nana's recipes. I made everyone sing Happy Birthday to Taz before they could get a slice of birthday cake. It wasn't quite like I had planned. I wouldn't be wearing the silk and lace lingerie while he blew out the candles. Even if I did have the self-confidence to pull it off, that gift was private, for Taz's eyes only. I hoped to convince him to unwrap his other present in the bedroom later. The cake had turned out muy delicioso. The guys got a kick out of the character on the cake, and I could tell Taz was pleased.

"Feliz Cumpleaños," I said, rubbing some frosting off his beard stubble with my thumb. I sucked the frosting from my finger. "I have another surprise for you later," I whispered in his ear.

Taz's face heated. I wonder if he had seen what I had in store for him. Someone had checked my bag because everything was out of order when I looked through it earlier. They were probably looking for tracking devices or bugs. Either way, I was

ST. LOUIS SECRETS

ok with it not being a surprise. At this point, I believed surprises were overrated. I had enough shocks to last a lifetime.

Two days later, I was sitting in a small room in the courthouse awaiting my turn to give testimony. I tapped my foot nervously under the table. Taz was standing at the door watching me with hawk eyes. I let out a breath and searched through my purse. I pulled out my lipstick and compact, freshening up my warpaint. The suit I wore was conservative, but the purple silk blouse was feminine enough to make me feel pretty. Taz had made sure to get the correct size. I didn't want to feel self-conscious on top of how nervous I already was.

"You're going to be fine," he said. "You look great."

I smirked at him. "I know, but I still wish I had a gun."

Sam had escaped with Taz's gun. I'm sure Taz had a tough time explaining how a fugitive now had his service weapon or at least one of them.

"Nothing is going to happen. Luís can't hurt you."

I nodded. I knew that.

"I'll protect you."

I wanted a hug, but Taz was keeping his distance. I understood that it would look bad in the courtroom if he had his arm around me, but we were in this room all by ourselves. I glanced up at the ceiling. I guess there was a surveillance camera. Maybe that's the reason.

The door abruptly opened, and Taz was there blocking my view. My shoulders tensed. He relaxed his stance after a few seconds. The paralegal, Lisa Winters leaned around him.

"We're ready for you."

I shook out my shoulders, trying to loosen them.

"I didn't get dressed up for nothing," I said as I got to my feet.

ZIZI HART

I followed Lisa out the door and down a corridor. Taz came up behind us. A security guard stood outside two large doors. She nodded to the guard and opened the door to the courtroom. The chatter abruptly stopped. I felt like I was the one on trial. I gulped. I could see the Attorney Dick Chambers at the front of the courtroom on one side. Luís and his lawyer sat at another table a short distance away. I thought the two tables were way too close to one another.

"Your Honor, the court would like to call our next witness, Ms. Rosa Lorenzo to the stand."

I walked steadily on my four-inch heels. Lisa had told me not to look at my cousin, but I couldn't help it. He was in one of his designer suits. Prim and proper, but his eyes betrayed him. They burned flames of retribution as he glared at me. His lawyer cleared his throat. Luís stared at the man and seemed to realize his mistake. His gaze softened. But I had seen it, and I hoped those on the jury did as well.

I walked past the rows of seats. The room was filled. Standing room only. My cousin sure could pack in a crowd. Dick patted my shoulder and signaled for the bailiff to escort me to the stand. I stood while they swore me in and took my seat. I sat up straight and stared at Dick, giving him my full concentration. His smile was warm and reassuring.

"Ms. Lorenzo, can you please tell the court your relationship with the defendant and how long you've known him?"

"Luís Lorenzo is my cousin on my father's side and I've known him my whole life."

"And you worked for him as well, correct?"

"Yes. I was employed by him in Santa Fe at a nightclub called Club Cuervo."

"Did you know that he was dealing drugs?"

"Yes."

"Why did you go to work for him if he was involved in a criminal enterprise?"

ST. LOUIS SECRETS

I licked my lips. This was tricky because technically I was involved in the family drug business back in Colombia. Dick had assured me that the deal I had with the federal government meant they couldn't prosecute me for anything in the U.S., but I also didn't agree to give testimony against the other Lorenzo brothers. I made it clear, I was only going to testify against Luís.

"He promised me that he wouldn't recruit his nephew, so I was willing to work for Luís to keep him safe."

"Did you feel threatened when working at Club Cuervo?"

"Yes. Back home they call him El Lobo Rojo for a reason."

"Objection, Your Honor." The defense lawyer said. "Relevance?"

"Establishing the nature of their business relationship, Your Honor." Dick Chambers said.

"Overruled." The judge stated.

"Why do they call him El Lobo Rojo?"

"They call him the Red Wolf because of the blood he spills. How he silences those who betray him. Everyone at the club feared him. Most of those working at the club came over from Colombia. They knew his reputation."

I glanced at Luís. He couldn't contain the gaze of hatred in his expression.

"You were afraid for your life?"

"Yes."

"Objection, Your Honor. Leading the witness."

"Sustained."

"Would you consider him a threat to society?"

"Absolutely. My cousin is out of control. He's an animal and should be caged behind bars."

I met his gaze of hatred with my own.

Luís stood before anyone realized what was happening and lunged for the stand.

ZIZI HART

Taz was there in front of him, jumping over the small wall dividing the gallery from the rest of the courtroom. I knocked the heavy wood chair on the witness stand over in my speed to get away. I stood with my back plastered against the wall and my arms raised to protect myself. I had learned to react quickly around my cousin. The courtroom was in chaos. Taz had Luís pinned to the ground. Luís was swearing in Spanish, promising his vengeance. His expensive lawyer closed his eyes and shook his head. He must have realized the defense's case was over. The cool as a cucumber businessman had always been a facade. Luís and his temper had proved that and there was no un-ringing that bell. The jury had witnessed it all. I should have felt vindicated by my cousin showing his true colors, but my pulse still pounded in my throat.

It didn't take long for the jury to deliberate. With all the evidence against him, they found him guilty on all counts. The judge revoked his release status because of his outburst in court. It was clear the man was a danger to society. Luís would be detained in jail pending sentencing. Taz explained that wouldn't take place for a few months, but he'd be behind bars. He felt like the judge would give the maximum sentence and Luís would be in prison for the rest of his life.

After that, we headed out to celebrate the conviction. The six of us; Mari, César, Jac, Sofía, Taz, and I all went to City Foundry Food Hall in midtown to grab dinner. Taz called it a foodie paradise. The industrial warehouse-style space was filled with so many food stands that it was hard to choose what to eat. Too many culinary delights. That had been my downfall since I had been in St. Louis. My waistline had grown in the months since I had been here. Not that I minded so much now. I wasn't trying to pry myself into a next-to-nothing cocktail waitress uniform.

ST. LOUIS SECRETS

That part of my life was done. And besides, Taz didn't seem to mind the extra weight. I hadn't been hungry before the trial, being too nervous to eat. My stomach had been twisting and turning, but now that the trial was over, my appetite returned with a vengeance. We all got something different; Caribbean, Cajun, BBQ, Mediterranean, Asian, and Hawaiian. Everything was delicious, and we ended up sharing.

"I have a surprise," Taz said escorting me out of the food hall. We had walked through the outdoor mall on our way in, but instead of stopping at any of the shops, he led us over to an unmarked door with a red light. Taz's eyes danced with mischief and I wondered what he was up to. Inside the door was a large floor-to-ceiling panel with levers and blinking lights with Danger and High-Voltage signs.

"I think you might have gone into a maintenance closet by mistake," I said.

"Where are you taking us?" Mari asked.

Taz grinned. Jac and César seemed to be in on the joke. Whatever it was, Mari and Sofía were just as confused as I was.

A window in the panel suddenly opened and I took a step back.

"What the," Sofía said.

It had surprised her, too. The man in the window reminded me of how the guard at the entrance to Emerald City in The Wizard and Oz had greeted Dorothy and her crew. I couldn't help but grin. My crew, the six of us, were on an adventure as well. The man asked Taz for the name on his reservation. Once we were checked in, the panel opened. We traveled down a ramp, stairs, and a graffiti-filled brick corridor with pipes along the ceiling. It was another of those underground tunnels that apparently, St. Louis was famous for. At least this one had more lighting than the last one I had been in. It also didn't have a psychotic assassin leading the way. The industrial door at the end of the labyrinth opened and we were greeted by a hostess welcoming us to None of the Above, a speakeasy-styled cocktail lounge. I glanced around the space, to my left was a dark leather couch and red velvet chairs around a small table. Rich wood-grain tables with brass table lamps were sporadically placed throughout the room. A glistening bar with accent lighting was on one side. Along the other walls were deep blue velvet booths. Couples sipped cocktails whispering to one another. Vintage pictures and ornate mirrors covered dark navy walls. Soft jazz played in the background. It gave an intimate vibe to the luxurious setting.

    The hostess walked over to a tall mirror on one side of the bar. It turned out to be a hidden door that opened into a secret room called the Library. Gold pipes from the ceiling glowed in the warm lighting from the brass sconces. Coordinating leather and velvet furniture filled the space. She led us to a seating area in front of a large bookcase. Sipping one of their signature cocktails, I felt myself relax back into the plush velvet chair. The men were joking about something, and the girls were gossiping. I took a deep breath for what seemed like the first time in a very long while. I felt all the tension leave my body and I realized this was the first day of my new life. I had been sequestered in WITSEC since the drug bust over six months ago. In all that time I hadn't been living. My life had been on hold. Even before that time, back in Colombia, I always felt like I could never let my guard down. I experienced a feeling I wasn't accustomed to. In this cozy lounge surrounded by these people, I felt safe. With Luís behind bars, I could move forward. It didn't matter that I didn't have a clue what the future held. But it no longer filled me with dread. Now, I had hope. Clinking glasses with my girlfriends I joined in on the conversation. This is what my life had been missing. I raised my glass for a toast.

    "Hacia un futuro con mucha esperanza." Toward a future with much hope. Now that was something to live for.

Chapter 29

Taz

'El Lobo Rojo was found dead in his cell.'

    I re-read the text message again for the third time. How had that happened? Not that I felt particularly sorry for the bastard. I wondered how Rosa would respond to the news. I could never predict her reactions to anything. I grinned. Life with her would never be boring. That's for darn sure. She kept me on my toes. It was one of those things I loved about her. Strange, that concept. Love. I never would have imagined having that kind of emotion for someone outside my family. Although, she was family now too. I may not have put a ring on her finger yet, but I felt that connection down to my bones. And people knew not to mess with what was mine. Come hell or high water, I'd protect her. I had said as much the moment we met, and those feelings had multiplied in the short time we'd known one another. Rosa finished packing her bag, but she looked a little lost. I had told her she'd be relocated to Texas, but I hadn't filled her in on the details. She was moving in with me. Or at least I hoped so. She had every right to bolt. I might even have done the same in her place. But on her own, she was at the mercy of those after her.

    Even with Luís gone, Rosa still had enemies out there. I needed to convince her to stay with me. I had to get back to my father's ranch now that the trial was over. My brother called saying the bypass surgery went well, but he needed my help. He couldn't manage it all on his own, especially while working full-time with the Harris County Sheriff's Office. Brenda even stepped in to do what she could, but being in a wheelchair meant many tasks weren't possible. Of course, that didn't stop her from trying. Tenacious. That was Brenda. But it was my place to step in. I was the eldest brother. It was my responsibility. I was almost glad the Attorney General had given me an ultimatum, Rosa or the job. I had picked Rosa without hesitating. Although the St. Louis job had always been temporary. If it had been my old position back in Houston, I'm not sure it would have been as easy of a decision.

"So, when are we heading out?" Rosa asked. Her hip was cocked, and she gave me one of her patented glares.

"You anxious to see Texas?"

She shrugged. "Not sure. I've never been there."

"Well then. I reckon that will be changing real soon."

Rosa sighed. "I wonder if I will ever tire of you stating the obvious," she traced her fingers down my chest. "Although you say it so darn cute with your Texas accent."

"Cute?"

She grinned. Rosa knew that cute didn't fit me at'all.

I opened my mouth, ready to blast her, but a knock at the door interrupted me. I looked through the peephole and there was a delivery truck. A man with a small package stood waiting.

"Stay here," I warned Rosa and stepped out onto the porch.

"Delivery for a Ms. Rosa Lorenzo. I just need a signature."

I lifted my jacket to pull out the scanner, and my weapon flashed in the sunlight. The man's eyes bulged.

"That's ok sir. I'll just scribble something down."

He held up the box, but I didn't take it from him. Instead, I used the scanner on it and the guy visibly shivered.

"What the hell am I holding, man?"

The scan didn't show any electronics, or bugs that I could detect. Having a bomb sent to a witness was extremely rare, especially since she had already testified. Not that I was willing to take any chances. But the fact that someone had this address was a worry. Perhaps it was from someone at the office or it could have been from Mari or Sofía. They had returned to New Mexico a few days ago. After I felt confident the package was safe, I allowed the guy to place it in my palm. He ran like hell back to his truck. I had scared the poor delivery man. Oh well. He'd have a good story to share with his buddies at the delivery terminal.

The light box was wrapped neatly in brown paper and twine. Only Rosa's name and our temporary safe house address were listed on the label. I should have gotten a notification from the office if they were routing me or Rosa a package, even if I had been removed from my position. I felt like hiding the package or opening it myself, but Rosa and I had discussed this sort of thing before. She called me heavy-handed. I called it protective. We fought about it, and she had somehow managed to win that argument. I had agreed that she could be part of the decisions regarding her own safety. As much as it grated on my nerves, I knew that she needed some semblance of control, otherwise she'd go mad.

When I came back inside, Rosa's eyes were as big as saucers.

"Did they find me?"

"You got a package."

"What?"

She gave a nervous laugh when I handed her the small box. "It's not a bomb, is it?"

"I scanned it. You're safe."

She plopped down on the sofa. Rosa eyed the box like it was some hideous spider that had crawled onto her lap and she was just waiting for the thing to bite her.

"You don't have to open it," I said.

"What do you mean by that?"

"I can open it for you." I shrugged.

She licked her lips. "That would be the easy way out. When have you ever known me to do things easy?"

I laughed. It was true. The woman was contrary in the extreme.

Rosa shook her head like she was having a conversation with herself, building up her nerve. "No. I don't need your help," she looked up at me and blinked those gorgeous eyes. "I appreciate it, but I got this. I'm just mentally preparing myself for the worst."

It killed me that something so simple would tear her apart like this.

Rosa strode over to the desk and grabbed a pair of scissors. She cut the twine. In seconds, the brown paper was ripped off and the lid of the box was thrown open. Inside was a jewelry case. Her eyebrows rose.

"This isn't from you, is it?" She asked.

I grinned. "I almost wish, by your expression, but no. I didn't send you anything."

She popped open the case. Rosa's face paled and she collapsed into a chair.

"What is it?" I asked, trying to get a peek inside the jewelry box.

There was a man's ring. I frowned. It was on a severed finger. No wonder her legs had fallen out from under her.

"It looks like there's a note," I said.

She nodded at the slip of paper peeking out from beneath the case's satin lining. I went into my suitcase, found a pair of latex gloves, and handed them over to her. I should have had her put them on earlier. I didn't want this for her. Was this Luís' brothers promising revenge? Rosa set the box down on the side table. She slid the gloves onto trembling fingers and pried the satin lining up, slipping out the note. Rosa opened it and read the text. It was a small piece of paper. It couldn't have that many words. She must have read it multiple times.

"Huh," she said tilting her head.

ST. LOUIS SECRETS

"What does it say?" I asked.

"Very little. But I think I understand the meaning. It's not hard to figure out if you're a Lorenzo."

"I'm sorry," I said, wrapping her hand in mine, wanting to comfort her from anything her family had to say. No doubt it was some sort of threat. Why had I let her open it?

"It's unexpected. It might even be good news."

"Come again?" I asked. "How could a severed finger ever be a good thing?"

She shrugged. "I guess you need to know my family. With them, it's all in perspective."

I leaned over and read the words. No rata. No lobo. No problema.

"No rat. No wolf. No problem?"

"I didn't rat out the Lorenzos. I only ratted on Luís. He's the wolf. El Lobo Rojo. Because I didn't rat out the family, and the wolf is now gone, things are square between us. The family must have decided that Luís had become a liability. They cut ties, by severing a finger."

"The finger's not a threat?"

She shook her head. "No. It's Luís' finger. See his ring."

I glanced at the highly detailed etched wolf head in black gold. The ring looked extremely expensive and one-of-a-kind.

Rosa sighed. "Have your people test it if you want? It will be his fingerprint."

I knew she wanted this thing to be over, but I also knew nothing was ever that simple. If it helped her not worry so much, so be it. I wouldn't press the matter.

"Let's get out of here," she playfully slapped my behind. "You promised me Texas. I sure hope it's warmer than St. Louis."

"It usually is, but even if you're cold, I'll be there to keep you warm." I pulled her closer.

"Hmm. I just bet you will."

I kissed her until I felt her go liquid in my arms. She licked her lips when we pulled apart. Her eyes were on fire. I bet they matched my own. I was anxious to get on the road. I wanted to get her safely tucked away back home at our family ranch. It was north of Houston. I'd check the details surrounding Luís later. No one had mentioned a missing finger in the text, but they probably didn't think it would be sent as a gift either. Since I had turned in my resignation, and handed off the files to my deputies, it would be in someone else's hands now. I'd notify them from the road to pick up the package. It was no longer my responsibility. We needed to get to the airport before we missed our flight. My family was waiting for us back home. I said my goodbyes to St. Louis and held out my hand to Rosa. She was my life now. Somedays I couldn't believe I had fallen for a Lorenzo. I had sworn revenge against the family. The irony was not lost on me. Rosa had allowed me to see past bloodlines, to what was really important, deep down. I only had one thing to worry about now and that was Rosa and our new life together.

Chapter 30

Rosa

"This is your father?" I asked. My eyes must have been practically bulging out of my skull.

The man in front of me had big beefy arms, broad shoulders, with a worn leather face that looked like he lived out in the sun. He could have been the same height as Taz, maybe a few inches shorter, but the hat he wore made him look like a giant. I had never seen a taller Stetson in my life. This man didn't need the height advantage. He must have towered over almost everyone. In my heels, I still had to look up and up.

The man took off his hat. Nope. Didn't help. The man was still huge.

"Name's Lee Bennett. It is mighty fine to meet 'ya."

He shook my hand, and I felt like my arm was going to fall off.

"Easy Dad. You don't know your own strength." Taz frowned.

"Oh sorry, dear. I'm still on meds. Can't feel much."

"Well, you look fantastic. And you just had surgery?"

"Those darn doctors kept me in the hospital too long, and my daughter makes me take those pain pills that make me all discombobulated," he put his hat back on and took a seat back in his recliner. "It makes me tired, and there's too much to do."

"You're supposed to take it easy." Brenda rolled into the room in a luxury wheelchair with hot pink racing stripes down the sides. She moved about the room with ease. The woman had long brown hair with blonde highlights and stunning light hazel eyes. She wore soft pink sweatpants with a matching pink sweatshirt. The sweatshirt had hot pink lipstick prints all over it and it said kiss my ass or kiss off. I loved her immediately.

She shook her head at me, "You'll have to forgive my dad. He's ornery on the best days. But he can't sit still."

I bit my lip, worried that she might blame me for her injuries.

"Come here and let me get a good look at you?" She asked. Brenda spun around me in her wheelchair.

"The woman who won my big brother's heart. Of course, she'd be a knockout," she grinned at me. "I'm his little sis, Brenda."

She reached her hand out to shake mine, and it looked like it took effort. I could tell that Brenda's body was still fragile, even a year after the injury. I shook her hand gently and smiled.

"It's good to meet you."

"Let's get some iced tea out here," she yelled. "What are you going to do?" She held out her hands. "Just can't get decent help these days."

A few seconds later another huge man came in carrying a tray of tall glasses filled with ice and a pitcher of iced tea. He was close to Taz's size. This one had short blonde hair, and the same hazel eyes as his sister. He must be Blake. Taz had told me about him on our flight into Houston. There was quite an age gap between the three siblings. Taz was 45, his brother was 30, and his little sister was 22. His parent's marriage had been a tumultuous one, fraught with fights and reconciliations. Even though they both dated, neither had remarried after the divorce. I

ST. LOUIS SECRETS

wondered if Josie, Taz's mother would make an appearance. I had heard so much about her too.

"So, this is the criminal you're dating?" Blake asked checking me over.

"Reformed criminal." I grinned.

Taz shoved his brother's arm.

"Be nice."

"Make me," he said.

It appeared both brothers had the same warped sense of humor and fighting spirit.

"Don't mind Blake," Brenda shrugged, "He's just upset because his girlfriend broke up with him."

"How did you find out about that?" He asked.

"Just because I'm in a wheelchair doesn't mean I can't find out what's going on. I think the words she used on social media described you as emotionally bankrupt."

"Ouch," Taz said. "That's brutal. Which one is this?"

"You don't know her," Brenda said. "Blake has been blowing through women like tissues."

"Geez. Why don't you just air all my dirty laundry for our guest?"

"You were the one making her feel awkward," Brenda chuckled. "I just thought I'd show you how it felt."

"I apologize," Blake said to me. "I didn't mean anything by it. I was just ribbing Billy."

"Billy?" I asked.

Taz shook his head. "My real name is William, but the family calls me Billy."

"Billy Bennett." I chuckled. "Well, I guess I should give you my full name, Rosa Alejandra Lorenzo Rivera. Although you probably already know that from my file. But you can still call me Mrs. Connor."

"I'd rather call you Mrs. Bennett."

"Woah. What?" Brenda whistled.

"You want to marry this woman?" Lee asked.

He had been half asleep in his recliner during most of the conversation, but I wondered if it had just been a ruse. The man seemed wide awake now.

My eyes felt like they would pop out of my head. That was the last thing I expected Taz to say. I had never imagined getting married. That dream had been crushed long ago.

The front door opened, and Josie walked in. She looked just like her picture on the fireplace mantle. Josie had long auburn hair and freckles and wore jeans, cowboy boots, and a blue plaid flannel shirt. She looked around the room in shock. "What did I miss?"

"Billy just proposed," Brenda said. "We are all waiting for Rosa's response."

I blinked back tears. Taz had gotten down on one knee. He was doing this in front of his family. I bit my lip to keep it from trembling.

"So, what do you say? Feel like making things official and getting married for real?"

He held out an amethyst and diamond engagement ring.

It was gorgeous, the stones sparkled in the light from the fire. Taz knew that purple was my favorite color, and he had chosen something that fit my personality. How long had he been planning this?

I glanced around the room at the Bennett family members. I had lost contact with my family back home, severing my relationship with my relatives in Colombia. I didn't realize how it would affect me, not having any support system. Being completely alone. Somehow getting a fresh start, and joining a new family filled me with hope for the future. Things were going to work out. I grinned at Taz's expectant expression.

"Yes. Pendejo. Of course, I'll marry you."

"Did she just call you an A-hole?" Blake asked.

"Yes, she did," Taz said, sliding the ring on my finger and kissing me.

ST. LOUIS SECRETS

"She really must know him," he said.

The rest of the family roared with laughter, but I was too busy kissing the man of my dreams.

Epilogue

Taz

I was reading an action-packed spy thriller by a famous author but had lost interest after the fourth chapter. My life had been like the main character until recently. I tried to concentrate on the story when Rosa snuck up behind me. Or at least tried to. Rosa must have thought she was being stealthy, but I could have told her it was pointless. Too many years of training and the art of not being surprised was ingrained in my DNA. I could have allowed it, placated her ego, and made her think she got the better of me, or I could have a little fun. Guess which one won out? My mischievous side won the battle. I dropped the book to the table and tackled her to the floor.

"Oof. What the…"

She only managed those few words before my lips met hers and she melted in my arms. It was a full minute before we came up for air. She finally pushed on my chest and wiggled free.

"Stop," she panted. "There's a call for you."

I had left my phone in the kitchen so I wouldn't have any distractions from my book, not that I got many calls these days.

She got up on her elbows and blew out a breath. Her hair was a mess, and all I wanted to do was kiss that surly smirk off her face, and maybe mess up that hair some more. I started nibbling on her shoulder and up her neck.

"Taz. The call. The guy said he was the President."

"What?"

I hopped to my feet and pulled Rosa up beside me in one smooth move.

"I thought it was maybe an old friend playing a joke. But it's still not cool to make him wait."

I moved quickly to the phone. What Rosa didn't know was that I actually did know the President. I had met the man twice before. The first time was early on in his political career. When working for the Southern District of Texas, I was assigned to the Missing Child Unit at the US Marshal Service. The unit had rescued his daughter after she and a friend had gone missing.

"Mr. President?"

"It's about goddamned time. What do you think I have all day? They got my ass in appointment after appointment. You know my insane schedule."

"I'm sorry sir."

He grumbled and swore under his breath.

"I know that you took time off to be with your father after his heart attack, and have been taking care of the family ranch. I get that. But now that he's better, we need you back."

"I was forced out. You should know that from the AG."

"Don't worry about Henry. I'll deal with him."

"I'm not going back to St. Louis. I'm needed here in Texas."

"The St. Louis position is already filled, but you are right about being needed in Texas. I'm calling because the Chief Deputy for the Southern District of Texas is retiring."

I had heard about that, but I didn't think I'd be considered as a candidate considering my disgraceful exit from the US Marshal Service.

"I need someone to step into the position. Someone I trust. Someone with experience."

ST. LOUIS SECRETS

"But what about my transgression with the witness?"

It was the main reason I had quit. The Attorney General made it clear that I couldn't stay in the position after that. If I didn't resign, I would be removed. He had pressured USMS headquarters to expedite my disciplinary hearing.

"He won't give you any trouble. Plus, I saw a picture of that witness. I don't fault you for falling for that woman. She's mighty easy on the eyes."

"I'm not giving her up."

"Damn it, I'm not asking you to," he chuckled. "Do you trust her?"

Glancing at the expectant stare Rosa gave me, I admitted the truth. "I do."

"You sure do know how to pick 'em."

"We're engaged now."

"Wow. You work fast. And the threat against is her resolved?"

"It is."

I had confirmed through back channels, but I still had feelers out there to give me a heads up if the Lorenzo brothers changed their minds and wanted her dead. I was also concerned about Sam, or rather Ground Zero since he had disappeared after Mari's sniper had been found dead. Rosa seemed certain neither the Lorenzos or Sam would come after her. She had officially declined the services of WITSEC, but we'd still be cautious. Rosa wouldn't be traveling to Colombia anytime soon.

"So how about it?" He asked.

I thought about the possibilities. I had been bored at the ranch, even though I kept busy. I missed the demands and challenges that came with working for the US Marshal Service.

"Your country needs you."

"Yes sir," I said, barely able to contain the excitement in my voice.

"Good." The President blew out a breath. "Headquarters will call you next week with the details."

He hung up. I stared at the phone for a moment before setting it down.

"That really was the President of the United States?" Rosa asked.

"Yeah."

"Wow. You must be quite the badass if El Presidente calls begging for your return."

"We have a history. My team rescued his daughter. I had been first on the scene. Lindsay had been traumatized, but I had talked her through the worst of it. I made the little girl laugh."

"Humor therapy. It works."

I chuckled. "Her parents were grateful, to say the least. I'm still on their Christmas card list."

"So, what will you do?"

"There is an influx of violent fugitives in Texas. I led several task forces in the past. I'm guessing that's what he wants me to focus on. They must need help if he's willing to bend the rules to get me reinstated."

"Isn't your brother working on some task force with the Marshal Service?"

"Blake works for the Sheriff's office, but yeah, he is on a task force with the Marshals. How did you know about that?"

"Your mother, Brenda, and I go shopping. They like to gossip. Brenda seems to know everything about everyone, including the town's dirty little secrets. Like the one where Blake and some female deputy from the US Marshal's office have been hooking up."

"I hadn't heard that rumor."

"Are you going to tell him that work romances don't work?"

I chuckled. "He'd probably tell me to mind my own business."

"Or he'd put you in a headlock." Rosa grinned.

ST. LOUIS SECRETS

"He might try. But he'd fail. Whose side are you on anyhow?"

"Yours always. Mi corazón," she chuckled. "It would be nice to see you and your brother working together. You had some falling out in the past, right?"

I didn't want to get into it. "It's complicated."

"Isn't it always when it comes to family?"

"Not when it comes to you." I tapped Rosa's nose.

She rolled her eyes. "You think you have me all figured out?"

I pulled her into my arms. I didn't have a clue. Figuring out what made the most interesting woman in the world tick would challenge my investigation skills, but I was up to the task. I was willing to put in the time. A lifetime, in fact.

I kissed her instead of answering.

She mumbled something in Spanish. I think she called me a chicken for avoiding the question.

"This task force. You said violent fugitives. That's going to be dangerous?" She bit her lip.

"What do you think?"

She sighed. "It was more of a rhetorical question. Are you going to do it?"

"If it's all right with you."

Rosa shrugged. "I appreciate you asking. But that is who you are. You protect. I'd never ask you to change. Although I'd like you to promise me something."

"Anything," I said.

"Limit the risks, when possible. I've lost too many in my life, and I can't lose you too. Te amo."

"I love you too. And don't worry. I have plenty of reasons to make it home every night. Because I know you'll be waiting for me."

Rosa grinned. "Every night. And I will always make it worth your while."

Book Club Questions

- What did you think about the main couple's chemistry and compatibility?
- How was the heat level in the book? Did it need more or less spice?
- Which tropes did you find in the book? Do you have specific trope favorites?
- Did the characters' sense of humor enhance or distract from the story?
- How likable and relatable were the main characters?
- Did you have a favorite or least favorite side character? How did they contribute to the story?
- Are there other side characters you wished would have been explored in more depth?
- What did you think of the villain? Was he complex and realistic?
- Did you agree with the decisions the characters made?
- Was there enough tension in the book?

- Do you feel the book moved along at a good pace?
- Did the author balance the romance and suspense? Or do you feel it leaned one way or the other?
- How did the author explore the complexities of the character's life choices? Did you feel the mistakes and consequences were dealt with?
- Did you learn something you never knew before? If so, what?
- How were the author's descriptions of the settings? Were there locations in the book you now want to visit?
- Did the setting enhance or distract from the romance?
- How was the ending? Did it come to a satisfying conclusion, or did it leave you wanting more? Were there any unresolved issues or questions?
- What do you believe happens to the main couple after the novel ends?

Appreciation

Thank you to everyone in my life who has contributed in one way or another to the writing of this book. My insanity or lack thereof is entirely your fault. Just kidding. I appreciate your acceptance of me just as I am, and allowing me to bury myself in my office/cave and not come out for days on end. To my parents, kids, and friends for your support, and endless supply of laughter that keeps me going. To my fellow author friends who understand that writing is our therapy and for being my sounding board whenever I need it. I'm amazed and humbled by your creativity and so grateful for your friendship. And lastly, for those within my inner circle that join me on the journey into the depths of the villain psyche. You always have a rope ready to pull me out if I ever go too far. I owe you more than you can ever imagine.

About the Author

Zizi Hart likes to sprinkle sizzle on her sass. Her muse takes her down shadowed, twisted paths, into her imagination and if you are brave enough to join her on the journey, you won't be disappointed. She writes a mix of fantasy, romance, science fiction, suspense, and adventure, wherever her muse takes her. But no matter what, you will always get a touch of humor and a feel-good story with a lot of heart. In her off-time, she travels the world connecting with nature and animals, getting distracted by decadent chocolates and is forever in search of the perfect brownie sundae.

www.ZiziHart.com

Thanks for reading!
Please add a short review on Amazon.
I'd love to hear your thoughts!